THE TIME WE MET

Timing is Everything Series, Book 3

CHRISTINE MILES

For the book nerds.
You are my people.

Books by Christine Miles

ADULT CONTEMPORARY ROMANCE

Timing is Everything Series

Last Time We Loved (Book One)

First Time We Laughed (Book Two)

The Time We Met (Book Three)

This Time It's Forever (Book Four)

YOUNG ADULT

Pacifica Academy Drama Series

Me, Shakespeare and the Anti-Love Club (Book One)

The '68 Camaro Between Kenickie and Me (Book Two)

Teddy Brewster's Hold On Me (Book Three)

Silver Bells for Me and (Saint) Nicolas (Book Four)

You and Me Dancing to Gershwin (Book Five)

Summer in Winter Wonderland (A Cozy Mystery)

Chapter One

CAMPBELL SLID her gaze from left to right, taking in the quiet students focused on their phones. A combo of guys and girls easily several years younger than her, though she could hardly call herself old at twenty-eight.

A nearly full classroom of young strangers pretending to be absorbed by their social media lives or checking e-mail or texting someone important in their world.

Day one of classes on a college campus had arrived.

She shrugged out of her coat and pulled off her red beanie cap with its bright-white pom pom. It had been a Christmas gift from one of her roommate's to go with her new heavy, dark gray coat that had been a gift to herself for making it over a year-and-a-half in a life she never envisioned. But enrolling in the spring semester at Jefferson County Community College had been a way to head back into the life she *had* originally planned ten years before.

She shoved those thoughts—the past—back into the deepest place in her mind.

Revisiting the past, even briefly, always equaled a huge waste of time and energy. After such a surprisingly amazing last year,

Campbell wanted this new year to be the same, if not even better. That meant fully crawling out of the dark and into the light.

Committing herself to finishing school had actually been Step Two. Her massive Step One had happened in the fall when it came to her personal life, so returning to school had been the next huge step forward.

She reached into her backpack purse and withdrew a notebook and pen. She placed both on the desk, then sat back and eyed the rather plain classroom—five rows of desks facing a bare whiteboard and brown desk. The sunlight streaming through the windows lining the left side gave the room a burst of warmth and life.

As excited as she felt to finally be back inside a classroom, required American Literature would probably be less than thrilling. The feeling, however, didn't stop a small smile from playing with the corner of her mouth while she again glanced at her classmates. Most of them were several years younger than her, but maybe by the semester's end in May she'd walk out of here with a couple of new friends? Something she wouldn't have remotely wanted after she moved to Denver over a year-and-a-half ago. But the Campbell Grey sitting in this room no longer resembled the woman she'd left in Durango. It was also a new year, full of possibilities.

Positive possibilities.

She'd witnessed too many miracles last year to think otherwise.

The classroom's door opened and…a man strode into the room. A tall, striking man wearing dark jeans and a snug white, V-neck shirt under a brown leather jacket. He also had a head of thick, rich copper hair cut stylishly short for his age which had to be thirty-ish? Maybe a little older.

Campbell's mouth inched open at not only his good looks but also at the feeling she knew him from somewhere. And according to the schedule this literature class had a woman assigned as the instructor.

She frowned and glanced at the girl sitting to her right who flashed Campbell a wicked smile before putting her phone down. The girl's grin an obvious indication as to what *she* thought of the man.

Campbell refocused on him as he placed his laptop bag on the desk. He then unzipped it and withdrew a stack of papers that had to be the syllabus.

He straightened and smiled. "No, you aren't losing your minds. This is Darcy Neilson's class, but I'm clearly not her." He paused, gave himself a quick once-over, and shrugged. "Or maybe I do look like a Darcy Neilson, but I swear that isn't my name."

Some of the girls giggled, including the girl sitting to Campbell's right.

The hair color. His eyes. The smile. Why did he look so damn familiar?

If they had crossed paths—maybe at a wedding or event— wouldn't she have remembered him? Yes. She'd been avoiding most of the male species before going on a blind date in October. Still, it's not like she'd been dead the last few years.

"I'm Scott Mayhew."

Campbell froze.

"Darcy was in a recent skiing accident. She's going to be fine," he swiftly added, "but she'll be out for weeks for recovery and rehabilitation. As such, I'm afraid you'll be stuck with me this semester." He leaned forward. "I'm not as nice as Darcy."

"I sure hope not," the girl mumbled. "I'd be happy to be stuck with him anywhere."

Campbell squinted at Scott Mayhew.

That's why he looked so familiar. He was Felicity Mayhew's *brother*.

While he passed out the syllabus, her mind rewound to March of last year.

Felicity, the most sought after wedding coordinator in the Denver metro area, had walked into Daisy's Bouquets, the flower shop she worked at, and changed the business's future to the fantastic in a matter of minutes. During the visit, she'd mentioned her brother *Scott,* the ultimate reason Felicity had ended up at Daisy's Bouquets.

Campbell grasped the syllabus the student sitting two desks in front of her handed over.

Felicity's head-turning-hot brother would be her lit professor for the next sixteen weeks?

He sat on the desk and held up the extra copies of the syllabus. "Now for the fun part. Going over in depth what you signed up for from now until May."

Campbell stared at the first page which had his name at the top in bold, black print with the course name underneath; his work e-mail and office phone number were the third line.

"This is a required course," he continued, "but I do hope at least a quarter of you like to read since you'll be doing quite a bit, starting tonight. First reading assignment will be due when we meet again on Thursday. But we'll talk more about it when we get to the assignment section of the syllabus."

The girl expelled a quick sigh, then her phone went off.

Scott's gaze shifted to Campbell, and their eyes locked.

Her breathing slowed before he focused on the girl and grinned.

"This would be a great time to address phones in the classroom."

The girl's face became the color of Campbell's hat.

"We're all adults here with busy lives," he easily began. "And shit happens. But for the sake of respecting this classroom as a place of learning, please put your phones on silent. If for some reason keeping your phone on silent isn't possible, we can talk about it after class."

Campbell joined her classmates in silencing her phone.

"Excellent." His grin grew. "Top of page one. That's me, the course name, and my contact info. I also have my office hours listed here. You can call me Scott. I don't hold a doctorate in English, so no Dr. Mayhew. And please no Mr. Mayhew, either. Way too formal."

"Think *Scott* offers private tutoring during his office hours?" the girl softly asked Campbell. "This might end up being the first semester I come to every class."

Campbell gave her a slight smile.

She planned on coming to every class, but for different reasons. As he reviewed the course description, though, she couldn't escape the fact that having a professor like Scott Mayhew would make a class like this much more bearable. He didn't know it, but they did have a connection, too. Not a super strong one by any means.

"Page two"—Scott flipped his copy's page—"assignments, projects, tests, and quizzes."

Campbell eyed him while he discussed their first reading assignment.

His eye-catching looks aside, Scott seemed like a genuinely nice guy. Affable. Outgoing.

What would she have to lose by saying hi, and introducing herself and her connection to his sister? It's not like Campbell expected preferential treatment for knowing and working with Felicity. It was also a new year, full of possibilities.

Positive possibilities which included no longer lingering in the shadows of her past life.

She softly smiled and focused on again being a college student. Excitement then wound through her as he went over the rest of page two.

SCOTT REACHED into his laptop bag and withdrew his phone while the students filed from the classroom. His eyes widened at his missed call and started to return it when he heard "Hi" from right behind him.

He turned at the soft voice.

A petite woman, easily in her mid to late twenties with large, bright blue eyes and long, dark-blonde hair poking out from underneath a red hat, gave him a tentative smile.

"I know you," she said, followed by a quick laugh. "I mean, I know of you through two people who do know you."

He raised his eyebrows. "I get that a lot."

Her cheeks flushed as she released a quick breath. "I'm sorry. That didn't make any sense, did it?"

His phone buzzed once, indicating the caller had left a voice-mail he really needed to check. At the same time, the woman in front of him was not only his new student but for some reason seemed nervous. So he sat on the desk's edge and said, "It made perfect sense. I'm also intrigued by how you know of me through two people who do know me."

She sighed and held out her hand. "I'm Campbell Grey."

Scott grasped her hand and gave her ice-cold fingers a quick squeeze. "You may have to wear gloves during class. They don't keep these rooms very warm."

"My hands are always cold. I'm always cold. But anyway"— she released his hand—"I work at Daisy's Bouquets. We work with your sister, Felicity, quite a bit."

He nodded. "Gotcha. It's nice to meet you." And because his sister knew at least half the Denver metro area's population, it had only been a matter of time before someone in her working sphere would end up as one of his students. But the shop's name did sound vaguely familiar. "Daisy's Bouquets. Why do I know that name?"

Campbell smiled. "You met my boss, Alyson, at a wedding at the Ritz-Carlton last year. She's the second person I know you through who does know you." She cringed. "She doesn't *know* you like your sister does, of course."

Scott couldn't help but grin at her cheeks flushing once more. Coupled with her deep red hat, it was quite…appealing.

She stepped to her right. "In any case, I just wanted to say hi and introduce myself."

He blinked twice.

Appealing? Where the hell had that come from?

Suddenly, his memory presented the Ritz-Carlton wedding Felicity had dragged him to almost a year ago as a way to piss off a *delightful* woman he'd dated for far too long who became his sister's ex-florist following that day. And all because a woman dressed like an iconic character from an iconic story had captured his attention.

"Right," he answered. "The Ritz-Carlton wedding. It's all coming back to me. But I believe at that time your boss, Alyson, was going by the name Holly Golightly."

Campbell lifted her shoulders. "Yes. And I never did get the full story from Alyson or her business partner, Jillian, who's my other boss."

"It was definitely an interesting day," he added under his breath.

"It sounded like you're ultimately the reason Daisy's Bouquets ended up partnering with Felicity." She gave him a blinding smile. "Thank you for whatever you said to your sister."

"All I did was tell her the truth. But you're welcome." He paused before saying, "Alyson and Daisy's Bouquets. *Holly.* Is she the one who just got married? Felicity mentioned something about it when I saw her at Christmas."

"That was Alyson. She and her husband actually just came back from their honeymoon."

"Very cool." Scott stood and grasped the strap of his laptop bag. As much as he genuinely enjoying talking to students—genuinely liked the fact Campbell had introduced herself—he had a call he needed to return. But still not wanting to be rude, he asked, "Are you a returning-to-college student or new to school?"

"Finally returning to college after being away too long."

They fell into step beside one another.

"Nice. Are you looking forward to the class? It gets better after today."

"Honestly?"

He followed her from the room. "I thrive off of honesty from students."

She stopped and faced him. "I think it's going to be boring. No offense," she hastily added. "I flipped through the text books and most of the stories and poetry and plays were written by dead *white guys*."

Scott fought a smile as he said, "True. But after going over the syllabus, you know we will be reading and discussing several black and women writers, as well."

She smirked. "True. But not nearly enough."

He stopped fighting his smile.

"I'm not saying any of this because I hate reading," she continued. "I love reading. I'm a total book nerd. Reading literature isn't the same thing, though."

"Okay. Argument understood." He leaned forward. "So what do you like to read?"

Her cheeks flushed for the third time.

He laughed. "I think I can guess by the look on your face and you don't have to be embarrassed."

"I don't only read romance," she mumbled. "I love almost all genres of fiction. The point is, I read because I want to be entertained. Transported to another world and life."

"I believe that's why most people read," he challenged. "It's certainly why I love to read. I promise you can do that with classic literature." He grinned. "You'll see."

"Maybe." She stepped backward. "I have to get back to work. But thanks for the chat. I'll see you Thursday." She turned from him.

Scott couldn't stop himself from saying, "Campbell?"

She stopped and looked at him over her left shoulder.

Their gazes snapped together.

Something deep inside of him fluttered before he said, "You've heard of Jane Austen?"

"Of course. I've just never read her books."

He stepped back. "Well, you like romance and as a literature professional, I'm making the statement she—along with the Brontë sisters—could be considered the first romance novelists. Especially Austen and Charlotte Brontë."

She grinned. "So as a literature professional, you're recommending their books?"

"If you find yourself with some spare time, yes. But this class will keep you pretty busy." He took another step back. "And on that note, happy reading." He turned and walked swiftly in the opposite direction.

Flutters weren't allowed. Never allowed. So where the hell had the flutter come from? On top of being his *student*, she wasn't even his type, physically speaking.

He'd been lonely too long.

Was there a song title in there somewhere?

Scott shook his head.

It's where this had to be coming from. He'd also always enjoyed passionate conversations about literature and reading. Okay. Campbell Grey happened to be a beautiful woman with the biggest, bluest eyes he'd ever seen in his life. He viewed her opinion on classic literature as an unspoken challenge, too, especially since she'd called herself a "book nerd." And he'd always liked a good challenge.

His steps slowed while he tapped the voicemail icon.

Right now, however, something way more important needed his attention. But as he listened to the message, he closed his eyes and released a heavy sigh.

The rest of his day wouldn't be going as planned.

Chapter Two

ALYSON AND JILLIAN stared at Campbell with round eyes from where they stood on the opposite side of the shop's backroom work table.

"Anyway"—Campbell stuck a white rose in the anniversary bouquet she was creating—"crazy, right? Scott seems really nice, though. I think the class will be okay." Only because he happened to be the instructor. She'd also be lying to herself if she didn't acknowledge his strongly spoken words about classic literature offering escape had piqued her curiosity a bit.

Jillian shook her head which caused her dark ponytail to flip back-and-forth. "How can the Denver metro area be so damn big and small at the same time?"

"I don't know, but he remembered *you*." Campbell used a red rose to point at Alyson.

Her boss's incredibly tan face from her honeymoon in Maui turned the color of the rose Campbell held as Jillian laughed.

"Are you two ever going to tell me the truth about that day?" Campbell asked. "It is the reason Felicity walked in here and changed everyone's lives in a matter of minutes."

Jillian glanced at Alyson. "After stepping up in the fall while I was gone and while you were on your honeymoon and me *again* while Jackson and I are in Argentina, I think she's earned the whole story."

Alyson gathered her long, auburn hair, then twisted it into a knot on her head which she fastened with a hair tie. "Definitely," she said while nodding.

Campbell smiled, put down another white rose, and leaned forward.

"Drinking needs to be involved, though," Jillian added. "We'll do a girls night when I get back? I have so much to do between today and Thursday."

Campbell's shoulders slumped. "Fine. But I'm not going to let this go." Recalling her conversation with Scott not an hour earlier, she said, "Scott did mumble something about it 'being an interesting day'."

Jillian arched her right eyebrow and focused on Alyson, who focused on Campbell.

"I promise you'll get the whole story when Jilly's back in a couple of weeks," Alyson vowed. "In the meantime, we have something—"

Campbell's phone dinged and buzzed. She pulled it from her back jeans pocket.

How'd it go today, Miss College Student?

"Could that be *Niall*?" Jillian asked with a wicked inflection.

Campbell shot her a tight smile and nodded.

Really well. Talk later? I'm at work.

She shoved her phone back into her pocket and picked up the white rose she added to the enormous bouquet.

"I'm really glad you two are still having fun." Jillian gave Campbell a warm smile. "I honestly wasn't sure if you two would connect, but it's obvious you have."

Campbell could never put the word connected with herself and Niall Donnelly.

When Jillian had approached Campbell for the third time in late October about "having some fun with Niall," followed closely by encouragement Campbell had received from her roommates, she'd acquiesced, wanting to take a substantial step forward in her Denver life. A blind date with Niall had happened soon thereafter. Despite being beyond easy on the eyes and a good kisser, she and Niall had very little in common. But since her last choice in a guy had ended up as a horrible and bitter disappointment, she hadn't remotely been interested in anything serious the last few years. So "having fun" with Niall had seemed like the right choice.

A few months later, however, it no longer felt right.

Her phone again dinged and buzzed with his response, but she remained focused on the anniversary bouquet scheduled to be delivered later to the woman's office.

"As I was saying," Alyson continued, "Jilly and I have something for you."

Campbell lifted her gaze from the bouquet to find her bosses giving her huge smiles.

Alyson presented her with a card sealed tightly inside a red envelope. "We meant to give this to you at Christmastime, but you know how *insane* everything became around here."

Yes. Between the weddings, including Alyson's to her now husband David on New Year's Eve, holiday parties, and the everyday bouquets, the shop hadn't experienced a moment of quiet until New Year's Day when they'd been—thankfully—closed.

"Then David and I left for our honeymoon, and I wanted to be here for this."

"Open it," Jillian urged around a quick laugh.

Campbell giggled, tore into the envelope, and withdrew a Christmas card with a "thank you for your hard work" message on the front. She then opened it and—

She inhaled sharply at the check written out to her from Daisy's Bouquets *and* the hugely generous amount they'd given her.

"Oh, my God." She looked up and caught their eyes. "What is this?" It had to be so much more than a belated Christmas gift from her bosses.

Jillian grinned. "In corporate America they call it a yearly bonus."

Campbell's mouth inched open.

"But we're calling it a *Daisy's* bonus," Alyson interjected, "which you more than deserve after last year."

A year with a couple of extreme lows but several incredible highs.

"We're giving one to Hayley, too, but you're our only other full-time employee." Alyson leaned forward. "You especially saved the shop *and* us the last few months of the year, too."

"*Absolutamente*," Jillian murmured.

Tears burned Campbell's eyes which turned the card and hugely generous check she held into a watery blur of gray and white and red.

For the first time since relocating to Denver from her hometown of Durango, located several hours away in the southwest corner of the state, guilt nearly knocked Campbell to the floor. The feeling so overwhelming she lost her breath. "Thank you," the whispered words were all she could manage at that moment.

Alyson and Jillian wrapped her in a tight hug which Campbell readily returned.

At some point, Alyson Douglas—now Preston—and Jillian Castillo had become more than her bosses. More than her friends, even; friendship being a gift she hadn't possessed in her previous life. Just like Campbell's roommates, Alyson and Jillian had become her Denver family.

The realizations caused another round of guilt to envelop her as Alyson and Jillian pulled away and gave her affectionate smiles.

"Alright. Back to business." Alyson faced Jillian. "With you leaving in less than two days and being gone two weeks, we need to come up with another schedule now that we have two lovely employees in college."

Campbell sniffed a few times, placed the card and check on the work table, and swiped underneath her eyes.

"Campbell, we'd love your help with writing that schedule," Alyson added. "It's pretty quiet around here right now, but Valentine's Day is less than a month away…on top of the weddings and everything else."

"I'd love to help," Campbell softly said. "Thank you for asking."

Alyson and Jillian headed for the desk in a front corner of the backroom. A tight fit with the work table taking up a good portion of the room. But any spot in the back offered an uninhibited view of the actual shop decorated with bright pink and red flower arrangements, and balloons and stuffed animals, for Valentine's Day. This space, located on a semi-quiet street in the Sloan's Lake neighborhood, was cozier than their last place in the Highlands. At some point, though, Daisy's Bouquets had become Campbell's second Denver home.

Amazing, loyal friends who'd turned into a second family.

A job she loved so much she considered the place a second home.

A guy in her life for the first time since well-before leaving her actual family in Durango.

A college student for the first time since another guy turned her life upside down.

Campbell took a shaky breath as the truth hit.

She'd created a second life in Denver over the last year-and-a-half and no one knew the *real* Campbell Grey. Or the real reason she'd ended up here.

A new year full of positive possibilities…that would have to include giving them the full story, sooner rather than later. But all she wanted at this moment was to continue reveling in the goodness she'd cultivated after leaving Durango.

THE PRINCIPAL GAVE Peyton an encouraging smile, then quietly asked, "Would you like to tell your dad what happened?"

Scott glanced at his daughter sitting in the chair next to him and his heart splintered at her red, tear-stained face as she continued to sniffle.

She vehemently shook her head at the principal's question which made her strawberry-blonde pigtails slap her wet cheeks.

He slid his gaze back to the older woman who turned her smile on him.

"There's a boy in Peyton's kindergarten class who likes her which is how this began."

Scott eyed his daughter still sniffling; her trembling, tiny body clothed in a bright pink dress she'd picked out when he'd taken her shopping for school clothes in August.

A boy liked her? *Already*?

Yeah. In Scott's eyes, she was definitely the cutest, funniest, smartest, five-year-old girl on the planet. But he sure as shit wasn't ready for this…and probably never would be ready.

"According to what Peyton told the teachers on recess duty," the principal calmly continued, "the boy was chasing her around the playground."

So little boys still thought chasing girls around at recess would win their hearts.

"And trying to kiss her," the woman swiftly added.

Scott straightened.

Okay. He'd never done that at the age of five. Any age, for that matter.

He again glanced at his beautiful, innocent daughter whose face had turned even redder while tears started to stream from her chestnut eyes once more.

"I'm confused"—he faced the principal—"as to why Peyton's in your office since she was the one experiencing the unwanted attention from a boy in her class." More like being harassed by a persistent little shit.

"I'm getting to that." The woman folded her hands on her desk. "Please know Peyton did the right thing by letting the teachers know what was going on since that behavior is unacceptable. We will be talking to the boy and his parents, as well."

Scott slowly nodded while somehow stopping himself from saying, "*Better you than me.*"

"Unfortunately, after the teachers spoke to the boy there was another incident between him and Peyton."

"He…he called me…a s-snitch," Peyton said around a fresh wave of tears.

"Which is also unacceptable," the principal interjected. "But Peyton's response to that was to kick the boy in a…very sensitive spot."

Scott cleared his throat at the image. And to stop his laughter.

"We can't have behavior like that, either," the principal finished.

He paused long enough to swallow his remaining humor, then solemnly said, "I understand." More like he understood his daughter was—without a doubt—a Mayhew.

Her Aunt Felicity would especially love hearing this story.

"Peyton's been quite upset and doesn't want to go back to her classroom." The woman gave him a tight smile. "She told us she was with you this week, but when you didn't answer we thought it best to also call her mom. But she didn't answer, either."

"It's fine. Thank you for calling us, Mrs. Atkin." He scooted forward in his chair. "Her mom's out of town on business. I'll let her know what's going on." He stood, and the woman copied his actions. "I'll talk to Peyton about all of this, too." He held out his hand and they shook. "It won't happen again."

His five-year-old daughter had every right to stand up for herself to an obnoxious kid, but she did have to learn kicking boys in the balls wasn't necessary *most* of the time.

"We do love having Peyton here." The principal smiled warmly at his daughter. "Her teachers and friends absolutely love her."

Peyton came to her feet and picked up her Hello Kitty backpack and matching lunch bag.

"Thank you, Mrs. Atkin. I appreciate hearing that."

Minutes later, Peyton buckled herself into her booster seat situated in the backseat of his SUV. Then started sniffling once again.

Scott started the engine before facing her. "Honey, please stop crying. I promise you're not in trouble."

"But I was in...Mrs. Atkin's...office," she managed around her choppy breathing.

He went into his glove box where he kept tissues, retrieved one, and handed it to his little girl he wanted to pull into his arms and hold for as long as humanly possible.

"Peyton, you heard Mrs. Atkin say you did the right thing by telling the teachers what was going on."

She wiped her nose with the back of her hand holding the tissue. "I hate boys."

Good girl. But he said, "Not all boys act like that." It was mostly the truth, too.

"Did you?"

"Of course not." Though he had chased a girl or two around the playground, but not in kindergarten. And he'd never chased a girl as a way to get a kiss. Only persistent little shits behaved that way and deserved to be kicked by girls. He still had to say, "It's good you stood up for yourself, but you shouldn't have kicked him anywhere. You can't do that again, okay?" Not in a situation like this, anyway.

When she became a teenager, however, this conversation would be wholly different.

She released a heavy sigh. "Okay. But I was mad. Daddy, he called me a snitch."

That did seem harsh for kindergarten. Was the word "tattle-tale" now obsolete?

He opened his mouth to respond when his phone burst into song inside his coat pocket.

"I just got off the phone with Mrs. Atkin's assistant who said you two had left," Peyton's mom and his ex stated after he answered. "What happened? Is she okay?"

Scott put his SUV in drive, pulled out of the parking spot, and launched into the story.

When he finished, she said, "That boy deserves to be suspended for treating a little girl like that."

He kept a sigh in check. "Shannon, he's also five. Maybe six. And Mrs. Atkin assured me they're handling it."

"Fine." A long pause fell on her end before he heard, "Peyton was well within her right to defend herself, but she still has to learn resorting to violence isn't appropriate."

Violence? It's not like she'd organized and participated in a playground rumble.

"I took care of it," he answered.

"Good. Give her a great big hug for me. How was the first day of classes?"

The memory of two big, beautiful blue eyes drifted through his head—

Scott stopped the image, shoved it to the back of his mind, and buried it.

He needed a damn life outside of fatherhood and Jefferson County Community College.

"I only have the one lit class on Tuesdays and Thursdays, but it'll be good. Mondays and Wednesdays are my busy days this semester. How's the conference?"

"I'm learning all about the latest drugs that will make a person's life their idea of perfect." She laughed. "There's a new and even better drug for erectile dysfunction causing some pretty heated chatter among the female pharmacists. Of course, I instantly thought of you."

He plastered a smile on his face and said, "You must have me confused with your current boyfriend. But it's always a pleasure, Shannon. I'm hanging up now." He lowered his phone and ended the call.

If not for Peyton, he would have come back with something much more colorful for his ex who just couldn't help herself when it came to her "friendly" teasing.

"I owe you a big hug from your mom when we get home."

Peyton continued to stare glumly out of the window. Which meant at this point only one thing would put a smile back on her face.

"It feels like that time, don't you think?"

She turned her head ever so slightly in his direction. "Disney karaoke?" Her eyes, already a bit brighter, met his in the mirror. "Can we sing 'Do You Want to Build a Snowman?'"

He nodded. "Perfect choice, too, since it's supposed to snow tomorrow."

They were singing their third song, "Hakuna Matata," as he drove into his garage when his phone again burst to life.

He cringed at the caller's name while putting his SUV into park.

"Baby," he said to Peyton still loudly singing, "hit your pause button for a sec. I need to answer this."

She switched to quietly humming along with the music while he lowered the volume.

"I'm really sorry I missed the staff meeting," he answered. "It couldn't be helped."

"Don't worry about it," his boss, Johanna, replied. "Is Peyton okay?"

"She'll be fine. What'd I miss?"

"It's actually why I'm calling. Turns out there's going to be a big opening in the department after spring break."

Scott halted.

"It's official. Marisol won't be coming back after she has the baby."

He sat back. "Wow. She decided to leave?"

"She wants to be at home with her kids. That means I'll need an assistant department chair when we come back from the break. I know this is only your second semester with us, but you've already made quite an impression. Stepping in for Darcy without hesitation helped. You interested in pursuing it?"

He loved teaching, but the atypical work hours, and the hours upon hours of grading, were starting to become tiresome. The assistant department chair position, on the other hand, would be less teaching and grading, more administrative, and come with better hours *and* pay.

"Scott? Did I lose you?"

"No, I'm here." He caught Peyton's eyes in the rearview mirror which were back to bright with happiness. He smiled, then said, "And yes. I'm very interested. I have a break tomorrow between eleven and one. Can we meet up for lunch and talk about it?"

The better hours and less grading ultimately meant more time with his daughter.

"You're on. Let me know where and what time."

"Will do." He ended the call.

Scott Mayhew, M.A., Assistant English Department Chair did sound pretty damn good in his head, too, and his smile grew as he climbed out of his SUV.

Chapter Three

CAMPBELL'S EYES drooped as she tried to read Walt Whitman's "Song of Myself." Scott's assignment hadn't been to read this particular poem. He'd told them to choose one of the many Whitman poems in the book and come prepared on Thursday to discuss it in class. Wanting to challenge herself, she'd chosen "Song of Myself" which had to be the longest, most boring poem she'd ever tried to read. Between that and the fact she didn't like poetry—at all—she seemed to be failing miserably at her first assignment in years as a college student.

She sighed, shut the heavy book with a *slap*, and put it aside. She then reached right and swiped her phone off of her nightstand.

Campbell needed to hear her voice. She also had something heavy on her mind.

"Hi, Sweetie," her mom answered. "I was hoping I'd hear from you today. How was your first day at school?"

Campbell grinned. "I'm back in college, Mom. Not kindergarten."

"Okay," her mom amended, "how did it feel to be back in a college classroom? Is that better, smart aleck?"

"Much." Campbell nestled into her pillows. "I'm not super excited about the class, but the instructor's very cool." And very hot. "He's actually Felicity Mayhew's brother."

"Oh. She's the fancy wedding planner?"

"Yeah."

Campbell couldn't help but think he had to be younger than Felicity since she had such a take charge, commanding presence. When she entered a room, everyone knew it. Scott, though definitely confident, gave off a much more mellow vibe. Felicity had also said some things about Scott the day she'd walked into the shop strongly implying she was his protective big sister.

Something Campbell understood.

"Well isn't that a fortuitous twist. And how's the shop?"

Her grin slipped, though she said, "Really, really good." She paused for two breaths before adding, "Mom, Alyson and Jillian gave me a huge bonus because of how crazy last year was, especially the last few months."

Her mom laughed. "Sweetie, that's wonderful. And so nice of them, too. I hope you save the money for a retail therapy day with Blaine."

Campbell cracked a smile at picturing the look on her roommate's face when she told him about the bonus. He probably would suggest shopping and expect her to buy lunch. But she had something way different in mind for the money.

"Actually," she said, "I want to pay for you and Evan to spend a week here in Denver. You two could come during spring break in late March."

Her mom fell silent.

"Please?" Campbell persisted. "I miss you guys so much and I'm still bummed you couldn't get here for Christmas." She also hadn't seen her mom and brother since leaving Durango due to everyone's busy lives and work schedules, as well as other reasons.

"We miss you, too, but that money is yours. I can't let you spend it on me and your brother. You *earned* it and should spend it on yourself." She released a quick laugh. "I'm not sure we could get Evan to leave Durango. You know he's in love yet again and is enjoying his job."

She nodded. "I know, but I have everything I need."

"You know, you could use it as a deposit on your own place," her mom quietly suggested. "I know how much you love having Blaine and Lance as roommates, but I do remember you saying that Alyson and Jillian gave you a substantial raise last summer."

Campbell frowned. "I'm going to need at least one more raise before I can think about having my own place. And I do love living with the guys." They were part of her Denver family.

Just like Alyson and Jillian. She and Hayley had even become close the last year or so.

Guilt again settled itself onto Campbell's shoulders, followed by another thought.

"Then I'll come home for spring break."

Probably risky. But only because her ex-bastard had returned to the Durango area, where his family still lived, after being gone for months to receive "emotional and mental help." That's all she knew, too, as it had happened quickly and quietly. She wanted to see her family, though, and a break from the Denver area wouldn't be a bad thing. It'd give her a chance to get away and clear her head which could be exactly what she needed.

"I'd much rather you spend some of your bonus to bring yourself here for a week than bringing your brother and me to Denver," her mom admitted. "But are you sure you're really ready to come back here?"

No. She certainly wasn't sure, but she'd take the chance to see her family. And maybe…just maybe…going back home to Durango as an entirely different woman would be another huge and necessary step forward.

"It's just one week and I'll keep a very low profile." She'd sacrificed way too damn much to get away from her ex and his inability to let her go to stop being careful now. Still, she added, "I need and want to see you guys. If you won't let me pay for you to vacation here in Denver for a week, than me coming home is the only other option."

Silence fell on her mom's end before Campbell heard, "Nothing has to be decided right now. It's only mid-January. So promise me you'll give it some thought first?"

She expelled a frustrated sigh. "Fine." Though she absolutely understood her mom's hesitancy at both suggestions Campbell had offered, a huge part of her had foreseen this conversation going in an entirely different direction.

A knock on her closed bedroom door, followed by, "Are you decent?" caused her to grin.

Lance's deep voice had, from day one, reminded her of a grizzly bear. If, of course, a grizzly bear had the ability to speak.

"Yeah, come in!" To her mom she said, "Lance is here. Talk in a few days?"

"Of course. Love you. Tell your roomies I said hi."

"Love you, too. Give Evan a hug for me the next time you see him."

With a heavy breath, Campbell ended the call.

Lance walked into her room holding two half-full wine glasses in hands so large they reminded her of a grizzly bear's paws. In fact, Lance's overall hulking size, bald head, and semi-thick, dark beard gave off a whole grizzly bear image.

He handed her a glass. "How's Mom doing? Is she sending more cookies any time soon? Or did you forget to ask?"

Grizzly bear on the outside. Total teddy bear on the inside.

"I forgot to ask, but I can make those cookies. All you have to do is ask nicely." She sipped her wine as he rolled her desk chair toward the right side of her bed. "My mom says hi, by the way."

"Hi, Mom." Lance straddled the chair and pointed at the three books stacked neatly on her nightstand. "I thought you were taking an American Lit class."

She slid her gaze to her newly purchased books and back to him. "I am." She pointed at the textbook on her bed. "Assignment number one is to read a poem by Walt Whitman."

He focused on her. "Then what's with the three books by British authors?"

Jane Austen, and Charlotte and Emily Brontë.

"My lit professor recommended them to me." She peered at him. "I'm also super impressed you know the women were British."

He lifted his thick shoulders. "Just because I didn't finish college doesn't mean I didn't learn anything." He took a large swallow of his wine. "My ex-wife's favorite book is *Wuthering Heights*. She loves the movie, too, but I always fell asleep."

Campbell pressed her lips together and nodded once.

Lance rarely talked about his ex or divorce, the reason he'd ended up here in the house.

He gave his head a hard shake and smiled. "You must like your professor if you rushed out to buy more books that he recommended after only one day of class."

She explained Scott being Felicity's brother and swiftly added, "I do like him. It'll be good." Boring poetry and stories aside, she really believed it.

Lance narrowed his eyes. "He must be good-looking."

Campbell again sipped her wine as she recalled Scott walking confidently into the classroom, dressed like he had been, and his infectious grin before he spoke to the class.

Lance groaned. "Your silence is all the answer I need. But what about the boy toy?"

She glared at him. "His name is Niall." He also happened to be miles away from being her boy toy even though she had a strong feeling he wouldn't mind the job. "Yes, Scott's good-looking but he's my *professor*. There are rules against that."

"A rule that's broken all the time," Lance countered. "No one talks about it, though. Is he at least single? Because if he's married, that would really be—"

"I don't know and we're not talking about this." Still, she hadn't remembered seeing a ring and something about his entire, charming lit professor package seemed to say single.

Lance shrugged and stood. "I have an important call to return." He shot her a huge smile. "Turns out my date from Saturday night didn't ghost me after all."

As he headed for the doorway, she loudly said, "I told you she wouldn't."

"Yeah, yeah," he said while closing the door behind him.

Campbell rested her head against the headboard. She then eyed her textbook and wrinkled her nose. Walt Whitman was patiently waiting for her to return to his "Song of Myself." She needed to be a good student and get back to the assignment.

She rolled her head right and stared at her new books, also calling her name.

Remembering Scott's piercing gaze while suggesting Jane Austen and the Brontë sisters, she reached for the top book.

She shimmied deeper into her pillows and opened *Wuthering Heights*.

With it only being Tuesday night, she could get back to Walt Whitman tomorrow.

SILENCE FILLED the classroom as Scott stared at his students staring at him with damn near blank expressions.

He grinned. "So reading Walt Whitman went that well."

A few students snickered, and his eyes locked with Campbell's.

She grimaced while the girl sitting beside her sighed.

"Don't take this the wrong way," the girl began, "but I was totally bored and really don't remember what I read."

He'd been teaching American Lit long enough that her statement didn't surprise him. Or her honesty. Most students couldn't get into ol' Walt Whitman.

"Something about beating drums?" she added.

Scott sat on the desk. "That would be 'Beat! Beat! Drums!'. One of my favorites, but why did *you* choose it?"

"Um…well…I guess I liked how it started? It caught my attention. All the exclamation points?"

"Exactly." He scanned the classroom. "Did anyone else choose that poem?"

A few hands inched into the air. He couldn't help but notice Campbell didn't raise her hand and—right or wrong—he really wanted to know which poem she'd chosen.

He also couldn't help but like how her light-blue sweater made the blue in her eyes stand out even more.

Scott cleared his throat and asked, "Is it safe to say you chose the poem for the same reasons as your classmate?" He needed to stay focused.

The students looked at each other, then shrugged and nodded.

"Well, it just so happens," Scott continued, "that poem was originally published in a book where Whitman introduced a new form of poetry—in free verse that he was also known for—where he begins in an exciting, *attention-grabbing* way."

The students continued to stare at him.

Holy shit, this would be a long class.

"Can those of you who read that poem tell me what he was writing about?"

"The Civil War," a guy sitting in the back left corner stated. "I read it in the footnote."

"We have a footnote reader. Excellent." Always a good sign when a student took the time to read the footnotes. "I want to hear from all of you today, so who's going next?"

Silence.

He held on to a sigh. "If no one volunteers, I'll be forced to point at you, make you stand up and introduce yourself, and present that way."

The students' eyes became wide while they looked at each other, and Scott somehow suppressed his laughter. Then, very slowly, Campbell lifted her right hand.

Fantastic.

"It appears we have a volunteer."

Her cheeks flushed and damn him for still finding it appealing.

"Do I have to stand up and introduce myself?" she asked.

"Not this time. Which poem did you choose?"

What the hell was wrong with him? He was a professional and always had been.

"I initially chose 'Song of Myself'. The first version in the book."

He raised his eyebrows. "That was certainly ambitious." Completely surprising, too, since she'd made it clear what she thought of this class. "How'd it go?"

She paused, angled her head toward the girl sitting beside her, and said, "I also got bored, don't really remember what I read, and couldn't even finish it."

He laughed. "That's fair."

"So I read 'Once I Pass'd through a Populous City' and not because it was extremely short." She grinned. "I really liked the title."

"Good. And what'd you think?"

Her grin became soft. "Honestly, I thought it was kind of romantic."

Of course she did. And damn him if he didn't find that appealing, as well.

"I read that one, too," another girl, sitting near the front, offered. "It's so simple, but beautiful at the same time."

"Yes. But did you read the footnote?" Campbell asked the girl.

A footnote reader, too, and yet another—

Scott grabbed his water bottle and took a swift drink.

This had to be a sign he needed to give app dating another shot.

The girl shook her head.

Campbell focused on him. "According to the footnote, the publisher made him change 'man' to 'woman'."

He nodded.

"So Walt Whitman was gay?" the girl asked.

The students went back to silently staring at him.

He lifted his shoulders. "No one knows for sure. But Whitman *was* an advocate for sexual tolerance and freedom, and explored these ideas in his poetry." He leaned forward. "A brilliant man and mind definitely ahead of his time, but didn't always make his poetry popular."

"That's cool and all," the guy in the back left corner interjected, "but what I want to know is why one of his best poems isn't in this book."

Scott smiled. "'O Captain! My Captain!'."

The guy pointed at Scott. "That's the one I was hoping to read for this assignment, but it's not in the book which is *weird*." He looked at his classmates. "*Dead Poets Society*. Best movie ever. Even if you don't like poetry."

At least two students who read footnotes and one who'd just

plugged one of Scott's favorite movies? Maybe this would end up being a damn good class as the semester progressed.

Okay. Experiencing an explicable…and inappropriate…pull toward a female student for the first time since becoming a college instructor hadn't been expected. But there was a first time for everything and he'd undoubtedly get over it.

"I'm glad you mentioned 'O Captain! My Captain!'." Scott picked up a stack of papers beside him on the desk. "Because we're going to shift gears for a bit to read and discuss Whitman's poem for Abraham Lincoln." He stood and pointed at his student. "By the way, I agree with what you said about *Dead Poets Society*."

The guy smiled and gave his classmates an "I told you so" look.

"If we've never seen the movie," the girl next to Campbell began, "can we get extra credit for watching and writing about it?"

Scott fought a smile as he started to hand out copies of the poem. He opened his mouth to answer her when a book on Campbell's desk caught his attention.

Based on the placement of the bookmark, she appeared to be a quarter of the way into the story. She must have bought the book some time between Tuesday after class and last night.

Well, *shit* if that wasn't another surprise from the woman who hadn't been at all interested in reading classic literature two days ago at this time.

"Soooo, what about the extra credit?"

He yanked his gaze from the book and went back to passing out the copies. "How about we talk extra credit if it comes to that? It's only Day Two of a sixteen-week semester."

The girl nodded and shrugged.

Campbell Grey definitely kept catching him off guard—in more ways than one—and he'd always liked a beautiful woman full of surprises. But instructors dating their students not only went against the college's strict policy, but his personal code of ethics.

All of it meant this would be the longest semester of his college-instructing life.

Chapter Four

CAMPBELL EYED Scott talking easily with the guy who'd mentioned *Dead Poets Society*. She'd heard of the movie, but hadn't seen it. Based on the title, and not being into poetry, she'd never felt the strong urge to give up two hours of her life to watch the movie.

She slid her notebook into her backpack with the copy of "O Captain! My Captain!" tucked safely inside. Just like "Once I Pass'd through a Populous City," she'd taken to another Walt Whitman poem. Since Scott also liked the movie where the poem seemed to be pretty important, maybe she needed to give it a chance, too.

Blaine, once he returned from his trip, would probably watch it with her. She couldn't imagine Lance sitting down to watch a movie called *Dead Poets Society*.

Scott and her classmate ended their conversation as she stood. She then headed Scott's way. As he packed up his laptop bag, she couldn't ignore how *good* he looked in his black, V-neck sweater with the sleeves pushed to his elbows, showing off his forearms with the perfect amount of hair almost the same color as the thick, deep copper strands on his head.

Her breathing slowed when she reached the desk.

He looked up and his chestnut eyes connected with hers.

"Hey. Good job today." He followed his compliment up with his infectious smile.

If Scott Mayhew was single, Campbell had no idea how that could be possible. He *wasn't* wearing a ring, either. At the same time, she had no business wondering about his personal life.

Him, professor. Her, student. There were rules against them being anything more. So end of story. Or stanza, in the spirit of poetry.

"Thanks. Today was a great class."

His smile grew. "I appreciate hearing that. I never know how it's going to go with students when it comes to good ol' Walt Whitman."

She laughed. A little on the loud side, too.

He raised his eyebrows.

Her face became the temperature of boiling. She needed to leave before she embarrassed herself by really turning into a teenage, college freshman mooning over her hot lit professor.

She was a twenty-eight-year-old woman who'd already lived one lifetime in Durango.

Campbell stepped to the right. "After this class, I'm actually looking forward to reading Emily Dickinson. See you Tuesday." She faced the classroom's doorway.

"Speaking of *Emilys*, how are you liking *Wuthering Heights*?"

She halted mid-step, turned, and smiled.

So he had seen the book where she'd intentionally left it after he'd walked into class.

"Honestly, I think Heathcliff is way too good for Catherine." She faced him. "I hate her."

Fighting a smile, he leaned forward. "But she does love him."

She crossed her arms. "She has a screwed up way of showing it. In fact, I hate most of the characters." He laughed, and she added, "Based on the way the book began, I'm going to probably end up hating Heathcliff, too, even though he's the victim."

"Not all victims act sympathetically. Especially in literature." He picked up his laptop bag. "You said you hate most of the characters, but what do you think of the book overall?"

They walked side-by-side until they reached the doorway where Scott paused to let her walk in front of him. Just like he'd done on Tuesday.

"It is a classic, British book," he continued, "and I believe you said something about not being entertained by literature at around this time on Tuesday?"

She fought a smile at the humor in his voice. "Is that your way of saying 'I told you so'?" They stopped outside the classroom as a few students walked by. "If it is, that's not very…*professorly*… of you."

"That's a cool new word, but are you avoiding the question?"

Campbell lifted her chin. "Yes, Mr. Mayhew. Even though I hate most of the characters and know this story won't end happily, Emily Brontë hooked me." She laughed. "I even like the dark, somber, cold setting." She paused before adding, "It fits their love story."

He grinned. "Excellent. But please don't call me Mr. Mayhew ever again. I honestly mean it when I tell students to call me by my first name."

She returned his smile. "Okay, *Scott*." Saying his name did sound much better.

Such a nice, strong name. *Scott*. And, dammit, she might as well be an eighteen-year-old college freshman.

Scott thumbed over his right shoulder. "I'm headed upstairs to my office." He stepped back. "I hope you like reading Emily Dickinson." He turned to leave.

"I also bought *Sense and Sensibility* and *Jane Eyre*."

Scott stopped and glanced at her. "That's great. I hope you'll let me know what you think of those books, too?"

"Absolutely." She hesitated, gave him a quick smile, then turned.

"Campbell?"

She faced him, her breathing once again slowing when their eyes met.

"Since you're expanding your reading world," he slowly began, "can I make another suggestion? Another female writer I think you'd really like?"

She nodded. "Yes. Of course." He did happen to be the literature professional and certainly hadn't steered her in the wrong direction when it came to Emily Brontë.

"Kate Chopin."

She frowned.

"We're going to be reading two of her short stories in a couple of weeks or so." The corner of his mouth lifted in a slight smile. "Since you seem to like strong female writers, I think you'd enjoy her book *The Awakening*."

She smiled. "I do like the title."

"I have a copy of it at home, if you're interested?"

"Really?" She laughed. "That'd be great. Thank you."

He took another step back. "I'll see you Tuesday."

Campbell paused long enough to admire how good he looked in his snug jeans.

Handsome, smart, successful, charming, and mature.

There could be no way in hell that man was single. It shouldn't matter to her, either.

As she walked in the opposite direction, though, Campbell couldn't help but imagine what it would be like to be with a *man* for a change; not a "boy toy."

And Scott Mayhew absolutely qualified as a man.

"DADDY, you need to wear a crown like I am."

Peyton presented Scott with a pale-pink, sparkly tiara that she then placed on his head.

He straightened and waggled his eyebrows. "How do I look?"

She released a series of high-pitched giggles he'd fallen in love with when she'd been a toddler. A sound he could never hear enough.

"Are you laughing at me, your Highness?" He reached out and tickled her which caused her to squeal. "The crown was your idea."

She wriggled out of his grasp and walked to the kitchen island counter where she picked up a pot. "I made us dinner." She carefully carried the pot back to the table.

"And what did you make us?" That she must have "made" while he'd been dealing with the laundry.

"It's a surprise." She set the pot on the table and smiled. "It's my own recipe."

He nodded, then leaned forward to peer inside the pot. To find what looked like all of the cookies from the jar filling most of the pot. They'd also been doused in chocolate syrup.

Obviously, he'd have to rethink where he kept the cookies and the syrup from this moment moving forward. Princess Peyton was not only growing but clearly getting very comfortable using the step stool he kept in the hall closet.

"It looks delicious," he said while trying not to wince at the fact "dinner" would be so much fun to clean up after she went to bed.

"How many scoops would you like?"

He paused to find the correct answer when he heard his front door open, followed by, "I'm here and I brought a little surprise!"

Peyton's face brightened. "Princess Belle." She turned and raced down the stairs.

Scott stared at the pot.

Saved by another woman in his life and *her* little princess Peyton had named.

Peyton reappeared cuddling Princess Belle. "Daddy, why can't I have a dog like this."

He sat back at the same time his sister, Felicity, cleared the last step. Though he felt tempted to say Princess Belle the tan, miniature poodle didn't qualify as a *real* dog, he went with his typical, "When you're older." And can handle taking care of a *real* dog.

Felicity, dressed in gym clothes and holding a takeout pizza, stopped and pointed at his head with her free hand. "Love it. Sparkly pink is definitely a good look for you." She held up the pizza. "I brought dinner because it's been an atrocious week."

Peyton hugged Princess Belle as she glanced at her aunt. "But I made dinner. Right, Daddy?" She faced him.

Felicity frowned.

He pointed at the pot. "And it still looks delicious, but I think it's really more dessert."

Peyton shrugged and focused on the dog.

Minutes later, she held a plate with one small slice of cheese pizza and asked him, "Can I go downstairs with Princess Belle and turn on Disney Plus?"

"Yes," he answered. "But please don't spill your food."

"And please don't feed Princess Belle," Felicity added, though they both knew it's what Peyton would do before checking to make sure no one was watching.

He and his sister had caught her doing exactly that a few times.

Felicity handed him a plate with two enormous slices of

pepperoni pizza and joined him at the table. She did, however, pause long enough to peer inside the pot.

She flinched. "I apparently arrived just in time."

"Yeah, I definitely owe you one. Do you want a beer?"

"*Please*. I'll probably need more than one after this week."

He removed the tiara from his head, stood, and went to the fridge. "Yet another rich and spoiled bridezilla driving the usually unflappable Felicity Mayhew to the brink of insanity?"

Though he more than admired the hugely successful business his sister had built from the ground up, Scott would never understand how she could work with the clientele who hired her to plan their ridiculously over-the-top weddings.

Felicity grasped the beer he handed over and took a long swig.

If her rich, spoiled clients saw the real Felicity sitting in his kitchen right now with her hair—the same color as his—pulled up into a messy knot while wearing gym clothes and drinking a beer, they'd probably go into sudden cardiac arrest.

"The bride decided this week—though her wedding is tomorrow evening—that she doesn't like the head table floral arrangements after all." She closed her eyes and inhaled. "But thank goodness I use a brilliant flower shop who can handle anything I throw at them."

Her striking, huge blue eyes appeared in Scott's mind and he couldn't stop himself from asking, "Would the shop be Daisy's Bouquets?"

"Precisely." She grinned. "It's so refreshing to know my little brother does listen to me."

"Occasionally." He took a swig of his own beer, paused, then added, "Campbell Grey is in my Tuesdays and Thursdays American Lit class."

Felicity was about to take a bite of her pizza but stopped. "Isn't that a fun, unexpected twist." She laughed. "You do remember her boss, the owner Alyson, is also—"

"*Yes*," he muttered. "Why the hell does that keep getting mentioned? It was almost a year ago and I talked to her for maybe ten minutes." More like practically threw himself at her since she'd captured his attention in more ways than one.

A beautiful woman full of surprises. It was his kryptonite and always had been.

He bit into his pizza.

Until now when it *couldn't* be that way.

"Campbell's an absolute darling," Felicity continued. "From what I've seen and heard, she doesn't get out and experience life nearly enough."

Which sounded like Campbell was single…and shouldn't matter to him one damn bit.

"She's also a little quiet and reserved."

Not while she voiced her opinions on literature. But Scott stayed silent.

"There's something about her, though." Felicity pursed her lips. "Something…off."

He glanced sharply at his sister. "What do you mean?"

She lifted her shoulders. "Just a feeling there's more to her than what she presents."

It's not like he hadn't experienced that in and after class yesterday. Yet, it sounded as if his sister could be referring to something much deeper than voicing strong opinions on literature.

"You still better be nice to her because I like her quite a bit."

He frowned. "Why would I be any other way?" Despite what he'd told his students on Tuesday about his colleague, Darcy, being nicer, they'd actually lucked out with getting him as their instructor. She had quite the rep in the department for being an intellectually sharp, yet tough and unyielding English professor. Thinking of the department and needing to get far off the topic of Campbell Grey made him say, "I had lunch with my boss,

Johanna, on Wednesday about a new position opening up after spring break."

Felicity smiled. "Really? And what might that position be?"

"Assistant English Department Chair."

Her eyes widened. "Give up teaching? You?"

He shook his head. "I'd still have a couple of classes."

"And probably a tiresome amount of administrative nonsense." She tilted her head right. "Is that really what you want?"

Not entirely. But he said, "Better pay, hours, and far less grading." When he envisioned the less grading, he smiled. "I love the sound of that."

"Certainly." She narrowed her eyes. "But you're too much like Dad."

His smile slipped and he focused on his beer bottle.

"I understand what all of this really means," his sister continued. "More time with Peyton. But you're not going to be truly happy unless you're in the trenches. Just like Dad was."

The big difference was their dad being in the trenches had cost him his life.

"Felicity, being a college instructor is nothing like being in the military. Or a cop."

Their dad had done both and the latter had taken him way too early.

She nodded. "True. But you were in the military first and being in the classroom—the trenches—with the students is where all the real work and brilliance happens." She gave him a soft smile. "It doesn't happen inside an office, sitting at a desk most of the day, answering e-mails and returning phone calls. Or going to one dull meeting after another." She sat back. "My prediction—if you decide to pursue the position and get it—is that you'll be bored senseless after one semester of being in your office more than the classroom." She swallowed some beer. "Mom and Leann will agree with me, too."

Scott remained silent, unable to argue with his sister's statement about the other two important women in his life siding with her on this topic.

He'd been outnumbered for years and in these moments he especially missed their dad.

Getting a male point-of-view rarely happened in his life. He was friendly enough with the few other male instructors in the department, but they were, on average, twenty years older than him. In completely different places in their lives. And most of Scott's real friends—*brothers*—were scattered across the state and country, living their lives. Some were still on active duty or had made a career for themselves in the military.

"Scotty, I'm not advising you to ignore this opportunity. It sounds wonderful."

He lifted his gaze and caught his sister staring at him.

"And I know it would mean better pay and more time with Peyton. But you're doing a fabulous job of balancing everything and she's doing fine." Felicity laughed and pointed at the pot filled with the cookie mess. "She's five and already making dinner."

He joined her laughter.

"She obviously gets her cooking skills from you, too."

He frowned. "Hey, I resent that since I *never* would have added the syrup."

She shook her head. "Just think about what you want—who you really are—before you make a choice?"

In actuality, he'd already made his choice, but he nodded and went back to his pizza.

Scott had nothing to lose, except being in the classroom full time, and too much to gain by going after Assistant English Department Chair. Johanna had made it clear during their lunch meeting the dean would prefer to promote from within, though they'd be posting the position externally. If anyone else in the department had expressed interest, she hadn't told him.

Better pay, better hours, and far less grading? Less classroom-student time aside, it all sounded damn near close to perfect.

If he ended up with the promotion, having more time with his daughter would be worth it.

Chapter Five

HEY. *Feel like getting some dinner tonight?*

Campbell stared at Niall's text and sighed.

She had to be the definition of insane to be reacting this way to a cute guy wanting to have dinner with her on a Saturday night.

Niall seemed to genuinely like her and they did have a few things in common, the big one being they were students. But he was in grad school, working on his MBA. She, on the other hand, happened to be just a college student, picking up where she'd left off several years ago…after meeting and falling for a *boy* who had been her first everything. Months later they'd ended up as husband and wife following a hasty marriage, and his true nature had emerged.

Her ex-bastard had been the charming, tall, handsome guy carefully hiding his dark side and she'd, due to her naiveté, had fallen for every bit of it.

Campbell shook her head which caused the bitter memories to disappear into the farthest place in her mind, right where they belonged. Her gaze then drifted back to her laptop with the Jefferson County Community College's English Department homepage filling the screen.

She couldn't ignore the fact that for the first time since escaping her ex and his obsession with her, a *man* had caught her attention. And the situation wasn't at all convenient. Still, could it really be considered cyberstalking if she wanted to know more about Scott who had to have a pic and bio on the site? It's not like she'd Googled him or tried to find him on social media.

She picked up her coffee mug, sipped, then clicked on the faculty link.

A Department Chair. Assistant Department Chair. Full-time instructors listed in alphabetical order—*Scott Mayhew*.

His e-mail, office phone, and office room number followed his name.

After a few seconds of hesitation, she clicked on the link.

Campbell grinned at the photo of him, dressed similarly to how he'd looked on Tuesday, standing at the front of a classroom and smiling. He appeared to be in the middle of teaching.

She scrolled down to where his bio began with his education.

B.A. in English, Metropolitan State University.

M.A. in English, University of Colorado Denver.

He'd been born and grew up in Colorado Springs where he'd been "raised by three of the classiest, smartest women he knew."

She frowned.

One of the women had to be his mom, one had to be Felicity, and the other…another sister? Maybe a grandmother? It did seem pretty obvious he was the youngest in his family, but no mention of his dad. He'd also—

Her eyes widened at the fact he'd joined the army after graduating from high school and completed his B.A. while in the reserves, having been based out of Fort Carson. A few years after being discharged, he'd enrolled in graduate school.

And nothing more when it came to his time in the military.

Campbell couldn't shake the feeling there had to be way more to his experience in the army than he'd included in his bio.

She pushed the thought aside and continued reading.

Up until last school year, he'd been an English instructor at Red Rocks Community College. He spent his spare time with "the most important person in his life."

She froze.

Scott Mayhew had a five-year-old *daughter*?

"Holy crap," she murmured. "Didn't see that coming."

No mention of a wife or fiancée or any significant other.

Could that make him a divorced, single-working dad?

She sat back and absently drank her coffee.

It would definitely explain why he gave off the single vibe. Campbell and her brother had always come first, having been raised by a divorced, single-working mom. In fact, their mom had rarely dated when they'd been kids.

Handsome, smart, successful, charming, mature, ex-military, and a dad. All of it made Scott Mayhew more than a man—it made him a real-life superhero.

And *way* out of her league, her lit professor or not.

She re-read Niall's text.

Though not her definition of a man, Niall did happen to be fun, a hard worker, and cute.

She typed, *Okay. I have a late wedding today, but I'll text when I'm done.*

Niall was also the first guy she'd been with since turning her life right side up after years of it being upside down. Perhaps fun was all she still needed and could handle right now?

"I thought you were working today."

Campbell turned at the sound of her roommate's voice from her bedroom doorway. "I am, but the wedding's not until six. I'm going into the shop a little later than usual."

Blaine released a huge yawn while running his hand through his thin, light-brown hair sticking up in several directions. "It's a good thing I'm off the next few days because I'm fried."

She swiveled her chair forward at the same time he collapsed onto her unmade bed, then stretched his lean body clothed in navy-blue pajama bottoms and a white T-shirt.

"I can't believe you're up," she replied. "What time did you get in?"

He grabbed one of her extra pillows off of the floor and placed it under his head. "About two a.m. It was the longest flight of my life."

She smirked. "It's what you get for partying in Miami Beach until dawn." She knew what he and his fellow flight attendants had been up to after seeing the photos on Instagram *and* Snapchat. "I don't know how you guys can party like that when you have to work a long flight home the next day." Her stomach twisted at the thought. Then again, she'd never been a partier.

In fact, her twenty-first birthday had been a hugely forgettable day.

"Recovery time is definitely getting longer and longer," he mumbled. "But South Miami Beach is the shit when you're gay and recently single."

Campbell buried the bleak birthday memory and shot Blaine a sympathetic smile. "Tim's an asshole and you were way too good for him." Saying those words reminded her of talking to Scott about *Wuthering Heights* on Thursday.

She'd said the same thing about Heathcliff when it came to Catherine. By the time Tuesday came, she'd be done with the book, too, and they could continue their conversation.

Maybe he'd even have the other book for her?

"I love you for saying that."

She finished her coffee. "I know you do. But it's also the truth."

"Speaking of single"—Blaine pointed at her laptop—"who's the hottie?"

Campbell peered at him. "How can you see that picture?"

"Honey, I'm exhausted. Not blind. Perfect vision, actually. Who is he?"

She opened her mouth, hesitated, then said, "Scott, my lit professor."

Blaine's brown eyes widened. "You lucky bitch. I never had a professor who looked like that." He stared at her for a handful of seconds before asking, "Are you, Campbell Grey, cyberstalking your hot lit professor?"

She lifted her chin. "Of course not." And she wasn't. "I'm on the English Department's page and checking out the faculty." She had scrolled through the other names.

Blaine shook with laughter. "You're a terrible liar. You should also see your face."

Campbell swiveled toward her desk, closed the page, followed by her laptop.

"So what'd you learn about him?"

"Not much." She faced him. "Get out of here so I can start getting ready for work."

He sat up. "Your lit professor is *adorbs* and you like him. Who cares? Campbell, it happens." His humor subsided. "And you know I like Niall—"

"You mean *looking* at Niall."

"That, too." Blaine gave her an affectionate grin. "But you're way too good for him."

She lowered her gaze to the floor.

"That doesn't mean I think you should start a torrid affair with Professor Hottie."

The crystal-clear image of being locked in a torrid embrace with Scott Mayhew landed in her mind with such force her breath caught in her throat.

Her phone buzzed with what had to be Niall's response.

Niall, who might be a better match for her. At least right now.

But if that were really the case, why couldn't she stop thinking about and researching someone else?

"He isn't married, is he?" Blaine asked. "That would make it a really forbidden, torrid affair and painfully cliché. You're way too good for that, too."

Forbidden.

"I'm almost positive he isn't married," she murmured.

That had to be what was happening with her when it came to Scott. That and the fact he was a *man* and she'd only ever been with boys. She'd also genuinely enjoyed talking with him about literature—books—another first in her life. And enjoyed hearing him talk about Walt Whitman in class and *Wuthering Heights* afterward. He also had to be a book nerd.

"I'm not sure it's a good sign you're almost positive about something like that."

Campbell raised her head and stood. She needed to get ready for work.

"Blaine, I was curious about my lit professor. That's it."

He leisurely rolled off of her bed. "Whatever you say. Will you be home tonight?" Blaine asked while she nearly shoved him from her room.

"No. I made plans with Niall." Blaine opened his mouth, but she swiftly said, "I'll see you later." She gave him a final, gentle shove into the hallway and closed her bedroom door.

Yes. She definitely felt drawn to Scott for many reasons. But feeling that way for him happened to be the definition of complicated. Even if it weren't, was she really and truly ready for anything deeper than *fun*? So when she saw him on Tuesday, she'd be friendly and polite during class and after while talking to him about *Wuthering Heights*. If he brought *The Awakening*, she'd graciously accept it, then leave. That's it.

Enough was enough when it came to Scott Mayhew.

SCOTT LEANED BACK and rubbed his eyes.

After reading through his now updated résumé three times, he'd started to see double. But the doc had to be perfect. He'd only been teaching full time for a few years. Compared to his colleagues, he was under-qualified for the position of assistant department chair. At the same time, his boss—the department chair—had brought the job to him which had to mean he had a legit shot at getting the promotion. Having a top-notch résumé would be key. Another huge step toward a future to keep him in his daughter's life. That had become his primary goal after finding out he would be a dad. And after the shock wore off since Shannon had been on birth control. Before that day, his life had been on a vastly different trajectory. He'd discovered a love for teaching while in the army. It still hadn't been his first choice, though he'd always been an avid reader. Now, he couldn't imagine doing anything but teach.

Like he'd told his sister the previous night, the promotion wouldn't take him completely out of the classroom and away from the students. He did love being in "the trenches." It would merely be a lighter teaching load which would equal a lighter grading load. The tests were never too bad. The English Composition papers, combined with the American Lit midterm essays, were what obliterated his spare time every semester.

It's not that he didn't like reading all of the papers and essays —getting to know his students through their writing—it had simply become time he didn't get to really focus on Peyton. Grading at night while she slept had proven to be a challenge following particularly long, exhausting days. And she was already five-years-old and in kindergarten.

How the *hell* had that happened? She'd just been an infant he could hold in one arm.

Being five and turning six in May, she'd been asking about dance lessons and gymnastics. Extracurricular activities Shannon had started to research. That meant eventual recitals and meets. Peyton could even develop an interest in school sports someday.

Scott wanted to be present for everything in her life as much as humanly possible.

Despite his personal life hovering around drought level the last year or so due to not making any real connections with the few women he'd dated, he also hadn't given up on finding *the one*. Getting married and having another kid, possibly two.

Giving Peyton what he and his sisters had lost in an instant all those years ago.

He refocused on his résumé, specifically on everything he'd accomplished academically and professionally since being discharged from the army eight years ago.

If not for Peyton, he would have ended up in a career never meant for *him*.

His phone burst into song and he swiped it off of his desk. At seeing Shannon's live-in boyfriend's name on the screen, Scott went for ignore. But curiosity at why the guy was calling caused him to tap accept. "Hey, Adam. What's up?"

"Not much. How's our little redhead?"

Scott narrowed his eyes. "Fine." And she sure as shit wasn't *our* little redhead. "She's at a friend's house. Was there something you needed?"

"Actually, yeah. You know Shannon's birthday is Monday."

"Yep." He still needed to ask Peyton what she wanted to get her mom for her birthday.

He and Shannon had gone their separate ways a few years earlier, but Scott still felt the responsibility of taking their daughter shopping to buy her mom a birthday present.

And either he took Peyton shopping or Adam the boyfriend would.

"Shannon will be back from the conference tomorrow," Adam continued, "and with her birthday being on Monday, I was hoping you could keep Peyton tomorrow night?"

Scott somehow managed to suppress an exasperated sigh.

It was fantastic to know his ex was getting laid on a regular basis.

"Of course. Anything else?" He needed to get away from his computer and go on a long, hard run before he picked up Peyton in a couple of hours.

It would also help him clear his head of *everything*.

"Yeah, just a couple more things."

Scott closed his eyes. "Okay."

"Shannon's car is still in the shop, so I'm taking her to work and picking her up, then surprising her with dinner at her favorite restaurant. She doesn't get off until four, and I have a meeting at three I can't reschedule. Can you also pick Peyton up from school? We'll swing by your place and get her on our way to the restaurant."

This being the main reason Scott couldn't help but respect the guy. From day one, Adam had shown he had no problem putting Shannon and Peyton first.

"I can do that." It's not like he'd ever say no to spending more time with his daughter.

"Great. Thanks. Oh, and one more thing."

Scott took a deep breath.

"I'm sure Peyton's already mentioned it, but just in case she didn't she told me she wants to get her mom a bunch of white roses for her birthday and paint them red." Adam laughed. "I'm not certain where that came from. I'm guessing she meant to buy her mom red roses?"

Actually, Scott knew exactly where Peyton had gotten the idea. But he said, "I'll take care of it. Thanks for letting me know. Is that it?"

"Yeah. We'll see you Monday."

Scott ended the call and put his phone down.

He released a quick laugh as he pictured buying a dozen white roses and Peyton painting them—*buying flowers*.

Campbell's eyes lit up with passion while sharing her opinion on *Wuthering Heights* drifted through his head.

He slowly swiveled his chair in the direction of his two packed bookcases.

Somewhere in that chaos was *The Awakening* which he'd read while in grad school. He'd never been able to discard a book—even take them to a used bookstore—the primary reason for the chaos. There were books on his shelves he'd received and purchased in high school.

Scott stood and within two steps he was closely scanning the titles that were in no particular order. When he found *The Awakening*, he nudged the book out of its tight spot and stared at the worn cover.

Would it really be so wrong to drop in at Daisy's Bouquets on Monday?

His daughter needed flowers for her mom, Felicity loved the place, he'd be supporting a local business, and Campbell had said yes to borrowing the book.

Wins all the way around.

As he went back to his desk, however, a faint, nagging voice said, "*Don't be an idiot.*" Unfortunately, he could at times be a little too good at ignoring that voice.

Chapter Six

CAMPBELL SIPPED her beer while sliding her gaze over the restaurant. In truth, popular college hangout would be a more accurate description considering she undoubtedly had to be the oldest person in the place.

Groups of University of Colorado Boulder students were gathered at the various-sized tables, talking and laughing loudly with one another. In spite of the overall volume surrounding her, she could still hear the alternative rock music blaring through the overhead speakers.

She focused on Niall reading the menu which was a trifold, nearly worn out piece of paper kept on the wood tables that weren't very well cleaned.

Niall was only a few years younger than her—undoubtedly the second oldest person in the place—but still managed to look as though he belonged here among all of the college kids. Ten years ago she would have definitely enjoyed being in a restaurant like this with friends. But she was no longer an eighteen-year-old girl with a big, exciting life ahead of her.

At least, that's what she'd thought at the time.

She'd become a woman with real-world experience and

should never have agreed to meet Niall in a restaurant right near a college campus on a Saturday night.

She forced her mouth into a pleasant smile and leaned forward. "This place seems cool, but why did you choose it?" She wanted to add *"out of all the restaurants in Boulder."*

Niall could have suggested a place on Pearl Street where the chances of being around an older, quieter crowd were more possible. A place where they could have talked without having to lean across the damn table and strain their necks.

He set down the menu and picked up his beer. "I know it's kind of loud in here, but I promise the food is great." He followed that up with a quick grin that didn't quite reach his hazel eyes. "Do you know what you want? I'll go put in our order."

While he stood at the counter, she tried to relax into her uncomfortable, plastic chair.

She couldn't deny Niall Donnelly was beyond easy on the eyes. Tall, lean, looked good in a blue button-down shirt and jeans. He'd received several salacious once-overs by girls in the short time they'd been there. Happened to be receiving them at this moment even. Instead of feeling jealousy, though, Campbell could only be amused. And awed at the fact the girls in here had way more confidence at their age than she'd ever experienced ten years ago.

No doubt another reason she'd fallen extremely hard and quickly for her ex-bastard at the oh-so mature age of twenty. Tall, blond-god good looks, charming, and he'd chosen *her*.

"So," Niall began after he sat, "you're really liking being back in school?" He shook his head. "Because I can't wait to be done with my MBA. I'm over all of the damn homework."

Homework. She still needed to read Emily Dickinson. She'd be lying to herself if she wouldn't prefer to be at home at this moment, curled up in bed with a glass of wine, and reading poetry. Doing the homework Scott had assigned on Thursday.

She really, really wanted to finish *Wuthering Heights*, too.

Campbell set her beer down. "With this class I'm taking, most of the homework is reading which I love." There were a couple of big writing projects, as well, but reading more than anything else. "My homework for Tuesday is reading poetry by Emily Dickinson."

Niall cringed. "That sounds like torture. I'm so glad I don't have to take another lit class for the rest of my life."

She gave him a tight smile.

Yes. She'd felt that way about literature and poetry not even a week ago. She still wasn't sure how it would go with Emily Dickinson. But it sounded as if Niall didn't like reading at all. Not a huge surprise, either. She'd never known a guy who liked to read.

Scott's handsome, grinning face while talking to them about Walt Whitman on Thursday drifted through her mind.

Correction. She'd never known a guy who liked reading until now. Her "*adorbs*" lit professor who happened to be a *man*...and would probably never take a woman to a place like this on a date.

She picked up her beer and took a drink.

"I was thinking we could hit a party after dinner." Niall picked up his phone. "My roommates are going and it could be fun. The house isn't too far from here."

Having roommates being the only other thing she and Niall really had in common.

Campbell eyed a pretty brunette wearing a pink beanie hat, tight jeans, and black top checking Niall out as he went into his phone.

These girls not bothering to hide their drool would absolutely call her bat-shit crazy for wanting to be anywhere but here at this exact moment in time. Still, she couldn't quell the longing for more than a burger and beer at a hangout crawling distance from an enormous college campus. Or wanting more than hitting a party where she'd probably still be the oldest person in the place.

She definitely wanted more than being with a guy with whom she shared almost no connection, him being easy on the eyes and a good kisser aside which happened to be all they'd ever done. She hadn't felt right about sleeping with a guy she could take or leave.

Jillian's heart had been in the right place back in October when she'd finally convinced Campbell to take a chance on Niall. After watching her bosses fall in love with men who adored them, Campbell had figured *what the hell*? She'd also, after living in Denver for well over a year, reached loneliness and craving human touch. So she'd taken a chance…and knew before her first date with Niall ended they wouldn't last. But she'd felt somewhat obligated to give him a real chance since Jillian had been pretty adamant he would be *fun*.

A burst of rowdy laughter, followed by loud, excited chattering from a nearby table caused her thoughts to scatter. It was in that moment her head began to hurt. Then what she needed to do —should have done weeks ago—hit with such force she leaned forward and strained her neck in Niall's direction.

"Niall?"

He looked up, and their eyes caught.

"Is this working for you?" She gestured at him and herself. "Please be honest."

He set his phone down and sighed. "Not really."

She quietly released a long breath.

"But we had some fun and it was worth a shot, right?" he added.

Some fun. The key word being "some."

"Yes. Of course." She again set her beer down. "But hopefully Jillian won't be too disappointed when I tell her. She's in Argentina with Jackson."

Niall absently nodded. "I should also tell you I…met someone in one of my classes. We sit next to each other and are connecting. We even swapped phone numbers." He winced. "I wasn't expecting to meet anyone. And I like you, too. But something is missing. Between us?"

More relief shrouded Campbell to the point she wanted to laugh. But she gave him a soft grin and said, "We're not right for each other. And there's nothing wrong with that." But being with him the last few months had definitely helped Campbell realize what she did want.

Scott's infectious grin while talking to her after class on Thursday appeared in her head.

Her pulse picked up its pace.

"I know." Niall turned his beer bottle in a circle. "The girl I met in my class is in the same program, so we have a lot to talk about. She also speaks fluent Spanish." He smiled. "I really like her. It could be something, you know?"

"I think that's great. You should ask her out." Every part of her meant those words, too.

His smile deepened. "Thanks for being so cool about this. I feel much better."

"Me, too." She hesitated, then said, "Spending time with you the last few months was really good for me." In more ways than he would ever know. "I'll see you, okay?"

He frowned. "You don't have to leave. Our food should be up any minute."

Campbell smiled. "Or you could call your new friend and see what she's up to tonight. Maybe even surprise her with dinner?" She stood.

He brought back his smile. "That's actually not a bad idea."

She turned from him.

"Campbell?"

She stopped and looked over her shoulder.

"When you see Jillian, will you tell her I said hi? And that I'm happy for her?"

Campbell grinned softly. "Absolutely." She swiftly left the restaurant.

She'd always suspected Niall had a little crush on her boss, but Jillian had made it no secret since getting back together with Jackson in late September how she felt about him. Setting Campbell up with Niall had probably been Jillian's way of helping Niall move on from the crush while also giving Campbell the push she'd needed to get herself back out into the dating world.

She'd never fault Jillian for it, either, since she couldn't stay stuck in the past forever.

Earlier today when Blaine had been in her room, she'd briefly thought of Niall as a better match for her right now. But the girl he'd met in his class would be a much better fit for him.

Campbell, on the other hand, was a woman who deserved and wanted to be with a man.

SCOTT STARED at Daisy's Bouquets through the windshield of his SUV.

"Daddy, what are you doing?"

"I'm thinking." More like calling himself a complete jackass for following through with this idea that had felt harmless enough Saturday afternoon.

"I thought we were going to buy Mommy flowers."

"We are." But he'd—without a doubt—become the definition of an idiot.

"What are we waiting for?" Peyton practically whined.

Now he really had no choice but to see his stupidity through to the end since they were running a tad on the late side due to all of the *fantastic* Denver traffic.

With a weary sigh, he hauled himself from his vehicle.

When they reached the shop's door, Scott paused to look at the book he tightly held with his right hand.

"Now what's wrong?" Peyton asked with a hint of attitude.

He glanced at his daughter staring at him as if tentacles were coming out of his ears. And he flashed forward ten years to when she'd be a sassy teenager.

Holy shit, this moment was only the beginning.

He opened the door. "After you, your Highness."

Peyton walked ahead of him, but stopped after three steps and shrank backward since a Siberian Husky—also known as a *real* dog—had leapt to its huge paws.

The dog trotted toward them, its mouth hanging open while wagging its tail, then stopped to furiously sniff Peyton not much taller than the animal.

"Hi! I'm so sorry," a woman said as she walked swiftly from the backroom. "Thatcher." She snapped her fingers, and the dog turned from them and headed her way. She stopped when she reached the counter that lined the shop's left side. "I promise he's harmless."

His eyes locked with the woman's who he recognized as *Holly*.

"Oh, my God," she murmured. "It's you."

Scott grinned. "I love it when I have that effect on women."

She laughed, eyed Peyton standing right in front of him, and looked at him once more. "I think we need to start over."

He nudged Peyton farther into the shop. "I'd like that."

Holly walked through the opening in the counter and held out her hand. "I'm Alyson Douglas—Preston." She shook her head. "I'm still getting used to the name change."

He grasped her hand. "Scott Mayhew. It's nice to actually meet *you*." He released her hand. "Felicity mentioned you got married recently. Congratulations."

"Thanks." She cringed. "And I really am sorry for deceiving you that day."

He laughed. "No worries. I promise." He glanced at her left hand. "I'm just glad the real guy gave you a ring."

Her tan face turned a deep red as she focused on Peyton. "Hi there."

"Hi," his daughter murmured. "I like your dog. He's really pretty."

Somewhere in the back a door opened and slammed shut.

"I hate driving in this damn city!"

Alyson grimaced as Campbell came marching into the actual shop from the back.

"Why is it every time I'm on delivery duty, I encounter some *asshole*—" She stopped when she spotted Scott, then Peyton.

Her face became that way-too appealing color which matched her hat; the same one she'd been wearing the first day of class.

She covered her mouth with her hands. "Oh, my God. I'm so sorry."

"You said a bad word," Peyton accused. "I can't say it, but I've heard my daddy say it—"

"*Okay*," Scott interjected. "If you haven't already guessed, this is my daughter. Her name's Peyton and she needs red roses for her mom's birthday."

"*White* roses," Peyton declared. "I'm going to *paint* them red."

Campbell and Alyson stared at him with wide eyes.

He slowly shook his head and mouthed "*Red roses*."

Campbell stepped forward and smiled at Peyton. "Painting can be very messy and you look awfully pretty in your pink coat. We wouldn't want you to ruin it, either." She lifted her gaze to Scott and back to Peyton. "So would it be okay if Alyson and I painted the roses for you? You could stay here and hang out with Thatcher."

Peyton nodded. "Okay. He's way bigger than Princess Belle."

Campbell frowned.

"You look like Cinderella." Peyton looked up at him. "Doesn't she?"

Scott's eyes locked with Campbell's, and the same flutter from Tuesday *and* Thursday returned while her face flushed for the second time.

"Yeah," he murmured. "I guess she does."

He really was a complete idiot for being here like this.

"Thank you." Campbell smiled. "It just so happens she's my favorite Disney princess."

Peyton giggled.

Alyson cleared her throat. "I'm going to head to the back and get started on those roses. How many would you like?" She'd asked Peyton the question, but focused on him for the reply.

"A dozen will be fine. Thanks."

Alyson disappeared into the back.

Silence settled between him and Campbell.

Give her the damn book.

He placed *The Awakening* on the counter. "That's for you."

She pulled off her hat and set it beside the book. "Thank you. I can't wait to read it." She peered at him. "You could have given it to me tomorrow."

Truth. But he said, "We needed flowers and coming here was the obvious choice. Dropping off the book at the same time was no big deal." Giving her the book today had been another reason to stop by because he was such a moron.

Peyton wandered toward Thatcher back on his massive, thick dog bed.

Campbell opened her mouth, hesitated for several seconds, then said, "This is none of my business—*at all*—but are you… married?" Her face flushed for the third time. "I mean, you don't wear a ring but the flowers are for Peyton's mom."

She'd looked for a ring? And had also just asked about his marital status.

More surprises from the self-professed "book nerd" who did bear a resemblance to Cinderella, mostly in the eyes. Those mesmerizing, huge aquamarine eyes.

Aquamarine.

He was definitely in trouble. The realization didn't stop him from saying, "I'm single. Peyton's mom is my ex, but we're on friendly terms."

Campbell gave him a soft smile. "That's good. Nice to hear, too."

That he was single? That he and Shannon didn't despise one another? Maybe both?

"Daddy, I have to go to the bathroom."

Campbell held out her hand toward Peyton. "It's in the back. I'll show you where."

Seconds later, Scott stood all alone in the shop, with the exception of Thatcher watching him closely. Protectively. As if he could read Scott's mind. Though his thoughts weren't inappropriate, the woman at the center wasn't appropriate in the slightest.

He knew what he needed to do. But it happened to be the opposite of what he wanted.

Chapter Seven

ALYSON LEANED BACK, away from the work table, and whispered, "She's *so cute.*"

Campbell nodded.

Just like her dad, too. In truth, cute didn't accurately describe Scott's daughter.

Her thick locks of strawberry-blonde hair. The bright chestnut eyes. Her smile and laugh.

Peyton Mayhew was a beautiful child.

Though she clearly favored Scott in a few ways, Campbell couldn't escape the thought her mom had to be stunning. Her mom who was on "friendly terms" with her dad.

If they stayed that way as Peyton grew up, she would be an extremely lucky young lady.

Peyton emerged from the bathroom, but stopped and pointed at Alyson putting together the lavish bouquet of red roses.

"Those are already red," Peyton stated. "You're not painting them."

Campbell exchanged a wide-eyed glance with Alyson.

Of course Scott's daughter would be a sharp little girl who noticed *everything.*

Campbell leaned forward and down. "I'll tell you a little secret. We paint many white roses in the mornings and sometimes have a lot left over." She glanced at Alyson who had pressed her lips together. "Is it okay if we use those in your mom's bouquet?"

Peyton eyed the roses. "I guess. They are really pretty."

Campbell straightened, flashed Alyson a quick grin, and followed Peyton into the shop.

Her steps slowed, however, at seeing Scott crouched in front of Thatcher and vigorously rubbing his head and neck. Thatcher, in turn, gazed at the human giving him the attention.

Campbell smiled.

Scott had clearly made a furry friend for life.

"Daddy, why can't I have a dog like this?"

Scott gave Thatcher one final rub and pat, then stood. "When you're older." He faced Campbell and grinned. "How's the painting going back there?"

His thick, beautiful hair. The chestnut eyes. His infectious grin. Successful. Smart. Charming. Most importantly, absolutely devoted to his five-year-old daughter. And he was single, probably due to his devotion to—

"Campbell?"

She blinked several times and found him staring at her with raised eyebrows.

It was in that moment she realized she had to be gazing at him much like Thatcher had seconds earlier. Her face warmed as she said, "Alyson's almost finished."

"Cinderella said they paint the white roses in the mornings," Peyton replied while petting Thatcher's head.

"Honey, the nice lady's name is *Campbell*."

Campbell smiled. "It's fine. I could get used to a name like Cinderella." Yes. She definitely could. "By the way, I finished *Wuthering Heights* last night." A topic that would keep her from thinking about his status as a single man.

He stepped toward the counter. "*And*?"

"It ended the way I thought it would."

Their gazes locked, and her breathing stalled.

"Not all love stories end happily," he quietly said.

No. They sure didn't.

"One could argue," he continued, "that some of the best love stories end tragically."

She narrowed her eyes. "I like the word *memorable* better than best."

He laughed softly.

"Heathcliff and Catherine. Romeo and Juliet—"

"Scarlett and Rhett," he inserted. "Gatsby and Daisy. Great books and a play." He leaned forward. "All of them characters in stories that are consistently listed as the best of all time though their love ends quite unhappily, sometimes tragically."

She crossed her arms. "So you're saying tragedy is what makes romance great?" She'd experienced an unhappy, almost tragic romantic ending and it had certainly not been great.

"No." His grin slipped considerably. "Just more compelling."

Something about the way Scott had said those words and his grin fading gave her the distinct impression he'd spoken out of experience. That's when she remembered his faculty bio.

He'd been raised by three "classy, smart women." No mention of his dad.

"Because you feel so strongly about tragic romantic endings," he slowly began, "I should warn you that *The Awakening*—"

She groaned. "Don't say another word." She stared at him. "I know you're a lit professor, but do you ever read books that end happily?"

He brought back his infectious grin. "I actually just finished reading a *riveting* story about a cat named Pete who learns how to be himself with help from his friends." He paused before adding, "There was dancing involved, too."

Campbell fought a smile while shaking her head. "Children's books don't count." Though picturing him reading the book with his daughter was more than a little heart melting.

"Oh. My bad." He leaned against the counter. "So what would count?"

"Any book written for an adult that ends happily." She lifted her chin. "Maybe you're the one who needs to pick up a Jane Austen novel? Or a Shakespeare comedy?"

He slowly nodded. "Good suggestions. I haven't read Austen since grad school. I took a Nineteenth Century, British Lit class." He straightened. "Okay. Jane Austen it is."

Campbell's mouth inched open. "Are you being serious right now?"

"Yeah. Why not?" His eyes became round. "Will it make me less of a man if I willingly read a classic, happy romance?"

She grinned. "Hardly. But being a lit professor, are you really worried about that?" She also knew he had to be joking based on the mischief within his eyes.

Mischief looked so incredibly good on him, too.

"Not at all." He shrugged. "I was just curious."

Alyson walked into the shop carrying the vase now over-flowing with deep red roses, green filler, and baby's breath.

"Wow." Scott looked over his shoulder at Peyton still petting Thatcher whose eyes were half-closed. "Baby, come here and see the flowers."

Peyton stood and joined her dad at the counter.

She smiled up at Alyson. "You're a very good painter."

Campbell shared a quick giggle with Alyson while Scott shook his head.

"Thank you," Alyson replied. "I was happy to do it."

After paying for the roses Alyson had deeply discounted, Scott picked up the vase.

"Thanks for everything." To Campbell, he said, "I guess we'll pick this up tomorrow?"

Yes. Tragic romances and endings and Jane Austen. His visit to the shop with his daughter a pretty enjoyable surprise on a quiet, late Monday afternoon.

"Sure." She picked up *The Awakening*. "Thanks for the book."

He stepped back. "Despite the ending, I think you'll like it. Chopin—a strong, female writer—crafted a strong, female heroine." He glanced at Peyton. "Honey, what do you say?"

She clasped his hand. "Bye. Thank you." She looked at Thatcher. "Bye, Thatcher."

He lifted his head and wagged his tail.

Scott gave them a swift smile, then they were gone, the bells over the shop's door tinkling with their departure until they fell silent.

"If Jillian were here," Alyson stated, "I know exactly what she'd say right now."

Campbell faced her.

"*Santo cielo.*" She tilted her head right. "You like him."

Without question. The thought made Campbell say, "Of course I like him. What's not to like? I mean, I know you're madly in love with David, but it's not like you're *dead*."

Alyson stared at her. "Campbell, you know exactly what I mean. And you're right." She released a quick laugh. "What's not to like?" She paused, then said, "But he's—"

"My professor," Campbell mumbled. "Al, I get that he's off-limits." And she sighed, the total unfairness of it all hitting her for the first time.

"Saying this is probably only going to make it worse," Alyson continued, "but I kind of got the impression he likes you, too."

Campbell fell silent, recalling his infectious grins, charm, and long gazes.

Had she managed to finally attract a *man*? If so, it only added to the total unfairness.

"I overheard a little bit of your conversation. About the tragic books? And something about him reading Jane Austen?"

Campbell lifted her shoulders. "I was giving him a hard time about all of the books he read ending unhappily. I suggested he needed to read Austen, too, and he agreed. That's it."

Alyson peered at her. "Okay." She smiled. "That was a lot of quick thinking on your feet. Painting the white roses red?" She laughed. "I wonder where she got that idea."

Cinderella. Princess Belle. Of course Peyton loved all things Disney.

"Probably from *Alice in Wonderland*. The Disney cartoon?" Campbell could clearly envision the scene since she, too, loved many Disney movies. "In the movie, Alice helps the cards paint the white roses red for the Queen."

"Oh. I haven't seen that movie since I was a kid." Alyson reached out and grasped Campbell's hand. "Anyway, promise me you'll be careful? I'm sure Scott would never do anything to intentionally hurt anyone."

Based on what Campbell had read in his bio, that was a huge understatement.

"But a situation like that could get…messy…very quickly," Alyson finished. "A friend of mine in college became involved with one of her instructors and it didn't end well for either of them. She withdrew from school, and I'm pretty sure he lost his job."

Campbell gave her a tight smile. "I swear you don't have to worry."

Alyson squeezed her hand and headed for the backroom.

Dammit. She hadn't meant to be so obvious. At the same time, there really was nothing for Al to worry about.

Campbell stared at the shop's door as frustration simmered inside of her.

It's not that she wanted anyone to worry about her choices, but could it be so wrong to want a little excitement? To enjoy Scott liking and seeing her as an attractive, single *woman*?

Recalling Alyson's story about her friend, the answer landed in her mind, swift and hard. Instructors dating their students could get more than messy for many reasons. Scott also exuded he had integrity. It didn't change what Campbell wanted as she lowered her gaze to the book.

The Awakening. A short novel—by the looks of it—written by a strong, female author with a strong, female heroine. Scott had also said the story ended sadly.

Still, the title had reached out and captured something deep inside of Campbell.

A KNOCK from Scott's office doorway, followed by "Hi," caused him to drag his gaze from the computer screen.

A familiar young woman—girl—stood just inside his office and gave him a shy smile. "I'm Kinsey." She stepped forward. "I'm in your morning Mondays and Wednesdays English Composition class."

That's why she looked familiar.

"Do you have a sec?"

He actually had to be in his American Lit class shortly, but he smiled and pointed at the empty chair in front of his desk. "Of course. What's up?"

She dropped her backpack to the floor, sat on the chair's edge, and pushed a lock of dark hair behind her ear. "I'm having trouble coming up with a subject for the first paper. Choose an influential person from the last fifty years that you greatly admire and explain why?"

He nodded.

"I really don't…admire anyone. At least, not anyone truly *influential*."

Every semester he had at least one student come to him stating the same thing. And every time, he said, "I seriously doubt that. What are your interests?" Because these same students seemed to think they had to write about a president or Pulitzer-Prize winning author or scientist, even though they needed to write about someone *they* admired and viewed as influential.

It was something he always made clear, too, but some students simply didn't believe him.

She shrugged. "I don't know." She nibbled her lower lip. "I like music."

"Excellent. What kind of music?"

She gave him another shy smile. "Mostly rap and hip-hop."

"Okay." Not surprising, either. "Are there certain singers you like?"

"Well, yeah. But I wouldn't call them *influential*."

"Why not?" He leaned back in his chair. "Rap and hip-hop are legit types of music with lyrics. Those lyrics can be considered poetry." Though not music and lyrics he tended to like.

She stared at him.

"My point is, there have been many rap and hip-hop artists over the last thirty or so years who revolutionized—*influenced*—that genre of music. My suggestion is to do some research on its beginnings and see what you find out."

She angled her head back. "You mean I can write about a rap singer?"

And there it was. The disbelief.

"The assignment isn't about who *you* think *I* want you to write about."

His boss, Johanna, suddenly appeared in his doorway.

He shot her a swift grin, but said to his student, "The assignment is about someone *you* think is influential and admire and explaining why. That's it."

Johanna adjusted her round glasses while fighting a smile.

"Oh. Okay. Very cool then." She went back to nibbling her lower lip. "I'm really liking your class so far. Even though I *hate* writing."

Also not surprising. But he said, "Thank you. I'll see you tomorrow?"

She gradually came to her feet and picked up her backpack. "Definitely. Thank you…Scott." She flashed him a final, shy smile and darted past Johanna.

His boss laughed. "Another coed has clearly fallen under the Mayhew spell."

He groaned. "Please don't say that." He cringed and shuddered at the thought.

Okay. The young women—girls—in his classes were legally adults. But at the end of the day, they were still nothing more than kids.

Her eyes filled with passion and the defiant lift of her chin while talking about tragic romances appeared in his mind. Yeah. His attraction to Campbell Grey was…inconvenient.

But she happened to be a *woman* full of surprises and who challenged him.

Johanna sat in the same chair as his student.

If the circumstances were different, he'd have her number and a first date set for the near future. If she liked him the same way. And he felt pretty damn certain she did. She'd also proven yesterday she liked and was a natural with kids, and would more than get along with his little girl who he hadn't introduced to any of the women he'd dated since splitting from Shannon.

"I know you have to get to American Lit, so I'll make this quick."

He shook his head. "What's going on?" *Focus*. "Did you get my résumé?"

"Yes. It looks great. We're hoping to begin interviews in the next couple weeks." She sighed. "March will be here before we know it."

What a massive understatement. Scott could hardly believe they were already at the end of January.

"But I thought you should know," Johanna added, "someone else in the department has also expressed interest in the position. This person has definite seniority, too."

Scott had a strong feeling of who it might be, but couldn't ask since it was none of his business. Unless his colleague told him, but she was out on medical leave.

He'd also been the one who'd taken over her American Lit class.

"Scott, in all seriousness," Johanna quietly continued, "you're quite popular with the students. *All* of them really like you."

"Thanks," he murmured.

A compliment for sure, but with an unspoken message. Him being seriously considered for the promotion could come down to the dean wanting to keep him as a full-time instructor.

He kept a sigh in check.

"But hang in there. Go through the interview process, keep being your magical self, and don't do anything stupid." She stood. "Coeds under the Mayhew spell or not, I know I don't have to worry about you breaking the school's policy when it comes to instructors becoming involved with their students." She laughed. "Or worry about you taking a group of your male students to a strip club."

Scott squinted at her. "What the hell are you talking about?

Did someone here actually do that?" He didn't always listen to *that* voice, but he'd never done anything defined as insane.

She waved her hand as if shooing a fly. "No. A story an old colleague once told me." She turned from him. "Get to class. We'll talk soon."

Scott stared at his desk.

Don't do anything stupid.

He packed up his laptop bag.

If only he'd met Campbell Grey in another time and place.

He stood and walked around his desk.

But he hadn't. And the school's policy about instructors dating their students was crystal clear. He also loved his career. Loved the life he'd made for himself since finding out he would be a dad. So no matter how damn hard it would be—especially feeling she also liked him—from this day moving forward he *had* to keep things strictly professional with the passionate woman who looked liked Cinderella.

He'd worked way too hard to get here to risk losing everything he'd achieved.

Chapter Eight
____

THE GIRL SITTING beside Campbell raised her hand.

Campbell glanced at Scott, but he focused on the girl.

Avoiding looking at *her* like he'd done throughout most of the class period.

"Yes?" he said to the girl.

"Don't take this the wrong way, but when are we going to be done with poetry? Because I just don't get why it's so flippin' important."

Scott smiled. "I like your honesty."

The girl grinned.

"And I understand what you're saying," he easily continued, "but there are many different poets who write different types of poetry. You'll meet some of these poets as we get further along in the semester, so don't give up on poetry yet."

She nodded and shrugged.

"But we are going to take a break from it for a little while."

"Thank God," the girl mumbled.

Campbell again tried to catch Scott's gaze as he scanned the classroom.

She frowned.

Something strange was happening here, but what? Outside of the obvious. Him, professor. Her, student. Still, he hadn't exactly been acting that formal the previous week, especially yesterday while he'd been at Daisy's Bouquets with his daughter.

"We'll be spending some time with Mark Twain."

"Oh, cool," *Dead Poets Society* guy said. "Are we reading Huck Finn? I saw the complete book is in the text."

Scott laughed. "I like where your head is at. And if this class lasted a full year, the answer to that question would be yes. But we don't have that kind of time, so"—he held up his copy of the textbook—"I want you to read the two stories I listed in the syllabus by Thursday." He paused, then said, "And there will be a quiz which will be your first real grade of the semester."

The girl released a heavy sigh as she closed the textbook.

"Happy reading."

Campbell leisurely packed up her backpack purse as her classmates filed out of the room. She spotted the book she'd brought for Scott, eyed him packing up his laptop bag, and withdrew it from her backpack. His odd behavior aside, he'd agreed to read a certain author and she wanted to return the book favor.

She stood, hooked her backpack straps over her right shoulder, and headed for him.

When she reached the desk, he zipped his bag up.

"Hi."

He straightened and gave her a quick grin. "Hey." He picked up his bag. "I liked what you had to say about Emily Dickinson's poetry having a way of cutting a reader off at the knees."

"Thanks." She smiled. "She had a way of saying a lot without using too many words." The main reason she'd enjoyed reading Emily Dickinson's poetry.

Maybe…just maybe…Scott had been right a week ago when he'd said she would be entertained while reading literature.

He nodded and stepped back.

"This is for you." She held out *Sense and Sensibility*. "Jane Austen. That was the deal."

Scott's gaze dropped to the book and went back to her.

"I know you said you read her in grad school, but I'm hoping it wasn't this book."

The corner of his mouth lifted in a tiny smile. "Actually, we had to read *Persuasion*."

She grinned. "Great. So you loaned me a book and I'm returning the favor."

Their gazes connected, but something unfamiliar flashed through his chestnut eyes.

Hesitancy? *Caution.*

Yes. Something had definitely shifted.

She lowered her hand. "But if you don't need the book, it's no big deal."

"No, I'll take it."

She hesitated before handing it over.

"I don't have this book and I've never read it, either." He slid the book into the front pocket of his laptop bag, the strap now hooked on his shoulder.

She lifted her chin. "Hopefully, you won't go into shock after reading *Sense and Sensibility* which ends happily. I've seen the movie version."

He released a quick laugh. "That's fair. But believe it or not, I don't have anything against stories that end happily." He slipped his hands into his pants pockets. "I'll have you know, I've seen every Disney fairy tale movie that's been released. About ten times. *At least.*"

Campbell giggled and, encouraged by him acting more like himself, said, "Peyton's definitely a girly girl. And so smart and beautiful."

His face softened. "I appreciate you saying that. She's a keeper for sure."

Their gazes met once more…followed by the flash of caution within his eyes.

At that moment, his phone started to ring.

He broke their eye contact and withdrew the device from his pocket.

"I should take this." He turned and said over his shoulder, "Thanks for the book. I'll see you Thursday." He veered left and disappeared from view.

Campbell stared at the empty doorway and released a deep sigh.

Dammit. He'd obviously realized, between yesterday after leaving the shop and class today, what she'd been telling herself the last week.

She followed his path from the classroom but went right.

The professor plus student relationship equaled a fine line which couldn't be crossed. At the same time, it was a line that could easily be crossed when the professor and student were a single man and woman. The fact he'd been noticeably cautious during most of their moment might also mean Alyson had been right yesterday when telling Campbell she thought Scott liked her, too. What else would be the cause of his drastic three-sixty?

Instead of being able to revel in the fact a man like Scott Mayhew did seem interested in her, Campbell could only grit her teeth.

None of this was fair.

For the first time in her life, she'd met the kind of man she'd envisioned for herself ten years ago. Then eight years ago her ex-bastard had dashed into a downtown Durango coffee shop during a raging thunderstorm and her life had changed in an instant.

He'd changed before the ink on their marriage certificate had dried.

Still, she'd stayed out of true love for the baby growing inside of her and utter powerlessness when it came to her controlling, possessive ex and his formidable family.

She pushed through the building's doors a little on the hard side and deeply breathed the frigid, dry air into her lungs.

Yes. She wanted to be with a *real* man, but it couldn't be Scott. Considering her past she'd kept to herself for so long out of embarrassment and her strong desire to forget, she also couldn't be certain if she was truly ready to have a *real* man in her life.

HE'D OFFICIALLY TURNED into a complete jackass.

Scott let himself into his office and dropped his laptop bag onto his desk. He then sat and shook his head.

He'd—without a doubt—blown Campbell off for his sister who hadn't even been on the line. Probably just a dropped call. But under different circumstances, there was no way in hell he would have ever taken a call from his sister while talking to a smart, beautiful woman about books, happy endings or not. And the look on Campbell's face when he'd blown her off? *Shit.*

She'd known since he'd seen the surprise and disappointment in her big, perfect eyes.

His phone again started to ring and he answered, "Hey. What happened?"

"I'm driving," Felicity replied. "I must have hit a dead spot. Did I catch you at a good time?"

Scott sat back. "Yeah. What's up?" He actually needed to get to work on grading some English Composition homework, but talking to his sister would be a much better distraction.

"I need you to come to the wedding this Saturday."

He reached into his bag's pocket and withdrew *Sense and Sensibility.* "Who's the lucky guy and why haven't I met him?" He stared at the book's simple cover.

"Ha! You know what I mean *and* that I'm still sworn off men."

After being married to the biggest dickhead on the planet, Scott couldn't blame his sister for feeling that way nearly two years later.

"There's someone I want you to meet at the wedding."

Scott sighed.

"I think you'd really hit it off with the maid-of-honor," Felicity continued in a rush of words. "She's quite pretty, has her own business, and has been such a lovely person to work with the last several weeks." She laughed. "I actually like her better than the bride. I showed her your picture and she wants to meet you."

He placed the book on his desk and rubbed his eyes. "Felicity, I love you and I know you mean well. But please stop showing my picture to random women."

"This is only the third time I've done it and how else are you going to meet someone? Scotty, it won't kill you to say yes for a change."

He refocused on *Sense and Sensibility*.

Using his common sense and sensibility was keeping him from a woman he genuinely wanted to get to know better. Something that hadn't happened in a long time. But he said, "I was thinking about giving app dating another try." Not a total fabrication of the truth since it had—briefly—crossed his mind last week.

"Because it worked so well the first time?" She groaned. "Please. You're also way too good of a catch for dating that way."

He grinned. "Thanks, but you're biased."

"Hardly. If I thought you were a *wanker*, you'd know it. I also wouldn't be trying so hard to set you up with a perfectly nice, intelligent, pleasant woman."

Scott laughed softly at his sister's slip into British which still occasionally came through because of her marriage to the dick-head, though she hadn't lived in London for over two years.

"Please come to the wedding and meet her? You have no excuse not to since Peyton's with Shannon this week. I promise you'll have no regrets."

He stared at the book. Campbell's book. The woman he couldn't pursue.

A substantial part of him—the *single man* part—did miss and want to be with a woman. It could be meeting this woman would be exactly what he needed to move on from another woman he couldn't have. At least, not while she was his student. He could wait until the end of the semester and hope for the best, but that would be absurd.

"Scotty, did I lose you again?"

He cleared his throat. "No, I'm here. And you win. I'll be there. Where and what time?"

What the hell did he have to lose?

"Brilliant! The JW Marriott in Cherry Creek. The wedding starts at five. And wear the suit you wore to the Ritz last year. That wedding when you met—"

"*Yes*," he muttered. "I remember."

She laughed. "Alyson told me you two started over yesterday when you were at her shop. It was quite sweet of you to give them the business, by the way."

Yep. *Sweet of him*. But not the wisest decision overall when he remembered Campbell's disappointment at him blowing her off minutes earlier…and after sharing a fantastic moment with her only yesterday afternoon in the shop.

"Love you! See you Saturday. Don't be late."

He set his phone down. He then picked up the book and softly grinned.

*You loaned me a book and I'm returning the favo*r.

He'd been so focused on being professional, he'd spaced

asking Campbell if she'd started *The Awakening* and what she thought. It was probably best he didn't know, though, when he recalled the story. An unhappy wife and mother discovering herself in many ways, including emotional and physical intimacy with men who weren't her husband.

Scott didn't know Campbell's story, but when he really thought about his interactions with her, something about her gave off a modicum of sadness. Some unhappiness, too. Except when talking about books. And he suddenly remembered what Felicity had said last week. About something being off with Campbell.

Maybe he and his sister were sensing those emotions from her?

He put the book aside.

It was none of his business, and he had grading to get done. As he pulled out the stack of homework assignments, however, he couldn't stop from imagining what it would be like to help Campbell Grey move past her sadness and unhappiness she couldn't possibly deserve.

Chapter Nine

BLAINE AND LANCE walked into the kitchen right as Campbell pulled the cookie sheet from the oven. She then set it on the counter.

"*Damn*, it smells great in here." Lance stood behind her. "Are those the same cookies your mom made us and sent for Christmas?"

"She made others, too, but yes."

He reached for a peanut-butter-chocolate-chip cookie, and she slapped his hand.

"Easy, Chef Grey." Lance glared at her. "I was only going to take one."

"They need to cool down." She shooed him backward. "Go away."

Blaine slid into a stool at the island counter. "Honey, what's wrong?"

Outside of the fact Scott had made it clear he was avoiding her when he left almost immediately to talk with *Dead Poets Society* guy? He'd also barely looked at her during class.

Still, she glanced at Blaine and replied, "What do you mean?"

Yes. Scott's behavior was understandable, given the situation, and for the best.

Lance refilled her wine glass and his, then sat beside Blaine sipping his red wine.

So why did she want to break something just to watch and hear it shatter?

"The last time you baked like this," Blaine answered, "was when your boss, Jillian, was in the hospital after that car accident she was in with her boyfriend."

Campbell nodded.

Unable to sleep that night while waiting to hear from Alyson, she'd busied herself by pulling out her favorite cookbook and baking until the sun rose. At about that time she'd finally heard from Alyson who'd told her Jillian had awakened. By then, they'd had enough cookies and brownies and whoopie pies—her personal favorite—for every neighbor on their street.

"I ask again," Blaine continued, "what's wrong?"

There was no way in hell she would ever tell her roommates she did in fact have the hots for her lit professor who had ignored her today which had more than hurt her feelings.

Even thinking it made her feel like a ridiculous, immature, naïve *girl*.

She sipped her wine. "I think I need a vacation."

A real vacation far from Denver, Colorado, would be absolutely perfect, too. Like to Maui or Argentina, two places she'd never been and would love to visit.

"Or now that you've finally moved on from Niall," Blaine offered, "give another guy a chance. What do you think about dating a flight attendant?"

Campbell held up her left hand. "Don't even think about it."

It's not that she had anything against flight attendants. But she'd seen enough of Blaine's activities on social media while away on trips to sense his friends were, for the most part, nothing more than *boys*.

"Why can't you take a vacation?" Lance asked. "You've worked at the flower joint long enough you must have earned some time off by now."

"And you know I could get you a flight to just about anywhere for almost nothing."

Blaine could do that for her, but the thought of taking a real vacation by herself filled her with more emptiness. It would be relaxing, yet also unexciting, and she'd reached beyond sick and tired of her mundane existence she'd settled into long before moving to Denver. She absolutely needed a break, though, and recalled the conversation with her mom over a week ago.

"I've pretty much decided to go home for spring break."

Her roommates gave her warm smiles.

"I miss my mom and brother," she softly added. "I need to see them."

Yes. Being back in Durango for the first time since leaving out of self-preservation would be challenging, but she had to see her family.

"I'm going to talk to Alyson and Jillian about it when Jillian's back from her trip."

Campbell couldn't imagine them saying no to her vacation request. Unless, of course, Hayley suddenly decided to go somewhere. She, too, had gotten a bonus.

Blaine raised his glass. "I think that's a superb idea."

"There are way worse places to go for spring break than Durango," Lance interjected. "Do you think you could talk your mom into sending you back here with cookies?"

Blaine frowned at him. "I never knew there was a Cookie Monster hidden inside all of that." He used both hands to draw a large circle to encompass Lance. "You know, you can buy all the cookies you want at this place called a grocery store."

"Not the same." Lance stood and headed for the cookie sheet. He picked up a cookie, placed it between his teeth, and scooped up a second one. "Thanks for baking," he managed to say. "Please don't ever move out."

Campbell grinned as he walked by her. "I love you, too."

Blaine walked to her side, placed his arm around her shoulder, and hugged her to him. "Sure nothing else is bothering you?"

She nodded while trying not to think about Scott ignoring her today.

It really was for the best.

"Okay." He released her. "I have to be at DIA before *dawn* tomorrow morning." He groaned. "I hate those six a.m. flights with a passion. But you can always call if you need me. You know I'll call you back."

"Thanks," she murmured. "And I will."

Once she was again alone in the kitchen, she faced the batch of cookies.

Reading or doing homework or watching television wouldn't be enough of a distraction tonight. With that thought, she went to the counter and found her favorite recipe in the cookbook.

Whoopie pies sounded incredibly yummy and necessary and chocolate was always a good idea in times of bitter disappointment.

Unfortunately, she knew this from way too much past experience.

SCOTT SCANNED the large room glowing with LED candlelight.

Rows and rows of chairs with white covers. Vases overflowing with colorful flowers. Archway, framing the officiate and perfect bride and groom, decorated with some kind of sheer fabric and clear lights. Overhead lighting set to dim.

His sister had once again outdone herself.

He sat back in his chair in the last row and eyed the maid-of-honor focused on the happy couple exchanging their vows.

Okay. Definitely attractive and more his type, physically speaking. On the tall side. At least while in heels. Brunette. Probably had dark eyes, too. Her strapless, burgundy bridesmaid dress fit her nicely in all of the right places.

She shifted from one foot to the other, casually turned her head right, and smiled.

But not at Scott.

He frowned, leaned slightly forward to see who exactly had earned her blinding smile, and halted. Some older gentleman with salt-and-pepper hair, dressed in a gray suit, happened to be returning her smile. Which seemed more than a little friendly. The maid-of-honor, his "date" for the evening, also hadn't looked in Scott's direction one time since walking into the room.

He sat back and shook his head.

What the hell had his sister gotten him into? What was he even doing here?

He clearly needed to have his decision-making rights temporarily revoked. He'd lost his common sense at some point the last couple weeks for one reason only—he wanted what the bride and groom had, minus all the pomp and circumstance, and the wrong someone had captured his attention. Now, he happened to be at a wedding in the JW Marriott in Cherry Creek, surrounded by strangers who had more money than he'd earn in his lifetime, because his sister had appointed herself as his personal matchmaker.

Holy shit, he needed a stiff drink. Two would be better.

His phone buzzed inside of his suit jacket pocket. It had to be his matchmaking sister finally texting him back.

Scott stood and surreptitiously left the room.

I'm dealing with a food emergency. What do you think of her?

He walked until he stood several steps outside the room where two beautiful people were pledging their lives to each other while surrounded by his sister's wedding perfection. He also somehow stopped himself from continuing his long strides out of the hotel and to the nearest bar.

She's cute, but I'm pretty sure she's unavailable. I'm going to the hotel bar to get a drink.

What he truly wanted was get into his SUV, go home, get out of this damn suit, order a pizza, and find a hockey game to watch.

With such compelling wants, he really couldn't question his status as a single man.

What are you talking about? And go to the ballroom to get one. You can check on Campbell and Hayley. They're having an atrocious day. Wait for me there.

Scott halted.

Campbell was here? How could that be possible? The wedding had started. Didn't the florist show up well before the wedding? He'd also seen flowers in the other room.

Her attractive face tilted up in her defiant way with fire in her eyes filled his head.

For some reason, Campbell Grey was in the ballroom and having a bad day. He'd never heard the other woman's name Felicity had mentioned. But knowing Campbell was so damn close reminded him he had American Lit quizzes to grade from Thursday's class where he had surpassed jackass and officially turned into an asshole after avoiding her altogether.

Hate seemed a little strong, but she probably didn't like him very much.

He hesitated for several seconds before typing, *Okay.*

Right or wrong, he wanted to see her and find out what had happened. It would also be better than watching strangers get married or drinking at the hotel bar. Or escaping to his SUV.

Within minutes, he strode into the massive ballroom filled

with a plethora of round, elegantly decorated tables. In the center of the room he spotted Campbell and another woman—girl—placing small vases of pale-pink and white roses on the center of each table, then rushing back to oversized carts to grab more vases.

He couldn't help but grin at Campbell's dark-blonde hair piled haphazardly on her head, sweatshirt sleeves pushed past her elbows, and jeans *hugging* her lower half.

Scott ran a hand through his hair.

He needed to focus. It did look like they were on overload, based on their stony expressions, and he headed for the carts.

Campbell swiped two vases from the lower shelf and stopped when she spotted him.

Her eyes, lacking their usual brightness, widened when he halted steps away from her.

"What the hell are you doing here?"

He grinned since he deserved that greeting. "It's nice to see you, too."

Her gaze slid down and up him, followed by her face turning that still way-too enticing shade of red.

Under completely different circumstances, Scott would have been highly encouraged by the fact she'd just checked him out.

"Sorry. You caught me off guard." She marched past him. "Are you here for the wedding?" She placed a vase on a table, then another table, and headed back in his direction.

"Sort of." He slid his hands into his pockets. "Felicity sent me in here to check on you two. She said you're having a bad day?"

"More like a crap ass day," the girl grumbled. "Our delivery van died."

She left as Campbell grabbed two more vases.

"But we didn't realize it," Campbell said, "until after we'd loaded it up with all of the flowers. So we called Alyson, but it went right to voicemail because she's been up in Winter Park, skiing with friends. Our other boss is in Argentina with her boyfriend." She darted away.

"We don't know any mechanics," the girl picked up the story, "and we don't have boyfriends. We also didn't have time to wait for someone to help. So all we could think to do was unload the van and use our cars to transport everything. But by then, we were running late."

"And of course there was an accident on Speer Boulevard," Campbell muttered when she reached the carts. "We were so behind, Felicity had to ask the staff to put the hotel's vases of flowers in the other room. But we—somehow—arrived minutes before the ceremony began, and the bouquets and boutonnières made it to the bride, groom, and wedding party." She left.

Atrocious day? *Shit*. That did seem pretty damn accurate.

When Campbell came back, he caught her frazzled gaze.

"How can I help?"

She stared at him. "Are you being serious right now?"

He smiled. "I'm good at a lot of things that don't involve teaching and reading."

She lifted her chin. "Okay. Help Hayley in here while I get the rest of the flowers."

"Whatever you say, boss."

Working together swiftly and quietly, they finished putting vases on all the tables, including the head table, right as guests started to filter into the ballroom. Still no sign of his sister, though. Or his so-called date.

"Hayley and I need to make ourselves scarce." Campbell gripped the handles of a cart. "Thank you so much for your help. Have fun tonight." She and Hayley, each quickly pushing a cart, veered right out of the ballroom and disappeared from view.

Scott stood near the bar fast becoming busy with people who were strangers.

He didn't see his sister anywhere due to no fault of her own.

She was working. And somewhere a maid-of-honor—who seemed to be here with another guy but had agreed to meet Scott—had to be taking picture after picture.

Campbell's weary expression, hair piled on her head, heavy sweatshirt, and snug jeans appeared in his mind.

Don't be an idiot. But Campbell Grey definitely deserved a stiff drink tonight, and he didn't belong here. Based on how the maid-of-honor and the guy had been smiling at each other, Scott wouldn't be missed, either. With that thought, he headed in the direction Campbell had gone with Hayley, then switched to a swift gait which damn near bordered on a jog.

He spotted Campbell in the lobby, to the left and away from the entrance-exit commotion. She shook her head while talking into her phone. Clearly still frazzled from her shit day.

"Okay. Thanks, Alyson. I'll see you Monday."

She hung up right as he stopped a few steps from her side.

Their gazes snapped together; the flutter deep inside of him followed.

"Hi." She slid her phone into her back jeans pocket. "Did you need something?"

He took a deep breath, released the air, and said, "You look like you could use a drink."

She laughed softly. "It's that obvious?"

"Just a little." He grinned. "Are you…busy right now?" His breathing slowed.

Okay. He'd officially turned into an idiot.

"No." Her eyes became round. "Are you…offering to buy me a drink?"

He slowly nodded. "Yeah. I am. But only if you can stand to be seen with me."

Campbell's shock transitioned into caution. "You're here for the wedding." She again slid her gaze down and up him. "Obviously," she added under her breath.

"I have to tell you the truth." He leaned forward. "I'm here because my sister has decided she's my matchmaker."

"Oh." Campbell crossed her arms. "So you're here on a *date*?"

"I'm really not comfortable calling it a date since I never officially met the woman." He paused before adding, "I'm also pretty sure she's here with another guy."

Campbell frowned. "I don't understand, but it doesn't matter." She stepped back. "I also don't understand why you want to buy me a drink after this last week. And is that even allowed?"

There it was. Yep. He'd officially become an asshole.

Scott sighed. "Can I explain this past week? After that, if you want to go home and forget today happened, I'll get out of your way and we can pretend this moment never happened."

She remained silent.

He stepped forward. "Campbell, I've only been a college instructor for a few years, and I always teach morning and day classes. To be at home with Peyton in the evenings?"

She nodded.

"I'm used to teaching kids right out of high school, not..." Not passionate, beautiful women with bright blue eyes. But he said, "Adults. I get few men and women in my classes."

Her expression softened. "I understand."

He released a quick breath. "This is new to me. *Liking* a student?" And wanting to help her forget all about her bad day, no matter how long it took.

She gave him a soft grin.

"I have absolutely no idea what I'm doing," he added. "Having drinks on a Saturday night with a student isn't technically against the school's policy. But it's not encouraged, either." He also had his hat in the ring for a huge promotion. "But I hate the idea of you going home after a day like you've had. And I love my sister. I know she means well. But I would much rather be somewhere else." Specifically with someone else.

Campbell continued her silence as she stared at him.

All around them, the hotel lobby pulsed with activity.

All Scott saw was her as he waited for her to answer.

She narrowed her eyes. "You look like you belong in Monte Carlo in a five-star hotel-casino at the high-stakes poker table while I look like"—she gestured at herself—"this."

He smiled. "Was that a James Bond reference?"

She took another step backward. "I need to move my car. I'm still in the loading zone."

"I'll go with you."

"No." She held up her left hand. "Just tell me where to meet you."

He rattled off the name of a nearby bar he'd been to a few times.

"I'll see you in a bit." She disappeared into a throng of people exiting the hotel.

Don't do anything stupid? Way too late for that. But the single man part of him wanted much more, and he could no longer avoid the obvious spark between him and Campbell Grey.

Chapter Ten

CAMPBELL'S STEPS slowed as she approached the bar tucked away in Cherry Creek North…which appeared to be the kind of place a *man* took a woman on a date. Though this could never be considered a date. Still, she stopped beside the doors and reached into her purse.

Once she held the compact mirror, she triple-checked her hair she'd released from its tight knot on her head, then swiftly ran her hands through the long locks. She next gave herself a quick once-over. After parking her car at the Cherry Creek Mall, across the street from Cherry Creek North, she'd covertly swapped her sweatshirt for a dark-blue sweater she kept in her car. But she couldn't do a damn thing about her jeans and black Converse.

It's not like she'd expected to end up at a nice bar on a Saturday night with a man dressed to kill while breaking hearts at the same time. She'd planned on heading straight home and right into the bathtub. Now she was here while *he* waited for her inside.

Scott Mayhew had been born to wear a black, formal suit. And—unbelievably—the handsome, smart, successful, charming, ex-military, single dad had basically admitted to being interested in *her*. Campbell Grey. A woman from Durango who'd been focused on having a new life in Denver. Scott had also implied them meeting up like this on a Saturday night went against the school's rules. Not surprising, but she refused to think about any of that at this moment.

She dropped the compact back into her purse.

Scott had been so incredibly honest with her earlier she'd have to return the favor. But she'd cross that path…street…interstate…when the time came.

With a quick breath, she headed inside the bar.

A dimly lit, quiet, cozy bar. Perfect for talking and getting to know a person.

She smiled and walked farther inside. And her smile grew when she spotted him, minus his suit jacket, sitting at a table in the actual bar area. He held his phone and it looked as if he were texting. His face appeared stuck in a deep frown, as well.

Her smile slipped while she approached him.

Oh, no. This night could not be over before it began. At the same time, it would be just her luck if that did happen.

Scott placed his phone on the table, looked up, and caught her gaze.

His eyes widened before he stood. "Wow." He laughed. "Now I know why you didn't want me to go with you."

She shrugged out of her coat. "I was a hot mess and wasn't about to show up here looking like that." She draped her coat over an empty chair as he pulled hers out for her. "Thank you," she murmured, then sat. She pointed at his phone. "Is everything okay?"

Everything *had* to be okay.

"My sister's giving me a hard time about leaving the reception, even though I explained my supposed date seemed to be there with another guy." He shook his head. "I'll talk to her about it later. What can I get you?"

"Chardonnay. Please."

Campbell closed her eyes and thanked the heavens Scott Mayhew would be staying right here. The thought, however, made her think of his daughter.

When he returned with her wine, she asked, "Peyton must be with her mom tonight?"

He sat. "Yeah. But just so you know Shannon—that's her name—isn't my ex-wife." He took a quick drink of what looked like whiskey. "She thinks marriage is unnecessary nowadays."

"Really?" She sipped her wine, debating whether to ask her next question since it might be too personal. After another sip, she figured she had nothing to lose and was genuinely curious. "Is that why you two broke up?"

He slowly nodded. "It was one reason." He lifted his shoulders. "We also work better together in the realm of friendly."

She frowned. "Don't you mean friends?"

"We're not friends." He sat back. "I don't believe exes can be friends."

"Agreed," she mumbled under her breath. "It's nice you two get along. Peyton's going to appreciate that when she's older." And nothing like Campbell had experienced with her parents.

"I hope so." He shot her his infectious grin and pointed at her wine. "Feeling better?"

"Yes. Thank you." She slid her gaze around the quiet, cozy bar, the only patrons a few older couples, some couples who were easily in their thirties, and a few people at the bar.

She wouldn't be surprised if she happened to be the *youngest* person in the place and couldn't stop herself from smiling at the thought.

"What's on your mind?" he asked, and she heard the humor in his voice.

"Nothing." She focused on him once more. "So I don't quite understand why your sister would set you up with a woman who already had a date for the wedding."

He smirked. "I'm sure it was just a huge miscommunication." His eyes locked with hers and his smirk eased back into a smile. "I'm not complaining, either."

Campbell took an unsteady breath, sipped some wine, again debated what to say next, then the word honesty landed in her mind. "I have to tell you the truth."

His smile grew. "I thrive off of honesty."

He'd said those words to her after the first day of class, but had added *from students*.

"I read your faculty bio on the English Department's webpage."

He raised his eyebrows. "Really?" He laughed. "I'm flattered you took the time." He stared at her. "But you officially know way more about me than I know about you."

Yes. She certainly did.

"That's not fair." He leaned forward. "I think we need to fix that."

His grin. The eyes. His hair. The clothes.

Scott Mayhew looked good enough to eat the rest of the night and well into morning.

She took a longer sip of wine. "Okay." It was time to share some of the truth. "I'm from Durango. I moved here the summer before last."

"I'm from Colorado Springs, but you knew that." He peered at her. "Durango. That's a spectacular area. What brought you to Denver?"

She shrugged. "I needed a change of scenery." Mostly the truth, too. "But I left behind my only family. My mom and younger brother, Evan."

"That's tough." He picked up his glass and drank. "I'm lucky my family is close. I try to get down there at least once a month on weekends I have Peyton." He paused before adding, "I didn't get down there this month because Peyton and I spent Christmas through New Year's with everyone. But we'll go next month for sure."

She folded her arms on the table. "And who is 'everyone'?"

His eyes widened. "I figured you could tell me that."

Campbell fought a smile while shaking her head. "Your mom and…another sister? Or grandmother. Your bio said you'd been raised by 'three classy, smart women'."

"Wow." He folded his arms on the table. "Did you take notes?"

She laughed. "Will you be serious?"

"Fine." His gaze found hers. "Everyone in Colorado Springs is my mom and eldest sister, Leann, and her husband and son. The 'three classy, smart women' who raised me were my mom, Leann, and Felicity." His smile faltered. "Our dad was a cop who was killed in the line of duty when I was twelve."

Campbell froze.

Though she'd thought it strange Scott hadn't mentioned his dad in his bio, she hadn't expected him to say *that*.

"Oh, my God," she murmured. "I'm so sorry."

He seemed extremely close to his mom and sisters, but it still must have been heart-wrenching for Scott to tragically lose his dad at that age. When he was almost a teenager?

"Thanks." He straightened. "You didn't mention your dad just now."

A portion of her heart splintered at the thought.

"Um"—she drank some wine—"he and my mom divorced when my brother and I were kids. Unlike you and your ex, my parents did *not* part ways on friendly terms." Nothing but the ugly truth. "Then he moved to Steamboat Springs and we only saw him during summer breaks." She shrugged. "Evan and I aren't terribly close to him and never have been." Also the truth. "But we still connect with him on the phone at birthdays and Christmas." She cracked a smile. "We have our mom who's definitely our superhero." And so much more than even that word implied.

"I can relate." Scott frowned. "I'm still sorry to hear you're not close to your dad. Friendly terms or not with Shannon, I couldn't imagine moving so far away from Peyton. And only talking to her a couple of times a year?" His frown deepened. "I don't get it."

Of course he didn't get it. Because Scott Mayhew qualified as a *man*.

"You know you're a superhero, too. Right?"

He squinted at her. "Where'd that come from?"

Her face suddenly felt as if she'd stuck it in an oven during the cleaning cycle.

His confusion eased into his infectious grin.

"You're smart and successful. From what I've seen, you're a great dad." She pointed at him. "You know how to wear a black, formal suit—"

"And that's extremely important."

"You were also in the military."

His humor slowly disappeared. "I think you're going to owe me a one-page autobiography after tonight."

That would never happen. But his transformation from easy-going smartass to seriousness at the mention of him being in the military could only mean one thing.

"You were in combat," she quietly stated.

He once again picked up his glass, but finished the contents. "Fifteen months in Afghanistan." He sighed. "It was a long time ago, and I've made peace with everything I saw and did." He stood. "I'm going to get another drink. Are you hungry?"

She smiled tightly. "I'm fine right now. Thanks."

Wow. There was way more to Scott Mayhew than she'd imagined.

Lost his dad at the age of twelve. Joined the army at the age of eighteen and had obviously seen and experienced way more than anyone under the age of twenty-one should. Anyone at any age, really. Ended up as an English college professor while co-raising his daughter whom he adored, giving her a life full of love and devotion and stability.

Campbell had no intention of writing a one-page autobiography and giving it to him. But she could give him more than what she had so far. Start out by crossing a path which would be another gigantic step forward since she also had a strong sense she could trust Scott.

A feeling that hadn't come easily since getting away from her ex nearly three years ago.

As soon as Scott sat, she said, "I didn't just move here because I needed a change of scenery."

He set his drink down. "I'm listening."

She pushed her hair behind her ears. "I was married and it didn't work out. It was also an ugly divorce because he didn't want it." Both confessions huge understatements.

Scott's eyes widened.

"Things—life—were messy for *a while*. But when the divorce was final, I decided it would be a great time to try something different in a new city." And that's all he needed to know.

Unless, of course, something deeper happened here. But it couldn't. Him, professor. Her, student. No. They certainly weren't acting like that now. In fact, it felt like they were on a date.

The kind of date she'd been imagining for months, only in her mind she'd been dressed much nicer than in a sweater, jeans, and Converse.

"Believe me when I say take this as a compliment"—Scott gave her a swift once-over—"that you don't look old enough to have already been married and divorced."

She lifted her shoulders. "And *you* don't look anything like a college instructor and single dad." He especially didn't look like either while wearing that suit.

He grinned. "Thank you...I think." He stared at her for several seconds before saying, "Would I be a complete ass if I asked you—"

"I'm twenty-eight. You?"

"Thirty-four."

She picked up her wine glass. "You're older than I thought."

He picked up his glass. "I think we should toast to the fact we're aging well."

They tapped glasses and drank.

"So what happened with the guy?" He tilted his head left. "Why didn't it work out?"

Here's where she'd have to be extremely careful with the truth.

"We were young and thought we were in love. And that combination makes you do such stupid things," she softly added while bringing her glass to her lips.

He frowned. "It sounds like you're being too hard on yourself. Campbell, people make mistakes. I've certainly made my fair share because I'm *not* a superhero." He shook his head. "I knew from the beginning Shannon's thoughts on marriage and continued to see her even though I do believe in marriage. Then she got pregnant, we had Peyton, and I stayed for *her*." He stared at a spot on the table. "At some point, what Shannon and I had wasn't enough. I also wanted to give Peyton more since I doubt Shannon will have more kids. On top of never getting married."

Campbell smiled. "It sounds like you—the lit professor who only reads books which end unhappily—have a sappy, romantic side." And, dammit, if that didn't add to his overall, almost irresistible package.

"I'm usually able to hide it so well, too." He shot her a

pretend glare. "I can't remember the last time I talked this much about myself."

"Well"—she propped her chin on her right fist—"I think you're an interesting person." Also not at all a lie.

"Same when it comes to you. But fascinating and riveting are much better words than interesting. Or what about intriguing? Engaging? I could keep going."

She giggled. "Enough, Mr. English Professor." Still, he'd said those words to describe her which made her smile deepen.

"You might also be *interested* to know I started *Sense and Sensibility* last night."

She leaned forward. "*And*?"

"It's good. Elinor and Marianne Dashwood actually remind me of my sisters since Leann is the practical one, like Elinor. And Felicity is outspoken and follows her heart, like Marianne."

Campbell laughed. "Felicity is definitely outspoken. And you might be *interested* to know I'm several chapters into *The Awakening*."

He leaned forward. "*And*?"

She took a deep breath and said, "I love it. A woman back then wanting more than to be confined by societal rules and norms created by a bunch of *men*? Edna has guts." She paused, then added, "Kate Chopin had guts for writing a story like that. I'm officially a fan."

Scott returned her grin. "Excellent. We'll be reading and discussing two of her—" He stopped and looked down. "I'm glad you're liking the book *and* Kate Chopin."

Silence fell between them for the first time since Campbell had joined him at the table. And it struck her. She'd had his undivided attention. He hadn't even glanced at his phone, much less picked it up to check if he'd missed anything. No. It hadn't gone off. But this kind of experience was exactly what she'd been envisioning and didn't want it to end anytime soon.

She had a strong feeling Scott felt the same way.

The thought gave her the confidence to say, "I'm actually a little hungry."

He glanced up, and their gazes met.

"Me, too." He stood. "I'll go get us menus."

Campbell sat back in her comfy, leather chair and stared at her half-full wine glass.

Yes. She could definitely get used to dating a *man*. Or more honestly, dating Scott Mayhew. But what would happen after tonight and it became tomorrow, then Monday, then Tuesday and they were back to professor and student? He'd just now stopped himself from slipping into Mr. English Professor.

She sighed as one simple word filled her head—reality.

That meant she needed to savor every bit of this night with him.

Chapter Eleven

SCOTT SIGNED the credit card slip, then eyed the chair across from him now empty because Campbell had gone to the restroom.

A beautiful woman full of surprises.

She'd definitely knocked him sideways by the fact she'd been married. It sure as hell didn't sound like it had been a happy marriage overall, either. Maybe that's where her sadness came from? And unhappiness.

Because his instincts were telling him she hadn't confessed the whole story.

Marrying the wrong person at a young age was hardly a new storyline, so her hesitation to talk about it didn't make a whole lot of sense. She'd really only confessed to being married after he'd halted the conversation about his time in combat.

Some life-changing events didn't need to be revisited, and he'd been completely honest when he'd told her he'd made peace with his time in combat years ago.

He shoved those thoughts aside.

Felicity had been right. There did seem to be more to Campbell Grey than she presented. It had also damn near sounded like she'd left Durango because she had no other choice. Though it was none of his business what had really happened with her ex-husband, Scott couldn't ignore the fact he liked Campbell—a lot—and not only wanted to know more about her, but wanted this night to continue for as long as possible.

Which meant he'd surpassed trouble and reached screwed. *Big time*.

Scott straightened when he spotted Campbell emerging from the hallway which led to the restrooms.

Before meeting him here, she'd fixed her hair and changed into a sweater as blue as her eyes. Her actions had to mean she liked him, too. Had wanted to make a good impression. Of course, she'd probably also done it because of the way he was dressed; not at all his norm.

He smiled, though, remembering how many times she'd checked him out.

Scott stood when she reached the table. "Are you ready?" Though he really wanted to ask her, *"Do you want to stay until they kick us out?"*

"Sure." She grabbed her coat.

As he shrugged into his suit jacket, he couldn't help but feel she'd probably say yes. Especially since her eyes, that had been bright the entire night, had dimmed a bit.

Once they were outside, Campbell paused to button her coat.

"I'll walk you to your car," he offered. "Where'd you park?"

"At the mall. And thank you." She laughed, her breath coming out in a white puff due to the below-freezing temperature. "I did *not* see the night going in this direction."

He leaned forward. "You and me both." Right or wrong, he wouldn't have changed a damn thing, either.

They fell into step beside one another and strolled toward the mall.

Silence fell between them.

Despite all of the little bars and restaurants, Cherry Creek

North seemed pretty quiet for a Saturday night. Then again, it wasn't exactly warm outside. They probably needed to walk faster so they wouldn't freeze by the time they reached her car. But Scott couldn't bring himself to pick up his pace, even though he'd probably resemble an icicle before arriving at his SUV still parked in the hotel's garage. He hadn't exactly dressed for a nighttime stroll in late January.

"Can I ask you a question?" Campbell suddenly said.

He glanced at her to find her eyeing him. "You've been asking me questions all night. I'm not going to stop you now."

She grinned. "How'd you go from being in the army to teaching college English?"

Holy shit, she kept catching him off guard at every turn.

"No one I've ever dated since Shannon and I split has asked me that."

She stopped and faced him. "How is that possible?"

He laughed. "Maybe they didn't find me as *interesting* as you do."

She shook her head. "I don't believe that. But seriously. I want to know." She paused before adding, "I'm sure you were a dedicated soldier, but you're a really good teacher."

Scott slipped his icy hands into his pants pockets. "Thanks. I like to think I have my moments of brilliance in the classroom."

They started walking once more.

"Teaching wasn't my first choice," he slowly began. "I've always been an avid reader, but when I was discharged from the army I was determined to follow in my dad's footsteps."

Campbell whipped her head in his direction. "Be a cop?"

Scott nodded. "He was in the army, too. I guess joining the police force was another way to be close to him."

She gave him a soft smile.

"My mom and sisters weren't on the same page, especially since I miraculously came back from Afghanistan uninjured." A few of his buddies—*brothers*—had not been so lucky. "It caused a lot of tension for a while."

"I get that they'd be concerned."

"Well, as it turns out," he continued, "their concerns were for nothing because my time with the Denver Police Department lasted a whopping three years."

Her steps slowed, as did his.

"I'm doing the math," Campbell murmured. "Shannon got pregnant with Peyton. Is that why you left the force?"

Smart, beautiful, and intuitive. How would he ever go back to normal after this night? Though he'd never liked the word normal. It was boring and overrated.

"Yeah," he quietly replied. "I'd never thought about being a dad and what it would mean until I had to the day Shannon told me she was pregnant."

"And life changed in an instant," Campbell stated.

"Without question." He stared at a spot over her shoulder. "I couldn't stand the thought of my kid—possibly—growing up without a dad."

She pressed her lips together and nodded.

"So I resigned soon thereafter and fell back on another passion. Reading." He lifted his shoulders. "I discovered I enjoyed teaching while in the army and it made sense to combine the two." He grinned. "And that's how I ended up in a college classroom trying to get students excited about reading poetry—among other things—written a long time ago."

She laughed.

He'd be a fool not to concede he'd throughly enjoyed watching the tension ease off of Campbell with each smile and laugh as the night progressed.

She leaned forward. "You're awfully good at it. You certainly got through to me."

Their eyes locked, then came the flutter.

"I can't believe I've enjoyed most of what you've assigned. Except Mark Twain." She wrinkled her nose. "I know he's supposed to be funny, but I didn't get it at all."

"He's not for everyone."

They again started to walk.

Scott had zero interest in talking about the American Lit class for obvious reasons. However, he was curious about something and asked, "You said the first day of class you were a returning-to-college student. Do you have a major?" He also had a strong feeling the failed marriage had something to do with why she hadn't finished school the first time.

"Business. But I'm focusing on the required courses right now."

When they reached First Avenue, he stopped them and caught her gaze.

"What are you planning on doing with a business degree?"

She smiled softly. "Being a small business owner, like my bosses. But I'd like to own a cozy bookstore that sells new and used books. Maybe even specialize in featuring local authors." She shrugged. "We'll see. I have a long way to go until I get to that point."

Scott returned her soft smile. "Yeah. But it's a very cool idea." And definitely seemed to fit her personality.

Her smile deepened.

"Is that what you've always wanted to do?" he asked as they crossed the street.

She shook her head. "No. I had no idea what I wanted to do or be ten years ago."

"That's fair. Pretty normal, too." It could be another reason she'd ended up in an unhappy marriage at a young age.

Under a minute later, her steps slowed while approaching an older Honda CR-V.

Silence fell once more.

Now what?

Under different circumstances this would be the part of the night, after connecting with a woman, Scott wouldn't hesitate to ask for her number.

Campbell faced him, her teeth quietly chattering.

"You're shivering." So was he, for that matter. "We should have walked faster."

"No. I'm fine. I'm always cold."

He raised his eyebrows. "*This* cold? Your teeth are chattering."

She stepped toward him. "Scott, I haven't told anyone the real reason I came to Denver."

Which meant his instincts were right. There was a whole hell of a lot more to her story than a marriage gone wrong.

"You don't like talking about your time in Afghanistan, and I completely respect that."

He remained silent. It's not like he could deny her statement.

"I don't like talking about the darkness in *my* past which is why no one else knows."

Darkness? A pretty strong word to describe something as common as a failed marriage between two people who'd simply been too young.

"But you're really easy to talk to, so I wanted you to know the truth."

"Thanks. So are you." He felt he had no choice but to add, "And I understand." Though he really didn't understand.

She smiled while her petite frame trembled from the cold. "Thank you for tonight. And all of your help in the ballroom. I had a great time."

"Me, too." Without a doubt. "You're going to freeze if you don't get into your car."

Instead of opening the driver's side door, she closed the small gap between them, stared up at him with those enormous blue eyes for a few seconds, then slipped something inside of his right pants pocket. Where she let her hand linger.

Her lips parted before easing into a grin with a hint of challenge. Defiance. The familiar passion flashed through her eyes before she removed her hand and stepped backward.

Every single cell inside of him sprang to life.

"Goodnight." She turned and opened her car door.

Scott clenched his hands inside of his pockets to stop himself from catching her hand, turning her toward him, backing her up against her car, and ending the night with his mouth pressed against hers for as long as they could stand it.

Campbell slid into her car and shut the door. Seconds later, and after a little wave in his direction, she drove away.

What the *hell* had just happened?

That's when Scott realized he happened to be gripping what she'd slipped inside his pocket. An action so damn hot he could still feel the warmth from her hand which had been uncomfortably close to another area that hadn't seen any action in an uncomfortably long time.

He deeply inhaled the bitterly cold air as a way to clear his head and stop what would undoubtedly be a painful hard-on. He then withdrew what felt like a piece of paper.

After walking into a stream of light provided by the parking lot lamps, he opened the small paper and—*holy shit.* She'd given him her number. She'd also written a brief message.

Because I want you to have it.

Scott shook his head.

She must have done this while she'd been in the restroom. She had taken her purse.

Between this, how she'd said goodbye, and their great night, what was he going to do?

He slipped the paper into his inside, suit jacket pocket and shoved his damn near frozen hands back into his pants pockets.

And tried *not* to think about her hand being inside the right one moments before. This was all his fault, too.

He turned and headed in the direction of the hotel.

If only he'd been able to control himself. But she'd looked so beaten down by the day while frantically placing the vases on the table. He'd wanted nothing more than to help her day end in a much better way. He'd succeeded, too, but now he officially had a serious problem.

For the first time in his college-instructing life, he wanted a woman who also happened to be his student. And he wanted her in *and* outside of his bedroom because they did have a connection. Chemistry. Tonight had only cinched it. Campbell obviously felt the same way.

Two words again appeared in his head.

Now what?

He really had a choice to make. Follow his heart or head. Of course, *that* voice deep inside of him quickly answered. The voice he'd rarely ever listened to when it came to matters of his heart. It could be the reason he was still alone. But what if this time turned out differently?

What if he'd finally met his match in Campbell Grey? If so, did it matter who she was right now? In fourteen weeks, she'd no longer be his student.

Not an ideal scenario by any means…but also not hopeless.

Chapter Twelve

"HI," Campbell's mom answered. "You read my mind. I was going to call you today."

"Well, I beat you to it." Campbell snuggled deeper into the flannel sheets and thick comforter on her bed.

Gray light filtered through her barely open window blinds and she could just see the snow flurries. The bitterly cold Saturday night had brought flurries into Sunday morning.

Saturday night.

The corner of her mouth lifted in a tiny smile as Scott's handsome, grinning face drifted through her mind.

"Are you working today?"

She blinked a few times and shook her head. "No. Unless it's a Felicity Mayhew wedding, we're off on Sundays now. But she rarely does Sunday weddings."

"Oh, how nice. When did that start?"

"Right before Christmas. And it has been nice." Especially when she also had Saturdays off which happened once a month. In fact, she would be off this upcoming weekend.

"How's your class going?"

Campbell's memory flashed back to the previous night when

she and Scott had been standing near her car, shivering, neither ready to say goodbye. Then she'd lost her mind for several seconds.

"I love it." Only because everything she'd told Scott about him as a teacher had been nothing but the truth.

"You must also like having Felicity's brother as an instructor?"

Yes. In fact, she liked him so much she'd walked up to him, shoved her hand into his pocket, and left the piece of paper with her phone number. She'd also lingered, mesmerized by the way he'd been looking at her with this odd combo of surprise and…*longing*.

"Yeah, Scott's really great." In truth, the word didn't come close to describing him.

Campbell still couldn't believe she'd done something so incredibly bold.

Where had the confidence come from? To not only give him her number—something which had to be a big no-no between a male professor and female student, and vice versa—but to also give it to him by slipping her hand inside of his pants pocket?

Her face became warm from the vivid memory.

"I'm glad to hear it. What else is happening? How are Blaine and Lance?"

And what would he do with her number?

She cleared her throat. "They're good. Blaine's been on trips the last few days, but will be home some time tonight. Lance has been pretty busy at night with his app dating."

They'd had such an amazing evening, Campbell couldn't imagine Scott throwing her number away. But there were rules they'd barely acknowledged last night.

Her mom laughed. "It's good Lance is getting himself out there." She paused before saying, "Something I think you should be doing. Are you still seeing the one guy? You haven't mentioned him in a while."

"No." She smoothed a wrinkle from her comforter. "It's over."

After last night, and no matter what happened between her and Scott, Campbell also knew she'd never go back to dating *boys*.

Thinking about her evening and telling Scott a highly condensed version of what she'd left behind in Durango, she said, "Mom, I've decided to come home for spring break. I can't and won't stay away forever." By continuing to do such a thing only gave her ex-bastard power, and she'd given him way too much already.

Still, if she hadn't left Durango, she never would have met Blaine, Lance, Alyson, Jillian, Hayley…Scott. With the exception of Scott, they were friends—family—she'd grown to love the last year-and-a-half.

"Okay, Sweetie. If you're ready to come back here, I'm certainly not going to stop you. This is your home and you're right. You can't stay away forever."

Campbell grinned. "I can't wait. I just have to talk to Alyson and Jillian when Jillian's back from her trip, but I'm sure it'll be fine." She laughed as some weight lifted off of her shoulders. At the same time, she shouldn't have let the weight linger for so long. "Do you think I could get Evan away from the newest love of his life long enough to get on Purgatory with me?"

She hadn't skied much since moving to Denver. When she'd lived in Durango, she'd nearly lived on the mountain during ski season and couldn't help but wonder if Scott skied.

"I don't know," her mom answered, "he's pretty smitten. Almost every time I see him, she's cemented to his side."

Campbell started to respond when her phone buzzed and dinged with a text.

Maybe…just maybe…*he'd* texted her?

"Mom, hang on a sec."

Campbell lowered her phone, went into messages, and saw an unfamiliar number.

Her mouth eased into a smile when she read what she could see of the message. She tapped the number, then laughed at what Scott had written.

So I should be grading, but Marianne just met John W.

She bit her lower lip to try and stop what would be a huge and ridiculous grin. Scott had also made it quite clear what he'd done with her phone number.

"Mom, I have to go. I'll call you in a few days?"

"Of course. Is everything okay?"

More than okay at this precise moment in time.

"Yeah. I just need to take care of something. Love you. Hugs to you and Evan."

"Love you, too."

Campbell hung up and paused to think about what she remembered from watching the movie version of *Sense and Sensibility*. And the memory appeared.

With a sly grin, she typed, *You'll probably like how their love story ends,* followed by the winking emoji. She then tapped send and settled deeper into her pillows.

Speaking of reading, she actually still needed to read what he'd assigned on Thursday. When he'd been avoiding her because he *liked* her. A student.

Her grin slowly faded.

What were they going to do? Where could this possibly go? No. She wouldn't be his student forever. But it was only the beginning of the semester.

Could she—they—realistically keep their obvious connection in check until May?

Thanks for the spoiler. And I told you I have nothing against happy endings. My favorite movie of all time is Tangled. But don't tell anyone.

Campbell giggled and wrote, *I thought it was Dead Poets Society.*

A movie she'd never been interested in seeing until now.

She closed her eyes and took a deep breath.

Surely their connection couldn't be seen as that wrong. They were single adults who shared a passion for reading and books. They'd also grown up without fathers, though his dad had been a hero whereas her dad hadn't been truly interested in fatherhood. She and Scott probably had even more in common.

Was it really so wrong they liked one another?

That's my second favorite movie of all time. How's Edna? Still think she has guts?

Campbell had still been coming off of her night-with-Scott high when she'd arrived home so she hadn't been able to concentrate on *The Awakening.*

I haven't read anymore yet, but I'm hoping to today.

As well as begin what he'd assigned, a story titled *Daisy Miller: A Study.* It sounded like it might be intriguing, unlike the Mark Twain stories they'd read last week.

Should we do a book check-in tomorrow?

Her goofy smile came back while she replied, *I'd like that.* She hit send as another message from him appeared in their thread.

I really do have to get some grading done before I pick up Peyton.

Her goofy smile transitioned into a soft and sappy one.

She hesitated before responding with, *Okay. Thanks for texting.*

The same question from moments ago reappeared in her head.

Could they realistically keep their connection in check until May?

Thanks for giving me your number.

Campbell re-read their thread, replayed choice moments from their evening including how they'd been staring at one another with her hand inside his pocket, and could reach only one answer. She had no idea what the realization meant in the long term.

She did, however, know she had no desire to douse the spark between them.

SCOTT SAT BACK in his office chair and eyed his phone.

He really wanted to shoot Campbell a text. Find out if she still liked gutsy Edna. But texting her while at work didn't feel right, already on the brink of playing with fire—actually, who the hell was he kidding? He'd lit the match Saturday night, and she'd added the fuel by giving him her phone number in a way he'd never forget. But he certainly didn't need to bring the fire into his office at Jefferson County Community College. So he picked up his phone and chose another woman's name because they hadn't spoken since their texting Saturday night.

"Okay," Felicity answered. "You were right about the maid-of-honor. Her ex was also invited to the wedding and she only had eyes for him that night. She later confessed to me they'd recently broke up, but weren't over each other. You still didn't have to leave like you did."

He sighed. "Felicity, why the hell would I have stayed?"

"The possibility of meeting another woman comes to mind."

He briefly closed his eyes and said, "I appreciate what you're trying to do. Really. But I never asked you to be my matchmaker." He shook his head. "I know you, Mom, and Leann think I've become somewhat helpless in dating since Shannon and I split *and* having Peyton every other week. But I've gotten this far without your help."

Yeah. He happened to be alone now. It hadn't always been that way, though.

"Scotty, I just want you to take a chance."

He was definitely doing that, and Campbell staring up at him Saturday night with her flash of challenge and passion filled his head. All while with her hand in his pocket.

"And I love you, but please stop playing matchmaker."

Her exasperated sigh reached him through the phone. "You drive me to insanity more than any bride I've ever worked with."

He grinned. "Bullshit. Are we friends again?"

"No. Not until you tell me where you went. I sent you into the ballroom to check on my florists and you vanished without a trace soon thereafter."

Scott stared at his desk.

Lying would mean he felt guilt and shame for meeting up with a beautiful woman who'd been having a shit day. Telling the truth would most likely earn him judgment from his strong-willed, mouthy sister. Something he had zero interested in hearing.

"If you don't start talking, I'll hang up and take you off of my Christmas shopping list. And you know I always give brilliant gifts."

He expelled a quick breath and said, "I met up with Campbell at a nearby bar to have a drink and we ended up having dinner." It had also ended up being one of the best nights he'd had with a woman in a long time.

Silence fell on his sister's end. Until he had to say, "Felicity?"

"Did I hear you correctly?" she asked. "You went on a date with Campbell? Campbell Grey from Daisy's Bouquets and who's in *your* class?"

"It wasn't a date," he stated, but then cringed at how absurd those words sounded.

"I'll admit I've been out of the dating game for quite some

time," she slowly said, "but I'm pretty certain a man and woman having drinks and dinner constitutes a date."

He became silent.

"Scotty, what are you doing?"

There it was. The judgment.

"It's not what you think. She was having a crap day and needed a break." He straightened. "I'm a single adult. She's a single adult. I know what I'm doing." But the other night he'd told Campbell he had no idea what he was doing which seemed closer to the truth.

"Scott Joseph Mayhew, if this ends badly and anyone—namely Campbell—ends up hurt, I will hunt you down and rip off the parts that make you a man. Am I being *perfectly* clear?"

He gritted his teeth. "Yeah. Got it. I'm hanging up now."

It's not like he'd expected any of this to happen. And, no, he wasn't handling it in the most professional way. Though he'd tried that route last week and had felt like a cowardly dickhead. But he'd definitely ended up on the opposite side of the spectrum.

Jeopardizing his career, not including a promotion, and livelihood undeniably fell into the category of playing with fire. Dangerous for sure. Then again, how in the hell could he ignore their connection for fourteen weeks? He'd never been a person who needed instant gratification. His upbringing and time in the army had shaped that part of him. But *holy shit*. Fourteen weeks?

At this moment, it sounded like fourteen months. With a promotion hanging on the fringes of half the semester, it sounded longer.

His phone burst to life and he glanced at the screen. He then narrowed his eyes.

If this call was about that same kid harassing his daughter on the playground, *he* would be requesting a meeting with the kid's parents and it wouldn't be cordial.

He managed to politely answer, "This is Scott."

"Hi. It's Mrs. Atkin. I hope I caught you at a good time?"

"Yes. My classes are over. Is everything okay?" He braced himself for her answer.

"Well, I'm afraid Miss Peyton has caught a bug going around the school. We have her in the office because she's looking a little flushed. She also has a slight fever."

Scott's shoulders fell forward.

Okay. He wouldn't have to turn into an outraged, protective dad after all.

"Since she has a bit of a fever, I'm afraid we do need to send her home."

"Of course. I understand. She was a little sluggish this morning, but wasn't warm and said she wanted to go to school." He stood. "I'll be there shortly."

"We'll keep Peyton here in the office. See you soon."

Scott packed up his laptop bag and strode from his office, closing the door behind him.

Right now, all that mattered was picking up his little girl and taking her home. Everything else could wait. Especially the *what* he would do when it came to the next several weeks.

Chapter Thirteen

"OKAY," Alyson said as she hung up the phone. "The mechanic just now finished looking over the van. It needs a new battery and while it's in the shop, they're going to change the oil and replace a few other things." She sighed. "That means I'm on delivery duty since we'll have to use my SUV the next few days."

"Or we can use mine," Campbell replied while adding a pink carnation to the birthday bouquet she was creating that also had to be delivered soon. "I don't mind."

Alyson stood and walked from behind the desk. "Thanks for offering, but it'll be a nice change." She shot Campbell an apologetic smile. "I still feel terrible I wasn't in town on Saturday to help you guys. What a mess."

Campbell added a white carnation to the bouquet. "Al, you deserve to have a life on your weekends off. It all worked out." She smiled softly at just how well it had worked out.

Alyson stopped at the work table and sat. "It was really nice of Scott to step up and help you guys." She laughed. "Felicity seems to get him to weddings which end up helping *us*. He's turning into our lucky charm."

Campbell joined her laughter while imagining how Scott

would react to hearing her words. Probably with his infectious grin, followed by a smartass comment.

"You've been in a really good mood today," Alyson added. "Did you and Niall do something fun this weekend?"

Her smile slipped since she hadn't yet told Alyson about ending whatever Campbell and Niall had been the last few months. She stuck another pink carnation into the bouquet. "No." She glanced up to find Alyson watching her. "Can I be honest with you?"

She really wanted to tell Alyson about her night out with Scott following the crappy Satur*day* she and Hayley had endured. But Alyson had been a voice of caution this time last week when Scott had shown up at the shop with his daughter needing "red roses" for her mom.

A situation like that could get messy very quickly.

She'd then shared the *messy* story about her college friend.

Alyson folded her arms on the work table. "You're not really into Niall."

Campbell's eyes widened. "It's been that obvious?" Or maybe her boss happened to be extremely observant. She could be the definition of a perfectionist.

Alyson lifted her shoulders. "To me, yes. Jilly was so distracted and excited this last month about her trip with Jackson —and busy being my maid-of-honor in December—that she's definitely been in her own little world."

Lucky-in-love cloud seemed more accurate, but Campbell simply nodded.

"Have you told him?"

"Yes." She added another pink carnation. "It actually happened over a week ago."

Alyson gave her a quick grin. "Good. I only met him the one time at the bachelor-bachelorette party, and he seemed nice enough. Just very…young."

Yes. A nice way of saying what Campbell had long-since accepted.

"Outside of helping you and Hayley on Saturday, how was Scott?"

Campbell picked up some filler and carefully added it to the arrangement. "Good." And he'd absolutely looked better than good. She cleared her throat. "Really good. Why do you ask?"

Alyson stared at her. "All day you've been smiling like you were when he was here last week with his daughter."

Wow. Between Alyson noticing her ambivalence to Niall and that she'd been grinning like a silly schoolgirl all day, Campbell clearly needed to work on her poker face.

"And, yes, I'm madly in love with David," Alyson continued, "but I do remember how Scott looked in a formal suit at the Ritz-Carlton wedding." She leaned forward. "I also remember how you two were looking at each other a week ago."

Campbell concentrated on finishing the bouquet as her face became the temp of desert hot…which only intensified when she remembered how she'd slipped him her number.

At that moment, her phone started to buzz before bursting into song.

She swiped it off the work table while thanking the universe for the interruption. But when she saw the caller's name, she halted.

Apparently, Scott the Superhero had a sixth sense.

Campbell glanced at Alyson, back to watching her closely, then slid off of the stool.

She held up her phone. "I should take this." She pointed at the bouquet. "I'm finished if you're ready to make deliveries."

Alyson narrowed her eyes.

Campbell walked into the actual shop and didn't stop until she reached the street door.

She paused, took a quick breath, and answered, "Hi." She then heard the back door open and shut which meant she was now—thankfully—alone.

"Hey," Scott answered. "How are you?"

"Good. How are you?" She cringed.

"I'm good." He laughed. "Wow. That was scintillating."

She also laughed. "I think I'd go with the word *awkward*."

"That, too. So," he slowly began, "I had to cancel tomorrow's class."

Campbell's shoulders drooped.

"I sent out an e-mail and posted the announcement to the class webpage, but I"—he sighed—"felt like I needed to actually tell *you*."

No doubt because of their amazing Saturday night together.

"Thanks. I appreciate that." She hesitated before asking, "I know it's none of my business, but is everything okay?"

"Yeah. No emergencies. Peyton's down with a bug she caught at school."

She stared at the floor. "I'm sorry to hear that."

"My neighbor normally helps me out in rare situations like this," he added, "but she's a retired teacher who now subs and has a job tomorrow."

Campbell fought a grin. "Super Dad to the rescue."

"Yep," he replied, and she could hear the smile in his voice. "All I need is my cape and Super Dad suit, but they're at the dry cleaners."

She shook her head. "That's too bad. I'll bet you'd look pretty cute dressed like—" She froze, then squeezed her eyes shut.

Had she really just said that to him?

Silence fell on Scott's end.

Where in the hell had her flirty reply come from?

"I'm sorry." She opened her eyes. "I shouldn't have said that."

"No, it's fine. Honestly."

She pressed her lips together.

Scott sounded genuine. She still never should have said something so flirty to him. At the same time, she had stuck her number in his pants pocket a few days ago and let her hand stay there a few seconds longer than necessary.

"I was taking a minute to picture myself dressed like that," he easily continued, "and I have to be honest. I think *cute* is way too generous."

She shared a quick laugh with him.

"I need to get back downstairs. I left Peyton with Elsa the penguin and the remote with the T.V. on Disney Plus. I have no idea what I'll be walking into after being gone five minutes."

She smiled softly. "Okay."

"Talk soon?"

Campbell started to say yes, but stopped when an idea popped into her head. A pretty risky, brazen idea. But she had more than enough to share and had never known a kid—even sick—who didn't like chocolate.

"Scott?"

"Yeah, I'm here."

"It just so happens I have the best remedy for a cold at home." She paused before asking, "Think you and Peyton might be *interested*?"

Silence again fell on his end as Campbell held her breath.

"*Intrigued* is a much better word."

She smiled.

"But I'm not sure it's a good idea. For a few reasons."

"I know," she murmured. "But I promise you and Peyton won't be disappointed."

Another long silence before, "I'll text you my address."

Her smile grew. "I'm off at five, then I'll swing home and head your way."

Campbell leaned against the door and ended the call.

Maybe she and Scott were losing their minds. Still, after

getting away from her possessive, entitled ex-bastard and essentially living an invisible life while with him and well before leaving Durango, how could any of this really be wrong?

She and Scott had an unmistakable spark.

Yes. The timing was far from perfect. It didn't change the fact she—they—deserved this spark which could end up being so much more. And if that happened, she'd absolutely have to face some truths. But not today.

Campbell straightened.

Today, she actually had something to look forward to after work. As much as she loved her job, the rest of the day would be her longest few hours since starting at Daisy's Bouquets.

SCOTT CLEARED THE LAST STEP, adjusted Peyton barely awake in his arms, and headed into her bedroom, a shrine to the color pink and all of the Disney princesses.

He carefully sat on her bed's edge, but she kept her arms around him.

"You know," he said, giving her a long squeeze, "you're almost getting too big for me to carry like this." Something else he couldn't believe.

She lifted her head from his shoulder. "I'm hot."

"I know, baby." He helped her under the sheet. "The medicine should work soon."

She laid her head on the pink pillowcase and rolled onto her side. "Where's Coco?"

Scott patted Peyton's twin bed until he made contact with the elusive stuffed animal. He slipped his hand underneath the comforter and withdrew the pink elephant she took from his hand and immediately hugged to her chest.

He grinned. "Anything else, your Highness?"

"Read me a *Pete the Cat* story," she mumbled as her eyes drifted shut.

"Not tonight." He leaned down and kissed her forehead that was indeed warm. "You'll probably be asleep before I leave." He straightened and stayed with her until her breathing became slow and steady. Which had taken about as long as he'd predicted.

Once in the hallway, he paused to steady his breath.

Campbell would be here any minute because she'd surprised *and* intrigued him during their quick phone call. When she'd knocked him sideways with her flirtatious comment, followed soon thereafter by her statement about having the best cold remedy.

Scott had no idea what she could be bringing, but it had been an excuse to see her and that's what he wanted. She'd also sounded pretty confident.

How could he not have been intrigued?

A beautiful woman full of surprises.

He ambled down the stairs and went into the kitchen.

But she couldn't stay longer than a few minutes. He would take whatever she gave him, be polite, friendly, grateful, and send her on her way…no matter how hard it would be to not pick up where they'd left off Saturday night before she slid into her car.

Okay. He had a plan. In the meantime, and as a way to keep himself busy before she arrived, he could clean up Peyton's dinner of chicken noodle soup and a grilled cheese sandwich.

He'd just started to wash the pans when his phone buzzed and burst into song from his jeans pocket.

Had Campbell changed her mind?

He withdrew his phone, but paused at the caller's name. He then released a slight breath of relief he had no business feeling at seeing another woman's name.

"Hey," he answered. "I just put her down because she fell asleep on the couch."

"How's she feeling?" Shannon asked.

He leaned against the counter. "Pretty puny. I had to cancel my class tomorrow so I can stay home with her."

"You didn't have to do that. I've told you when your sitter isn't available you can always call the woman we use."

He shook his head. "It's only one day since I have my sitter on standby for Wednesday, possibly Thursday. Is that it?"

She laughed. "What's your rush? Gotta hot date waiting for you?"

No, but he sure as hell wanted a hot date with Campbell Grey. And his memory once again replayed the way her mouth had been parted as she stared up at him with her hand inside of his pocket and incredibly close to—

"Actually, there is something else."

Scott blinked and rubbed his eyes. "What's up?" *Besides him.*

"Adam wants to get married."

Well that info sure as shit was all he'd needed to snap out of his Campbell haze.

"Doesn't he know you better than that by now?"

"You'd think. But I still find him pretty irresistible."

Scott stared at his kitchen table. "It sounds like you're considering it." Which meant the world had in fact flipped on its head in more ways than one since the spring semester began.

"It might be better for Peyton, too." Shannon paused before, "She'll always be *our* daughter, but Adam does love her."

Yet another reason Scott couldn't help but respect the guy.

"What do you think?"

He lifted his head. "It doesn't matter what I think."

Another pause, followed by, "You wouldn't be hurt if I said yes to Adam six years after saying no to you?"

Proposing had been the right thing to do after she'd told him she was pregnant. Looking back on that period of time, though, he really hadn't wanted to marry Shannon any more than she'd wanted to be married to any*one*. A truth he hadn't felt Campbell needed to know Saturday night. But he had been truthful when he'd confessed he'd wanted much more than what he and Shannon had settled into for far too long.

"If you had said yes," he quietly said, "we both know how it would have ended." She'd actually done them and Peyton a huge favor by saying no. No other way around the facts.

"True." She sighed. "I haven't made a decision. I wanted to talk to you and Peyton first."

Scott released a quick laugh. "Shannon, you and Adam have been living together for over a year. Nothing's going to change in Peyton's life. Or yours, for that matter."

"I'd be legally bound to someone. That's huge."

"It's a piece of paper." He thought of it as so much more, but Shannon had always been a pragmatist. "Stop overthinking it and do what's best for you and Adam."

His doorbell rang.

He cringed for two reasons, the first being hope the bell hadn't woken up his sick daughter. The second being the fact Campbell now stood outside his front door.

Holy shit, he'd lost his mind. No other way around that fact.

"I have to go." He walked toward the staircase. "I'll have Peyton call you tomorrow."

Before Scott headed down the stairs, he paused to look up at the third floor for signs of life from his daughter's room.

"Okay. Give her a big hug for me."

He waited another few seconds, but seeing nothing he rushed down the steps.

"Scott, thanks for listening and the advice."

He stopped at his front door. "It nearly killed you to say those words."

She laughed. "I do prefer to hurl *friendly* insults at you."

"And it's always a pleasure, Shannon. I'm hanging up now."

He shoved his phone back into his pocket and with a quick breath opened the door.

Campbell gave him a blinding smile which reached her eyes, then came the flutter from deep within. Only this time, it captured his breath. The fact she wore her red hat from the first day of class did nothing to help his breathing return to normal.

She couldn't stay longer than a few minutes.

Yeah, right. Who the hell was he kidding?

Chapter Fourteen

CAMPBELL LOST her voice at the sight of at home, single dad Scott.

Mussed hair. Colorado Avalanche sweatshirt. Snug jeans. Barefoot. Adorably rumpled.

"Hey." He gave her his infectious grin and stepped aside. "Come in."

She stepped into his townhome, and he closed the door behind her.

He definitely wore this look as well, if not even better, than a black, formal suit.

"Is that the best cold remedy?" he asked, pointing at the plastic container she held.

She cleared her throat, tore her gaze off of him, and glanced into what had to be the living or family room based on the big, sectional couch which looked comfy and the massive T.V. "Where's Peyton?"

"I had to give her some medicine and put her to bed early. She was fading pretty fast."

Campbell nodded and handed him the container. "Hopefully she'll feel up to eating one of those tomorrow."

He raised his eyebrows and opened the lid. "Wow. Those look damn good."

"Whoopie pies." She grinned. "They're my specialty and always made *me* feel better when my mom baked them when I was Peyton's age." It had probably been more than he'd needed to know, but she couldn't stop herself from sharing a piece of her untainted past.

Scott glanced at her. "You made these?" His grin grew. "Then I definitely need to try one." He reached for a pie, but she slapped his hand.

He shot her an exaggerated glare. "What was that for?"

Campbell closed the lid and took the container. "They're for Peyton."

He narrowed his eyes. "Correct me if I'm wrong, but you said on the phone Peyton and *I* wouldn't be disappointed."

She lifted her chin. "Peyton gets first dibs. You'll have to control yourself."

Their gazes locked for a few seconds before he said, "Fine."

Scott held out his hand. "I'll take them upstairs. Can I get you anything while I'm up there? I have apple juice, orange juice, milk—white and chocolate—water, coffee, and beer."

She laughed. "That's quite a beverage list, but I'll go with a beer." She started to hand him the container, but stopped. "Can I trust you not to eat one?"

His eyes widened. "You think I would actually steal a whoopie pie from my sick, five-year-old daughter?" He shook his head. "That hurts."

She fought a smile while letting him take the container.

"I'll be right back."

As he headed up the stairs, Campbell walked into the living room.

When she reached the chocolate-brown sofa, she pulled her

hat off, then shrugged out of her coat and placed them on the back of the couch.

She grinned softly at what must have been Peyton's spot, based on the thick, blue-and-white blanket featuring Olaf from the *Frozen* Disney movies, a pink pillow, and a stuffed penguin. Scott's spot was marked by papers he appeared to be in the middle of grading. And another Disney movie happened to be paused on the T.V.—*Tangled*.

Campbell quietly laughed.

It seemed clear in this space alone how much love existed in his three-story townhome.

She was lowering herself to sit in the only clear spot on the couch when pictures on the built-in shelving flanking the T.V. caught her attention.

Campbell stopped in front of the nearest shelves and leaned forward.

Pics of Peyton as a baby to what had to be her school picture, the definition of adorable.

A picture of him, which looked fairly recent, with Felicity and another striking woman who also had the rich, copper hair. His sister Leann?

Another picture of him with his sisters and an older woman with graying, auburn hair, the family resemblance unmistakable. She had to be the Mayhew matriarch. But a third family pic caused her to reach out and pluck it off the shelf.

Scott as a boy—maybe eleven or twelve?—wearing a huge, goofy smile while he stood beside a handsome man who had to be his dad; his sisters stood on the man's other side. A lake shimmered behind where they stood on the bank.

"Sorry that took so long."

Campbell whirled forward to find Scott standing steps away.

"I checked on Peyton." He held out a bottle of beer. "She's out. I think the cold medicine kicked in."

She grasped the bottle and held up the picture. "This is a cute photo."

Scott stood beside her and took the frame. "Thanks. It's one of my favorites with me, my sisters, and our dad." His grin slipped. "It was taken during our last camping trip together."

Campbell pressed her lips together as he placed the frame back on the shelf.

"When I look at that picture," he quietly continued, "I still can't believe three months later he was gone. Just like that." He glanced at her. "October is a rough month in my family."

She nodded, eyed the photo, then asked, "Did your mom ever remarry?"

"No." Scott drank some of his beer. "My dad was *the one*."

Campbell's heart cracked at his softly spoken statement. In that instant, she recalled their conversation in the shop about love stories ending unhappily.

He'd called them more compelling which now made complete sense.

"My mom knew, too. He wasn't home when we expected him and didn't call." His gaze strayed to the photo. "The doorbell rang and she *knew*. I—we—could see it in her face."

Campbell sipped her beer and hesitated because what she wanted to ask next qualified as extremely personal. Yes. He'd already shared more than she'd expected.

But reliving this kind of darkness wasn't easy, no matter how much time had passed.

"I know it's none of my business, but…" Her voice trailed into silence.

He leaned against the shelf. "A traffic stop that went horribly wrong. The guy was a career criminal with an arrest warrant and wasn't going to go back to jail without a fight."

Campbell's eyes widened.

"My dad opened the car door while his partner was calling for backup and the shit bag opened fire on them."

Her mouth inched open. "Oh, my God."

Scott took another drink of beer. "My dad's partner was hit pretty bad, but survived his injuries." He stared at the bottle. "I can still remember my mom opening the front door and at seeing my dad's boss she let out this...sound." He lifted his gaze which connected with Campbell's. "Like her heart had shattered and the pain was killing her."

She reached out, clasped his hand, and squeezed.

"I'll never forget it." He cleared his throat. "But they did catch the sonofabitch later that night and he's rotting in prison for the rest of his life."

She again squeezed his hand though she really wanted to take their beers, put them aside, and pull him into her arms. The desire so strong she gripped his hand a tad harder than necessary.

He straightened. "I'm sure you weren't expecting me to throw all of that at you after doing something as simple as picking up a picture."

Campbell gave him a soft smile. "It's absolutely fine. It's also not just *any* picture."

"No," he murmured. "It sure as hell isn't." He pointed at the photo of him with his sisters and mom. "In case you haven't guessed, those are the other two classy, smart women who raised me." He leaned forward. "So if there's something you don't like about me, it's all their fault."

She laughed which felt good after hearing such a tragic story. And it occurred to her where this part of his personality came from. Diffusing tension with humor. He'd probably learned it as a twelve-year-old boy who'd become "the man of the house" in an instant.

The thought made her say, "There's nothing about you I don't like—" She froze.

Oh, no. She'd done it again. Only this time with Scott standing in front of her.

What was wrong with her? She always thought before she spoke. That is, until she'd met Scott Mayhew.

She focused on the top of her beer bottle while a heavy silence fell between them.

"That's nice to hear, but you don't know me too well."

No. She sure didn't. But she wanted to know every part of him *extremely* well.

Campbell slid her gaze back to the shelf where yet another pic caught her attention.

She pointed at the photo of Scott as a young soldier with a shaved head while wearing a white T-shirt and his army fatigue pants. He stood beside another tall, equally handsome guy with light-brown skin and black facial hair. They had their arms hooked loosely around each other's necks as they grinned at the camera. "Who's that?"

His smile slowly returned. "My good buddy, Ian. He lives in Grand Junction. We were in the same unit and ended up being based out of Fort Carson together." He eyed her. "The guy who took the picture was another good friend of ours, but he didn't make it back."

Also not just *any* picture.

Another portion of Campbell's heart cracked at all the tragic loss Scott had endured in a rather short amount of time. The fact he shouldered all of it as well as he did seemed miraculous.

He absolutely deserved the title of superhero.

"Daddy?"

Campbell's eyes widened at Peyton's soft voice reaching where they stood. She caught Scott's startled gaze before he withdrew his hand from hers and turned toward the staircase.

He set his beer on an end table on his way to the stairs.

"Baby, what are you doing up?" he asked while jogging up the steps.

"Now I'm *sweating*. I feel yucky."

His and Peyton's voices slowly faded into silence.

Dammit. She really had no business still being here.

Her heart had been in the right place with the whoopie pies since they had always made her feel better as a sick kid. But she should have handed him the container and left. Not ended up pulled into his adorably rumpled, single dad world of Olaf blankets and stuffed penguins and Disney movies and grading and comfy furniture…and pictures which could make a person smile then break their heart seconds later.

She needed to leave, but she couldn't without saying goodbye. It would be beyond rude and hurtful. At least, that's how she'd feel if Scott did something similar to her.

Campbell set her beer beside his on the end table and grabbed her coat and hat. Once bundled back up, she went for the staircase and dropped to a step.

As she waited for Scott to come back downstairs, she focused on his living room filled with undeniable warmth and love. She then couldn't stop herself from imagining what it would feel like to be a part of his adorably rumpled, single dad world.

The image became so strong it brought forth a strange combo of contentment *and* disappointment. As much as she liked Scott— and vice versa—the price could end up being too high, especially for him. She had no idea where that left them, either.

***

WHEN SCOTT SPOTTED Campbell seated on the second-to-last step, wearing her coat and hat, he paused on the landing and kept a sigh in check.

He didn't want her to leave. Especially on the heels of him

sharing the darkest moment of his life; his time in combat had been the second darkest. But no matter how incredible it felt to have her in his home and how much he enjoyed talking to her—something so damn easy—having Campbell here had surpassed playing with fire.

They both knew it, too.

He also had a sick daughter upstairs who needed his undivided attention. He had a feeling it might be a long night. Peyton hadn't been this sick in a while.

Scott always meant it when he said he thrived off of honesty, so maybe it was time to address the elephant in the room?

He slowly walked down the remaining steps.

Campbell stood and faced him. "Is she okay?"

"Yeah." He stopped on the last stair. "Her fever broke. We changed her pjs, and I put a cold cloth on her forehead until she went back to sleep." He managed a slight smile. "It's always worse at night, right?"

She nodded. "Definitely. I should go." She stepped back. "My roomies will start to wonder where I am since I'm always at home on a Monday night."

He followed her to the door. "You have roommates?" For some reason, he'd assumed she lived alone in a studio or small one-bedroom apartment. Maybe because of her quiet, reserved side which did come out during moments she turned her way-too appealing shade of red?

The same shade as the hat she wore.

She grinned. "Yes. They are two of the nicest guys you'll ever know and have become my Denver family. We look out for each other."

"Very cool. You're lucky to have roommates like that." He leaned against the door. "The only time I ever had anything close to roommates was when I was in the army."

Silence settled around them.

He needed to stop being a coward and state the obvious.

"I guess I'll see you Thursday?" she asked with her hand on the knob.

Scott reached out and placed his hand on hers which earned him a wide-eyed stare.

"Campbell," he softly began, "we both know there's something here. Between us?"

She sighed. "Yes. But it's complicated."

He slowly nodded. "More than complicated since the school has a strict policy about instructors getting *involved* with their students."

"I had a feeling." She also leaned against the door. "How many more weeks are left in the semester?"

"Including this week, fourteen."

Campbell flinched. "Would it be wrong to say that sounds like forever?"

"No." He stepped closer. "Because it does." He paused to take a deep breath. There was no reason to stop being honest now. "But I'm not certain I can wait that long to see if there's something *real* here. Between us?"

Her lips parted.

Scott lifted his gaze from her mouth to add, "Can you? Because if you can, I'll shut up right now and we can forget this conversation happened until—"

She covered his mouth with her hand. "No. And even if I could wait, I wouldn't want to."

Yep. He—they—were in trouble. *Big time.* The realization didn't stop him from saying, "I like your honesty." Which came out muffled because of her fingers still over his mouth.

Campbell fought a smile while removing her hand.

"So maybe we should take this one extremely careful day at a time? Keep it professional during class and while on the campus?" Especially when he thought of losing his career and his livelihood…and his sister threatening his male parts.

But *shit.* A lot could happen in fourteen weeks. And what if now happened to be the only chance he and Campbell would get? They'd agreed there was something between them.

"I can do that." She leaned forward. "Scott, you have to know I would never do anything to jeopardize your career or what you have here"—she gestured at his home—"or the life you have with Peyton."

He grinned softly. "I know."

Campbell might as well have said, *"It'll be our little secret."* He despised the fact it had to be that way. It wasn't fair. But this situation wouldn't last forever, despite fourteen weeks sounding like an eternity.

"I liked texting you yesterday," she said with a coy smile. "About the books?"

"Then let's keep doing that."

She lifted her chin. The flash of passion within her hypnotic blue eyes quickly followed.

Scott's insides once again awakened.

"I'll expect an update on Marianne and John W. as soon as possible."

She opened the door, but Scott eased it shut.

Now that he'd accepted the fact he'd become an idiot who had lost his mind, he couldn't stop himself from doing something he'd been trying *not* to think about since Saturday night.

"Update as soon as possible. Done. I just have one more thing to say before you leave."

She smiled. "And what might that be?"

He hesitated before he closed the small gap between them, slipped his arms around her waist, and pressed his mouth to hers. Which opened beneath his with zero hesitation.

Their mouths moved together in a slow, perfect rhythm.

Everything around them became hazy. Until he gently guided her hips closer to him and deepened the kiss.

Campbell's soft moan filled his head, and Scott became aware of his body and hers. Her arms went around his neck and she hugged him tight. *Tighter*. And their kiss turned hungry.

She slid her fingers through his hair which she gripped, followed by another moan when he pinned her against the door. In that moment his common sense—reality—hit him with a vengeance. This wasn't the time and place to begin a make-out session with Campbell Grey.

Scott forced himself to bring their kiss to an end and pressed his forehead to hers while they caught their breath.

"I really liked what you had to say," she whispered.

He released a quick laugh. "And I would love to say more, but I can't."

"I know." Her eyes, filled with an odd combination of disappointment and lust, connected with his. "I need to leave. We're also supposed to be taking this one day at a time."

Right. His suggestion. But he'd needed to know if she tasted as good as she looked.

He hadn't been disappointed, either. Not even a little bit.

"It's not because I want you to leave."

She freed his hair from her grip, let her fingers linger, then slowly removed her arms from behind his neck. "I know that, too."

Scott released her waist and stepped back. "Thank you for bringing over your cold remedy. I'm sure it'll help Peyton feel much better tomorrow."

"You're welcome." She opened his front door. "Text soon?"

He grinned. "I promise. You'll owe me updates on Edna's *awakening*."

With a long, final glance at him, Campbell slipped out of his home.

After watching her climb into her CR-V and drive away, Scott expelled a lengthy, heavy breath as he closed and locked the door.

Holy shit, he couldn't remember the last time he'd kissed a woman and lost himself. In actuality, he wasn't certain such a thing had ever happened. That had to mean something. And not just the fact he hadn't been with a woman in an embarrassingly long time.

Sparks. Connection. Chemistry. The ability to talk as friends. They possessed all of it.

He faced his living room and leaned against the door.

Campbell knew it, too.

He—they—couldn't let this go. He knew firsthand about rare connections. How they could capture a person and never go away, despite tragedy and the passage of time.

One extremely careful day at a time.

He could do that. It was only fourteen weeks. A better way of looking at it, for sure.

They'd be smart while in class and everything would be fine.

It couldn't go any other way.

Chapter Fifteen

"WHERE HAVE YOU BEEN?" Blaine asked the moment Campbell closed the front door.

With Scott Mayhew.

Kissing Scott Mayhew.

Pinned between Scott Mayhew and a door while kissing Scott Mayhew.

"Running an errand," she replied with a quick smile for her roommates, sitting in opposite corners of the couch while watching T.V.

She could still feel Scott's warm, delectable mouth moving with hers in perfect unison, as well as his thick, soft hair in her fingers.

"What'd you buy?" Lance looked up from his phone. "Are you baking again?" He pointed at the television hanging on the wall. "It sounds like there's a huge snowstorm headed our way later this week. If we get snowed in, we'll need lots of snacks."

Blaine waved his hand at Lance. "Every time the weather people get this excited about a storm heading for Denver, it snows an inch. Maybe." He sighed. "I'm also on the schedule this weekend and would never be lucky enough to get out of a

Denver-to-Albuquerque-to-Phoenix-to-Salt-Lake-City-back-to-Denver trip." He exaggerated a fake yawn. "Snooze. *Cities*."

Campbell faced the staircase. "I have homework, so I'll see you guys later." As much as she would miss being in class tomorrow—seeing Scott—she'd barely started reading *Daisy Miller: A Study*. It had failed to capture her attention.

She probably wouldn't be terribly focused tonight, either.

"Are you baking this week or not?" Lance's question followed her up the stairs.

"Would you leave her alone and go buy your own cookies?" Blaine's response reached her as she walked into her room. "She's not a Keebler elf."

Campbell closed her bedroom door, tossed her purse onto her bed, and leaned back.

Wow. Bringing Scott the whoopie pies had certainly ended in an unexpected way. Though she would never in a million years complain about the way it had ended, they had definitely crossed a line which could become messy if they weren't careful.

In more ways than the obvious.

She removed her hat and coat, and headed for her bed where she dropped both.

He'd suggested taking it "one extremely careful day at a time." But after their head-blurring kiss—being wrapped in his strong arms—his words no longer seemed like an option.

Campbell lowered herself to her bed's edge.

She wanted him the way a woman desired a man. He'd made it absolutely clear, when he'd pressed her hips to his, he felt the same way.

Her breathing slowed and her skin turned warm from the memory of them locked together and against his front door. She became so warm she removed her sweater and laid back on her comforter, the cool, soft fabric easing her skin's heat.

She breathed deeply through her nose to settle her racing pulse.

Scott had proven he knew how to use his mouth in their brief moment.

Campbell couldn't stop herself from wondering what other talents he and his mouth and hands possessed. Her active imagination made her grin at the ceiling.

She couldn't ignore his entire package qualified as irresistible.

Smart, confident, talented English professor by day.

Devoted single dad by night when he had Peyton.

Fiercely loyal brother and son who'd been through more in life than was fair.

Charming, funny, *hot* single man who knew how to wear a formal suit and thoroughly kiss a woman before she left his house.

Four completely different Scott Mayhews and Campbell wanted to know each of them.

But what if the price did end up being too high for him?

Her grin faded.

"Forbidden love." "Secret love." It always looked and sounded so exciting in books and movies. In real life, though, the stakes were incredibly high and a tad scary. And if she and Scott, somehow, some way, were successful at carefully becoming something between now and May, she would have no choice but to face her past once and for all.

Yes. She'd already taken a huge step forward by deciding to spend spring break in Durango. Still, she didn't know if her ex was truly gone. He had faded from her family's life after being taken somewhere to receive his "emotional and mental help." Moving to Denver had helped keep him away from her family, as well. But not until she knew for certain he'd faded into oblivion would she feel total freedom.

Her mom and brother hadn't heard from him since he returned

to Durango, long after Campbell had moved to Denver. Definitely a good sign. It still didn't mean he was gone for good, though that's all she'd ever wanted after he'd, following months of playing games, signed the divorce papers.

For the umpteenth time, Campbell couldn't fathom how she'd been so stupid to get involved with him in the first place, much less let their relationship get as far as it did. At least what she'd told Scott on Saturday about being young had been the total truth. In hindsight, she should have added the word naïve.

You're being too hard on yourself. People make mistakes.

Scott had been so kind and supportive, then told her about his mistakes with Shannon.

If only marrying the wrong guy at a young age had been her whole story. Recalling the major parts of the whole story only brought back the humiliation and darkness she'd tried to leave in Durango. Darkness she had no interest in reliving unless she had no other choice.

And all because her ex-bastard wouldn't let her go to the point he'd become obsessed; emotionally and mentally unstable while refusing to leave her life. She'd then been forced to do something rather desperate after his parents quickly and quietly took him away.

Remembering her time with Scott earlier, from beginning to the memorable and idyllic end, she couldn't shake the feeling she might reach no other choice but to share everything. In fact, she probably needed to tell him the whole story before too soon became too late. But when?

They weren't exactly in a normal dating situation. They had to be extremely careful, especially during class, from this point moving forward. She could clearly imagine the judgment she'd receive from her roommates and Alyson if she told them the truth, and she sure as hell couldn't tell her mom. And what about Scott's side? He really couldn't say anything to anyone.

She shivered, sat up, and grabbed a nearby sweatshirt.

Forbidden love. Secret love. None of this was fair. They weren't the cliché older, married professor and young, inexperienced student. They were a single woman and man who weren't too far apart in age and had connected over a shared love of reading, among other things.

She shrugged into her heavy sweatshirt, then grabbed her purse and withdrew her phone.

Campbell couldn't stop from smiling as she read through her texts with Scott yesterday. When finished, her thumbs hovered over the keyboard to type one word—and a text appeared.

I think Marianne is way too good for John W. Something else that reminds me of Felicity.

Her smile slipped a fraction at Scott's comment about his sister as she replied with, *I have to agree with you.*

All Campbell knew of Felicity's past personal life was that she'd been married to a British guy and had lived with him in London, the reason she occasionally sounded as if she had an accent. But if the character of John Willoughby, the definition of a cad, reminded Scott of his ex-brother-in-law, he clearly hadn't been a good guy or husband.

Something Campbell absolutely understood, too.

You're agreeing with me? I hope you didn't catch Peyton's cold. The winking emoji completed his statement.

She'd better not catch Peyton's cold because she couldn't miss Thursday's class.

Actually, I'm feeling rather amazing right now.

She sat back, knowing Scott would understand precisely what she meant.

Yeah. Same. But I also like the word awakened.

Campbell's memory went to Edna in *The Awakening*, exploring the possibilities. Trying to connect with who she wanted to be despite the high stakes.

She wrote, *Even better. And Edna's making mistakes, but I still think she has guts.*

No matter the time—past, present, future—it took guts to be one's true self.

Maybe…just maybe…moving to Denver had been Campbell's way of connecting with who she'd wanted to be well before meeting her ex.

I have to agree with you. Book check-in tomorrow?

She hesitated before typing, *I can't wait.* She then added the one word, *Goodnight.*

On the outside, what she and Scott were moving into could be viewed as wrong and risky and foolish. But what about inside? What couldn't be seen?

This wasn't about breaking the rules and the excitement of rule-breaking and lust. Though now, for the first time in her adult life, she truly understood what that four-letter word meant. This happened to be about a man and woman who wanted to explore the possibilities.

Me, too. Goodnight.

She put her phone down.

Being a *them* couldn't be wrong, especially if it led them to the lives they wanted. Complications aside, she had to give this a chance and would face her past when the time came.

SCOTT'S PHONE buzzed and chimed with a text, and he swiped it off of his desk at work. His mouth curved into a smile as he read Campbell's message.

How's Peyton feeling? Has she tried the best cold remedy yet? She'd followed up her questions with the smiling emoji.

Since he had his office door closed, he felt zero hesitation quickly replying.

Her cold has hit pretty hard. Not sure when she'll be ready. He paused before grinning and adding, *But now I'm feeling under the weather, so I'll have to try eating some whoopie pies.*

His smile deepened while he waited for her to reply.

Complicated or not, it felt damn good to be texting a woman he genuinely liked and wanted. A woman he liked and wanted so much he hadn't been sleeping well due to his memory reliving their Monday night kiss. His active imagination had taken over several times when it came to the possibilities beyond a white hot first kiss.

I don't believe you. Stay away from those whoopie pies.

Scott started to respond when his phone burst into song, then he registered the caller's name which made him release a quick laugh. "Hey, man. What the hell's up with you?" He sat back. "You don't return calls. Your texts are no more than a few words. When did you turn into such a dick?"

Ian Stafford laughed. "Not too long after I met you. I learned from the best years ago."

Scott shook his head. "I think you have that backward."

"Whatever you say. How's life? And the most beautiful redhead I know?"

"Life's good." Even though it had become more than a little complicated. "Peyton's been pretty sick this week and is at home with my sitter."

"Well, give her a hug from her Uncle Ian later. So I have some news."

"Is this why you fell off the grid for so long?"

"Yeah. You could say that," his friend mumbled. "I'm moving to Denver."

Scott halted.

"I already have a job with DPD. Detective."

He smiled. "Are you shitting me? Ian, that's great." In fact, reaching detective grade had been Scott's goal when he'd been on such a trajectory.

It had also been a goal his dad had reached right before that dark day a long time ago.

"Why didn't you tell me you were looking to leave Grand Junction?" Scott asked. "And what does Candace think about all of this?"

A long silence fell on his buddy's end before, "Candace and I broke up right before Christmas."

Scott sighed. "I'm sorry to hear that." Especially since Ian and Candace had been together since high school and had managed to stay together despite Ian's time in the army. "What happened?" And could the break-up be the main reason behind what seemed like a sudden and huge life change?

"We were together way too long and drifted apart. It happens."

Scott frowned at his friend's flat voice and explanation.

"I've also wanted and needed a change for a while," Ian added. "That brings me to I'll be seeing you next week at your place, Professor."

Scott raised his eyebrows. "Did you just invite yourself to stay at my house?"

"I sure as hell did. I need a place to crash while I look for a place of my own. And your couch loves me as much as I love it. I'm going to meet my partner while I'm in town, too."

"What if I say no?"

"You won't." Ian laughed. "Peyton loves her Uncle Ian. More than you, I think."

"You really have turned into a dick." Scott straightened. "Fine. You can stay with me. But Peyton's with Shannon next week, so I'm afraid you won't be able to mesmerize my daughter with your corny magic tricks and that horse you call a dog."

"Hey," Ian deadpanned. "Watch how you talk about Stella who may end up being the love of my life."

He fought a grin while asking, "So when can I expect you two?"

"I was hoping to get there Sunday night, but according to the weather reports Denver's supposed to get nailed with a pretty big snowstorm. Grand Junction's only going to see the beginnings of it."

Scott nodded. "I've heard. But you know that doesn't always mean anything."

"Yeah. Keep you posted?"

"Sounds good." Scott paused, then said, "Ian, it'll be cool to have you in Denver." More like having a *brother* close by since being discharged from the army.

"Thanks. I know it'll be a good change. I'll see you soon."

Ian Stafford, who'd been on track to marry his high school sweetheart and live the rest of his days as a cop in his hometown of Grand Junction, had decided to relocate to Denver.

Scott had certainly not seen that change coming.

The world really had flipped on its head. He also couldn't help but wonder what exactly had happened between his buddy and his long-time girlfriend. The times Scott had been around the couple, they'd seemed perfect for one another. And perfectly in sync. He remembered this only because he'd experienced pangs of envy for what they shared.

Campbell's flushed face and eyes shining with an entirely different type of passion following their kiss appeared in his mind. That's when he remembered they'd been in the middle of texting when Ian had called and he went back into his thread with Campbell.

Okay. I'm back. On a different topic, is it wrong I want to punch John W. and Edward?

After noting the time, Scott stood and packed up his laptop

bag. He had a quick stop to make before heading home to his sick daughter.

He closed out of messaging, shoved his phone into his back jeans pocket, and headed for the door—where a knock stopped him.

With a slight grin, he opened it to find Johanna who smiled and pointed at him.

"Leaving us so soon?" She leaned against the doorframe. "I haven't had a chance to talk to you today. How's Peyton feeling?"

His phone buzzed with what had to be Campbell's reply, but he focused on his boss. "This bug hit her pretty hard. I have to swing by her school before everyone leaves for the day and pick up some work. I think I'm going to have to keep her at home the rest of the week. But thanks for asking."

Johanna smiled sympathetically. "I'm sorry. Poor little thing. I hope she feels better soon." She straightened. "I have an update on the position. Can I have a second?"

He backed up and lowered himself to the corner of his desk. "Of course." Based on her expression and tone, whatever she had to say didn't sound good.

"We were hoping to start interviews on Monday, but this snowstorm"—she released an exasperated sigh—"has become a serious impediment." She leaned forward. "There's some talk that the campus will be closing on Monday since this storm is supposed to last through Sunday."

And dump a shitload of snow.

If a college campus would be closed due to inclement weather, which rarely happened, it meant Peyton's school would definitely have a snow day.

"So now," Johanna added, "we're hoping to start interviews in the middle of next week."

Scott also, per the agreement, had to take Peyton back to Shannon on Sunday. It typically wasn't a problem at all having his little girl an extra day, but he'd had an extra day and night last week when he'd kept her Sunday per Adam's request. He'd definitely have to touch base with Shannon about Peyton staying with him through the storm or taking her back before it hit.

"The weather's looking very cold," Johanna continued, "but better overall after this storm passes through."

Scott nodded once. "Okay. Thanks for the update."

"Go home and take care of your daughter." She turned to leave.

A huge question suddenly popped into Scott's head which made him say, "Johanna?"

She stopped and raised her eyebrows.

He released a slow breath. "What are my chances of getting the position? You can be honest with me." Even though Scott wanted the better hours, pay, and less grading, he no longer felt confident jumping through the hoops would be worth his time if he didn't have a shot in hell.

Johanna had also made it a point last week to tell him how much he was liked as an instructor. *After* telling him his much more qualified colleague had expressed interest in the job.

"The applicant pool is quite strong," she quietly conceded. "Everyone's been pleased with what they've seen in the résumés. And someone else in the department—"

"I know." He stood. "I understand." He'd also asked for the truth and received it.

"Scott, you have nothing to lose by going through the interview process." She smiled. "You do have the Mayhew magic going for you, as well as many other strengths."

He forced himself to return her smile. "You're right. Thanks, Johanna."

"I'll see you tomorrow."

When she left, Scott stared at the empty doorway.

Maybe Assistant English Department Chair wasn't in his cards at this moment in time.

He removed his phone from his back pocket and seeing Campbell had replied, he couldn't deny the fact it might just be for the best. At least right now.

She'd texted, *You sound like a protective brother. And they do love Marianne and Elinor*. She'd also added the winking emoji.

As he re-read her message, the flutter deep inside of him returned.

It could be that right now something else in his life needed him more and vice versa. It's not like he despised being an instructor. Not even a little bit. He simply grew tired of all the grading by a semester's end. Felicity had been right, too. He did love being in the trenches.

Just like their dad.

He typed, *They love wealth and status more. Especially John W.*

That particular character had more than reminded Scott of Felicity's ex-dickhead—selfish, self-absorbed, and spoiled. And the bastard, like John. W. in the book with Marianne, had managed to charm his way into Felicity's life.

Scott shoved the thoughts aside, left his office, and closed the door behind him. He then went into an entirely different texting thread.

Hey. Give me a call when you can? We should talk about this storm and Peyton.

He sent the message to Shannon. As he left the building, Campbell's reply hit.

So that sounds familiar. A little like Catherine?

He laughed, paused, and tapped out, *Fine. You win. How's Edna?*

Okay. Connecting with a student…kissing a student…wanting a student…went against everything he'd signed up for when he'd become a college instructor. On top of going against the school's strict policy. At the same time, he'd never expected a woman like Campbell to be in one of his classes. Like he'd told her Saturday night, he mostly taught kids and the occasional adult.

But the previous, occasional adults had in no way been her. Not even close.

Scott stopped at his SUV and sighed.

They were certainly taking it one careful day at a time, like he'd suggested, but he wanted to know what it would be like to be on an actual date with her. Sooner rather than later. But he had his little girl with him this week and might have her through Monday due to the storm.

I finished the book last night.

He placed his laptop bag in the back and climbed into the driver's seat.

And?

The damn snowstorm which had everyone on high alert. It had been years since the last one rolled through. He'd been in the army and overseas, but his mom and sisters had been snowed in for a couple of days—*snowed in*. Damn him if the image didn't seem perfect with the right someone. He knew exactly who his right someone would be, sensible or not.

I hate that Edna did what she did because of ultimately being confined back then by the rules of society created by pompous men. It wasn't fair.

Scott sat back and shook his head. He could also imagine her big, bright, beautiful eyes lit up with the obvious passion in her reply.

If he wasn't careful, he could easily end up in way over his head with a woman like Campbell Grey. A rare connection. Spark. Chemistry.

True. But she did abandon her kids and husband.

He laughed quietly imagining what her reply would be to his

play as devil's advocate. And a realization hit with such strength his breath stalled.

He'd already reached way over his head and had been since Saturday night.

Scott let the thought linger as he drove away from the campus and in the direction of Peyton's school, also close to where he lived. Not until he reached a third red light did Campbell's message come through.

Fine. You win on that point. But it doesn't change the fact all Edna wanted was to be her true self and she couldn't without paying a huge price.

He stared at her response.

Something about this passionate reply told him she had to be speaking from experience. If that was the case, it undoubtedly had to do with her ex-husband.

Scott suddenly wanted to know the entire story.

I'm on flower delivery duty today. Text soon?

He quickly typed, *I promise.*

The light turned green, and Scott dropped his phone in the passenger seat.

Way in over his head? Nothing more than a massive under-statement.

Chapter Sixteen

"GREAT WORK TODAY WITH *DAISY MILLER.*" Scott held up the papers Campbell and her classmates had finished turning in to him. "I'm looking forward to reading your character studies." He set the papers down and opened his copy of their textbook.

Campbell eyed the clock on the wall for what had to be the millionth time in the last thirty minutes. Not until today had the last half hour of Scott's class seemed like forever. Replaying over and over the last time she'd seen him—Monday night at his house —wasn't helping. Still, she felt they'd done a rather impressive job at being nothing more than what they could be in this classroom. Him, professor. Her, student.

No. This situation wouldn't last forever. Fourteen weeks left, soon to be thirteen.

Scott held up the textbook. "Next reading assignment due Tuesday. There will be a quiz. I expect everyone to get a hundred-percent, too, since you'll have nothing better to do this weekend than read."

Dead Poets Society guy laughed. "Nope. I'm going snowboarding. Leaving tonight for Copper Mountain as a matter of fact."

"The campus will be closed on Monday, right?" the girl next to Campbell asked. "It could even be closed Tuesday."

Scott unleashed his infectious grin on the class.

Campbell's body became warm at the memory of them pressed against his front door, their mouths moving perfectly together. As if they'd been made to kiss each other like that the rest of their lives. He'd also given her the grin he currently wore.

"I have many superpowers"—Scott's gaze caught Campbell's for a second—"but I don't have the ability to predict the future." He lifted his shoulders. "At least I don't have that power yet. So, homework. Due Tuesday."

Campbell again slid her gaze to the clock and released a quick breath. Twelve-fifteen on the nose. Now she just had to leisurely pack up her stuff.

"Kate Chopin," he continued. "Another brilliant writer who was ahead of her time and didn't always make her or her work popular."

"Why's that?" the girl asked. "Because she was a brilliant *female* writer?"

"A brilliant female writer who wrote about things almost no one wrote about back then. Especially women." Scott leaned forward. "Her writing might make some of you blush."

Campbell smiled as some of the girls giggled.

He straightened. "You'll see what I mean after you read the two stories I listed in the syllabus. Be safe this weekend." He pointed at *Dead Poets Society* guy. "You can read on your way up to Copper and back."

The guy stood. "Not if I'm the one driving."

Scott laughed while everyone else started to pack up their bags which Campbell also did, but at a much slower pace.

Within seconds, she and Scott were alone in the classroom.

He looked up from packing his bag as she approached the desk. "Hey there."

She grinned softly. "Hi."

Silence descended between them for several seconds until they laughed.

"Would this be easier if I left and sent you a text?" he asked.

She continued to laugh. "No." She shook her head. "How's Peyton feeling?"

He eased onto the edge of the desk. "She's getting there. I kept her home again and will tomorrow. I'm off on Fridays, so I can stay home with her."

She lifted her chin. "Are there any whoopie pies left? Be honest."

Mischief flashed through his eyes as he fought a grin. "I only ate one."

Campbell narrowed her eyes.

"Okay, two." He met her gaze. "It turns out I have zero self-control when it comes to whoopie pies." He grinned. "They were fantastic." He paused before adding, "So really I have incredible self-control because I didn't eat all of them. I also don't want them to get stale."

"Of course not." She leaned forward. "How about I make more and give several just to you? I have that superpower."

His grin softened. "I'd like that. I'm hoping Peyton will feel up to having the two I left for her. I'm taking her back to Shannon a day early. Because of the storm? She'll most likely have a snow day on Monday." He leaned forward. "Do you want to hear a secret?"

Yes. But she wanted to pick up where they'd left off on Monday night even more.

"You have my complete attention." In more ways than one, too.

"I lied earlier," he whispered. "The campus will probably close on Monday. But the secret stays in this classroom."

She smiled. "I promise."

His grin slipped as he straightened. "I normally don't mind these big, Colorado snowstorms we get every decade or so, but this time…" He sighed. "I shouldn't be saying this—especially here—but I'd really like to take you out. On a *real* date," he murmured.

Campbell's heart pounded her chest. "I'd like that, too." Without question.

"But this weekend—"

"I know," she quietly finished. "Bad timing."

"That's one way of putting it." He stood and hooked his bag's strap on his shoulder. "So how will you be spending the weekend?" He frowned. "Do you have to work?"

"No. I totally lucked out by having this weekend off. Alyson and Hayley on the other hand—" She cringed. "Alyson's hoping she and Hayley can drop off all of the flowers at the hotel earlier than normal so they can get home before the snow really hits."

Scott slowly nodded, followed by another round of silence.

Not knowing what else to say and needing to get back to work, Campbell stepped right. "I should go." Though she wanted to stay right where she stood for as long as possible. "Text soon? I'll need my Dashwood sisters update." She'd especially been appreciating him reacting to the story as a protective brother.

Yet another heart-melting quality Scott Mayhew possessed. As he remained silent, however, she tilted her head right.

"Where'd I lose you?"

"Sorry." He cleared his throat. "You didn't lose me. Just the opposite, in fact." He concentrated on her. "What if I could give you the update in person?"

She squinted at him. "I'm not following."

He slipped his hands into his pockets. "I'm taking Peyton back to Shannon Saturday morning. There's a huge storm headed this way. It's going to be a long weekend." He hesitated before saying, "And neither one of us is working."

Oh, my God.

Campbell's breathing slowed at what Scott had inferred.

"That being said," he softly continued after a quick glance at the doorway, "do you want to get snowed in with me?"

Their gazes snapped together. As if two industrial-strength magnets.

Her mouth inched open while all of the delicious possibilities inundated her brain.

All alone with him—wrapped around him—for an entire weekend during a snowstorm? And no one would ever know until they had to know.

She had to be dreaming right now. Because this could not be happening to her, Campbell Grey. Then again, Campbell Grey was *not* the woman she'd left in Durango.

"Or is that too much, too soon?" He released a heavy breath. "I know we're supposed to be taking it one day at a time. I just don't think I can wait another week to spend time with you. The texting is fun, but it's not the same." The corner of his mouth lifted in a grin. "If what I asked is too much, too soon, I'll shut up right now and we can forget—"

"You're right." Campbell raised her chin. "The texting isn't the same. And no. It's not too much, too soon." She'd be bat-shit crazy if she said yes or no, so why not follow her heart?

Something she hadn't done in years which had ended badly. But she couldn't ignore the feeling this time would be vastly different.

Scott was a trustworthy *man*, and he liked and wanted her.

His grin deepened. "Is that a yes?"

She wanted to show him just how much of a yes it had been. But she went with a quick, wicked grin and murmured, "I'll see you Saturday at your place. Text me a time."

Her reply earned her his wicked grin which reached his eyes.

She had to get out of there and away from him before she did something really stupid. They'd probably been in here talking for too long, but thank goodness it always seemed pretty quiet in the building around this time of the day.

Campbell stepped backward, toward the doorway. "Thanks for the chat. I'm looking forward to the reading assignment this weekend."

"Right." He quietly laughed. "It was my pleasure."

Campbell shot him a final, impish smile and darted from the classroom.

Wow. That conversation had really happened.

She would actually be spending a snowy weekend, alone, with her—Scott. She had to start only thinking of him as Scott, a handsome, smart, charming, successful single dad and man who knew how to kiss a woman. He also had to know how to use his mouth in other ways.

Other delectable, unforgettable ways she would get to know this weekend.

She pushed through the building's door. Her pulse then amplified with all the pictures of them getting to know one another in an entirely different way filling her head.

How the hell would she get through the rest of today and tomorrow? And what would she tell Lance? She couldn't and wouldn't deal with any judgment. Blaine would be easier to tell, but his working weekend started tomorrow. He'd be gone until sometime next week. Maybe she'd luck out and Lance would spend the weekend in the mountains, skiing with friends? Or even his newest match on a dating app?

Once beside her vehicle, Campbell deeply inhaled the semi-warm, dry air. On sunny days like this one, when a person didn't need a jacket, it seemed hard to believe a snowstorm could be approaching. But this unpredictability was normal for a Colorado winter.

She slid into her CR-V, closed the door, and stared up at the bright-blue sky.

Somewhere a huge storm happened to be gathering force. Momentum. Getting ready to unleash near record snowfall in a short period of time. One weekend, to be exact.

She started the engine.

At that moment, a strong sense the storm would be bringing more than a substantial amount of snow settled around her. Maybe because she'd despised storms for the last several years. Meeting her ex during a raging thunderstorm had set the tone of their relationship.

Why was she even thinking about that day? Him?

She gave her head a hard shake and carefully backed out of the parking spot.

Starting at some point on Saturday, she'd have a smart, funny, absolutely delectable man all to herself for an entire weekend. *Two days*. It's all she had to get through.

Campbell had waited years—too many of them unhappy—for a Scott Mayhew to come into her life. She could wait another two days.

<hr>

SCOTT CLOSED the front door after making sure his neighbor made it back to her townhome across the narrow street from his. He then turned and headed back to the couch where he sat beside Peyton. Before he said a word, she crawled into his lap and curled into his arms.

He hugged her tight and kissed the top of her head.

During moments like this, he could barely remember his life before being a dad. And with the timing of the promotion no longer feeling as right as it had, he needed to start considering better ways to achieve more balance when it came to all of his work outside the classroom and time with Peyton. "How are you feeling, your Highness?" He didn't need to figure it out now, though.

"Okay." She picked up her stuffed penguin. "But now Elsa's sick."

Scott placed two fingers on the penguin's forehead and nodded. "Yep. She feels warm." He rested his chin on Peyton's head. "But I'm afraid I ran out of cold medicine for penguins."

"She'll feel better when it snows." Peyton looked up at him. "Can we build a big snowman and name him Olaf? It's gonna snow a lot."

His heart split a bit at her question when his mind backpedaled to two or so hours earlier. When he'd asked Campbell if she wanted to get snowed in with him and she'd said yes without saying the word. Which meant he'd be spending the weekend in a way he'd never imagined when the week began. Of course, the week had also started in a way he hadn't expected.

He glanced at Peyton staring up at him with wide eyes. "I'm taking you back to your mom's Saturday morning. But I know she and Adam would love to build a snowman with you. We'll make one next time."

She snuggled deeper into his arms. "Fine. But it's not the same. Adam doesn't know the words to 'Do You Want to Build a Snowman?'"

Scott couldn't stop himself from smiling.

Yeah. It made him an ass since Adam was a good guy. But Peyton's statement reminded Scott at the end of each day, if she was with him or Shannon, she'd always be his daughter.

Scott tightened his arms around her. That's when he remembered the two whoopie pies.

"So a good friend of mine," he slowly began, "gave me what she calls the best cold remedy ever just the other day. Do you want to try it?"

Peyton nodded. "Can I can share it with Elsa?"

He paused to find the correct answer, then his phone started to ring.

After working it out of his pocket with Peyton still in his lap, he glanced at the screen.

Saved once again by one of the many women in his life.

"Hi," he answered while shifting Peyton to his left. "Does this call mean we're friends again?" He stood and went to the staircase where he jogged up the steps.

"*Friends* is a bit of a stretch," Felicity replied. "I'm really only calling to see how my little niece is feeling. Shannon also told me you're taking her back on Saturday."

Scott walked into his kitchen and suppressed a frustrated sigh.

It was fantastic that his ex and sister had become close friends while he and Shannon had been together. They often talked more frequently than he and Felicity.

"Peyton's feeling better today."

"Wonderful. So this storm from hell is turning my bride into a *crazy* person."

He opened the container of whoopie pies and took one out. "I thought most of your brides were crazy." He stared at the dessert as Campbell's words replayed in his head.

How about I make more and give several just to you? I have that superpower.

It's not so much what she'd said, but how she'd said it. Intimate and sensual.

Saturday wouldn't get here fast enough.

"They are, but this bride did not start out that way." Felicity sighed. "It has taken all of my self-control during her many bitch sessions about the snowstorm—that I cannot stop—to not remind her she's the one who chose to get married in Colorado in *February*."

Scott set the whoopie pie on a cutting board and grabbed a knife from the drawer.

"Anyway," Felicity continued, "since you won't have Peyton, and I'll be in desperate need of wine by the time I get home on Saturday, do you want to come over?"

He stopped slicing the dessert in half.

"You bring the takeout, I'll provide the alcohol. We can find and watch B-grade horror movies on some streaming app and make fun of the atrocious acting."

He laughed.

"It won't be the same without Leann, but we haven't done that in forever."

His smile faded at remembering when he and his sisters had started the sibling "tradition." After they'd lost their dad in an instant. It had been a way to escape, and laugh, for a short period of time. But back then, alcohol hadn't been involved. The drinking while watching bad horror movies began when he'd returned from Afghanistan, no longer a boy.

"Scotty?"

He cleared his throat. "You're right. We haven't done that in a while. But let's plan for another weekend?" He had a guest coming over and wouldn't allow anything to interfere.

"Why? What else are you going to do?"

He finished slicing the whoopie pie. "I need to get caught up on some things around here." Like his personal life. "I have to go. Be safe on Saturday and don't kill the bride."

"I haven't killed one yet," she mumbled, followed by a long pause. "You're not telling me something." Another pause, then, "I promised myself I wouldn't utter a word about this, but does your *unavailability* have anything to do with—"

"Felicity, it's none of your business. I'm hanging up now. Talk next week." He ended the call and placed his phone back inside his pocket.

Scott loved his sister—loved his family—but sometimes the lack of privacy could be enough to make him wish they didn't live quite so close to him. Especially Felicity.

He turned to head back downstairs with half of the best cold remedy when his phone again burst to life. With a heavy breath, he once again removed his phone from his pocket, but had zero intention of answering the call if it happened to be his nosy, persistent, mouthy sister. At seeing a different caller's name, however, he grinned.

"Hey. What's the plan for next week?"

Ian sighed. "It looks like Stella and I won't get there until Wednesday now. The weather and roads should be much better by then. Is that cool?"

Not at all surprising and would definitely work out better for Scott and a beautiful woman he couldn't wait to have all to himself. But he said, "Yeah. Of course."

His buddy fell silent before, "We'll have to stay until I find a place. I'm sure it won't take too long. But the plan is once I get back to Grand Junction, I'll finish packing up the house, hire movers, and head to Denver for good."

Scott leaned against the counter. "That's fine." Something about all of this, however, seemed extremely fast. Almost desperate. It made him say, "Ian, I'm getting the feeling there's more to this move than breaking up with Candace." His friend would also be leaving behind a plethora of friends and some family since he'd grown up in Grand Junction.

Silence, then, "Just ready for the much-needed change."

Scott slowly nodded. "Okay then. I'll see you Wednesday." He ended the call and stared at his phone, knowing there had to be more going on than his buddy simply needing a change.

He couldn't imagine what might have happened with Ian to cause him to leave everything and everyone he knew for a new city and life.

"*Daddy*, what's taking you so long?" Peyton's raised voice reached him upstairs. "Elsa's getting sicker."

Scott straightened.

None of that needed his attention right now. He had a sick daughter and stuffed penguin waiting for him and the best cold remedy.

He once again shoved his phone into his pocket. But when he glanced at half the whoopie pie filled with white cream surrounded by the moist chocolate cake, he grabbed the other half which he popped into his mouth. He also couldn't ignore the fact Campbell Grey tasted better than her specialty dessert, and he grinned as he finished his half while heading down the stairs.

Chapter Seventeen

SO IT'S STARTING *to get bad out there and I'm home now.*

Campbell grinned at Scott's message and typed, *I'm leaving soon.* She added the smiling emoji and tapped send. She then faced her full-length mirror.

Because of the bitterly cold, snowy weather, she'd had no choice but to settle for a snug pair of jeans, black boots meant to be worn in the snow but were also stylish, and a black, heavy sweater. She'd fixed her hair to hang in long, soft waves and put on a little more makeup than usual. Certainly not the definition of alluring, but the best she could do given the horrible weather. She did have to brush off her car before leaving.

She faced her bed where she'd placed her overnight bag.

Getting snowed in with a handsome, irresistible man for an entire weekend was a decidedly new experience for her. As such, she had no idea what to pack. If everything went the way she'd been vividly imagining since Thursday, she probably wouldn't need pajamas. But she had to bring something comfortable to wear, so she went to her dresser.

Sweatpants. *Not a chance in hell.* Pink-and-black flannel pajamas. *Absolutely not.* More sweatpants. Yoga pants…She frowned.

A drawer full of clothes screaming she had no personal life and everything that went along with such a luxury.

Wow. She should have gone shopping yesterday after work.

Campbell sighed and settled on a pair of black yoga pants and a pale-blue top which had a tendency to slip off of her shoulder. Maybe *she'd* earn some irresistible points for the shirt?

Her phone buzzed and chimed with another message.

Text me when you're close so I can open the garage for you. No reason we should dig out your car after the fact when I have a two-car garage.

She brought back her grin, only this one had to be on the sappy side, while she tapped out, *I'll do that. And thank you.*

Campbell drew a slow, deep breath into her lungs and released the air.

She needed to stop overthinking what to pack and get the hell out of there. And, because more luck had miraculously ended up on her side, Lance had spent last night elsewhere and had yet to reappear. So if she could get out of the house before he came home, she'd only have to deal with check-in texts at some point the next couple days.

You're welcome. Drive careful. I'll see you soon.

Campbell swiftly placed another pair of snug jeans into the bag, a roomy T-shirt and sweatshirt, and a couple pairs of heavy socks. She then darted into her bathroom and grabbed her brush, toothbrush—an absolute necessity—and a few cosmetics.

As she zipped the bag, her phone started to ring.

Grinning, she reached behind to pull the device from her back pocket. But when she saw the call coming from a blocked number her grin faded.

A blocked number? Too weird since only those who absolutely needed her number, which she'd changed not too long after arriving in the city, had it. She never gave it out unnecessarily.

Not until this moment had she ever received a call from a blocked number while living here.

A hint of darkness slithered through her as her phone continued to ring.

Something she hadn't experienced since all of the unwanted calls from *him*.

When her phone stopped ringing, she waited to see if the caller left a message. She'd long since set her voicemail greeting to nothing more than saying her first name.

While she continued to wait, she grasped the strap of her overnight bag and hooked it on her right shoulder. She next grabbed her coat, hat, and gloves.

Still no message. At the same time, it sometimes took a bit for them to hit.

Campbell gave herself a final once-over in the mirror before leaving her bedroom.

By the time she'd picked up her surprise for Scott in the kitchen and *The Awakening*, shrugged into her coat, and put on her hat and gloves, no message had come through.

She allowed herself a quick breath.

Wrong number. That's all it had to be. There could be no other explanation.

She dropped her phone into her purse and shook off the remaining darkness.

Everything was fine. Better than fine when she refocused on the now.

Scott's scrumptious everything filled her mind while she opened the front door and headed into the snowfall which had become heavier. The wind has also picked up quite a bit.

Despite what would undoubtedly be tough driving conditions, Campbell smiled and closed the door behind her. There was absolutely no place on earth she wanted to be going but Scott

Mayhew's home and her smile grew as she carefully walked to her car.

SCOTT HIT the button which would close his garage door at the same time Campbell slid from her vehicle.

She'd arrived safely and of course wore her red hat.

He grinned at her bundled up in her coat and gloves while she removed a bag from the backseat. She then walked behind her CR-V and toward where he stood near the doorway.

She gave him a blinding smile and opened her mouth, but he cupped her face and silenced her with a kiss that swiftly turned hot, voracious…and lasted until she shivered.

He managed to bring their kiss to an end and asked, "How can you be cold? You're dressed to go hiking in Antarctica in the middle of their winter."

She pressed her lips together and stared up at him. "I didn't shiver because I was cold."

Scott laughed softly. "I like your honesty."

"I like how you say hello."

He lowered his hands, slipped his arms around her waist, and pressed his forehead to hers. "I'm really glad you're here."

She sighed. "That makes two of us."

After taking a moment to deeply breathe in her light, floral scent, he released her and straightened. He removed the strap of her bag from her shoulder and hooked it on his. "Ready for the tour? We also need to get inside and close the door. I think the temperature's dropped since I got back from taking Peyton to Shannon's." He clasped her right hand.

"Did Peyton make a full recovery?" she asked while he led her into his house.

"Pretty close." He closed the door. "You were right about the whoopie pies being the best cold remedy."

She lifted her chin. "So you didn't eat them all?"

He grinned. "You may be *interested* in knowing that I not only left an entire whoopie pie for Peyton, but also just enough for Elsa the penguin. She was pretty sick, too."

She laughed and shook her head. "And did they make *her* better?"

"She had more color around her beak the last time I saw her." He led her up the stairs.

"Another crisis averted?" She laughed again. "It also sounds like there's never a dull moment around here."

"Only when Peyton is with me." He shrugged. "I'm pretty boring by myself."

"That's not even close to true."

They cleared the landing, and Campbell paused, then sniffed the air twice.

"It smells incredible in here." She concentrated on him. "Are you cooking something?"

He shot her a fake, wounded expression. "That hurts. Why is it women assume most single men are clueless when it comes to cooking?" He pointed at the crockpot sitting on his kitchen counter. "I'll have you know it's my brilliance simmering in that pot." He leaned forward. "No recipe. No help whatsoever from my mom or sisters."

She narrowed her eyes. "I'm officially *intrigued.*"

Scott squeezed her hand. "I promise you won't be disappointed."

Their gazes locked for several seconds before he led her up the last flight of stairs.

He pointed at the first room. "Peyton's Pink, Disney Princess Palace."

"Do you mind if I look?"

"No." He released her hand. "It's a little messy because she was sick all week."

Campbell flipped the switch up and released a quick laugh. "Oh, my God. I would have loved having a room like this when I was her age." She glanced at him. "My favorite vacation of all time was when my mom took my brother and me to Disney World. I was nine-years-old and wanted to be a Disney princess."

Scott smiled softly as he leaned against the doorframe. "Well, Peyton was right that day. You do resemble Cinderella." Especially in the eyes.

Those beautiful, bright aquamarine eyes which could fill with passion in an instant.

"And I was being completely serious when I told her Cinderella was my favorite princess," Campbell continued. "Not because I think I look like her or anything. But because I actually met her while we were in the Magic Kingdom." She laughed. "She was so beautiful and sparkly and had this absolutely perfect smile."

Ironically enough, she'd just described herself. But Scott remained silent.

"You're going to think I'm crazy, but she gave me her autograph and I *still* have it."

He joined her laughter.

"Anyway"—she stepped backward—"this is such an awesome room."

"That was an awesome story. And I'll tell you a secret." Scott turned off the light. "If you were to tell Peyton you had Cinderella's autograph, you'd have a number-two fan."

She frowned. "Number two?"

Scott placed his head beside hers and murmured, "You've had my complete attention since day one of the semester while wearing that hat and calling yourself a 'total book nerd'."

He straightened and managed to tear his gaze from her mouth which had opened just enough to send his body into overdrive.

Like last Saturday night when she'd slipped him her phone number.

"Speaking of books," he said while grasping her hand once more, "my office." He angled his head toward the room to the left of Peyton's, but after the bathroom.

Campbell blinked several times, then glanced into the room. And her eyes widened.

She walked into his office, taking him with her since he refused to release her hand.

After turning on the light, she stopped them at his two packed bookcases.

"Have you read all of these books?" she asked while examining the titles.

"Every single one of them."

She whipped her head in his direction.

He lifted his shoulders. "I told you I'm pretty boring."

"Not boring at all." She gave him an affectionate smile. "But I knew you also had to be a book nerd."

"Yep." He returned her smile. "Want to be book nerds together? Could be an *insane* amount of fun." He waggled his eyebrows. "Especially if we read some Kate Chopin out loud."

She fought a smile as she stepped toward him. "You just reminded me I have a couple of things for you." She unzipped her bag, the strap still hooked on his shoulder.

"And I love surprises." Especially if a beautiful woman happened to be involved.

Campbell reached into her bag and withdrew a plastic container that had *The Awakening* on top. "These are for you. Thank you for loaning me the book." She paused before adding, "I didn't love the ending, but I did love the story."

"You're welcome." He picked up the book and placed it back

on his shelf. "The Dashwood sisters are starting to slowly recover from their broken hearts." He paused before saying, "But I still want to punch John W. and Edward. Especially John W."

She laughed.

Scott opened the container and froze.

"Those are all for you," she murmured. "You don't even have to share with me."

He looked up and met her eyes, shining with enthusiasm.

"I can't believe you made more of these for me."

"I told you I would."

"Right." He picked up a whoopie pie. "That you did. And I don't mind sharing." He took a careful bite, then held out the rest toward Campbell.

With a wicked grin, she leaned forward and also took a careful bite.

Scott placed the remaining chuck into the container and went to lick his thumb when Campbell caught his hand.

With her gaze connected with his, she leisurely slipped his thumb into her mouth, gently licked the skin for a few seconds, then slowly switched to his index finger and repeated her actions. All without breaking their eye contact.

Scott slowly nodded.

Okay. He and a certain area of his body had reached their limit of self-control.

He removed the strap from his shoulder and let her bag fall to the floor. He then turned and placed the container on his desk. When he faced her once more, she had pulled off her hat and was shrugging out of her heavy coat. Before it hit the floor, their mouths fused and picked up where they'd left off in the garage.

Scott shoved *everything* to the back of his mind except her and them.

Chapter Eighteen

CAMPBELL ENDED up pinned between Scott and the wall; her arms hooked behind his neck.

"I think," he whispered after a breathless kiss, "it's time I take you to the final stop on the tour." He tightened his arms around her waist.

"I think so, too," she whispered back before their mouths came together for a third time.

He lifted her off the floor and walked until the back of her legs made contact with something firm, but soft. His bed?

She opened her eyes and tore her mouth from his. "Your room." She grinned while taking in the dark-wood furniture and king-sized bed right behind her. "It's very…*manly*."

The breath from his soft laugh warmed the spot where her neck curved into her shoulder.

He placed airy kisses up her neck, then stopped at her ear. "You smell incredible."

She shivered, gripped the bottom of his T-shirt, and tugged it up and over his head. Within a millisecond, Scott stood in front of her, shirtless, and she gently laid her hands on his defined, smooth chest.

Campbell pressed her lips together while she admired every inch of his edible upper body, including his perfectly toned arms. That's when something caught her attention.

She grasped his left arm and angled him toward her. "You have a tattoo." She smiled at the American eagle above a banner with the words U.S. Army inside. "It's a little surprising." And beyond sexy.

Scott reached up and wound his fingers through her hair. "Why? Because I'm a book nerd?" He glanced at the tattoo and back at her. "Most of the guys in my unit got one, too."

She raised her chin and with a smile she removed her sweater. After tossing it behind him, she faced his bed and gathered her hair in a loose ponytail to show him her bare shoulder.

He laughed and ran his warm fingers across her skin. "Very cool. What do they mean? I'm afraid I don't know my Chinese symbols."

"Courage, hope, and strength." She looked over her right shoulder. "In that order."

Their gazes caught.

Scott opened his mouth, paused, but unleashed his infectious grin as he dropped a soft kiss on her shoulder.

Her eyes drifted shut at his lips leaving another trail of light kisses up her neck and down. She released her hair, leaned against him, and angled her head left to give him better access.

His warm arms went around her and he hooked his thumbs on the waist of her jeans. "These need to come off of you, but your boots have to go first."

She turned in his arms and grinned. "Then let's get rid of them." She sat on his bed and extended her right leg which he caught.

He gripped the bottom of her boot and gently tugged it off, followed quickly by the second one. Then she became stretched out beneath him while their mouths moved once more in perfect sync. Neither stopping until they had to pause for air.

Scott released a steady breath. "We need to slow down." He rubbed his thumb across her lower lip. "You taste as good as you look, and I don't do this very often."

She curled her fingers into his soft hair. "What? Fool around with a woman in your bed during a snowstorm?"

He nuzzled her nose. "Fool around with a woman *period*. I've been out of the game for longer than I'll ever admit out loud."

"Me, too." Campbell slid her hands from his hair, then lightly dragged her nails down his back which caused him to shiver. She giggled and brushed her lips against his. "And if it'll make you feel even better, you're the first real *man* I've ever been with."

Scott smiled as she brought his head back down to hers. In between one hungry kiss after another…and another…they managed to shed the rest of their clothing.

Campbell closed her eyes and grinned at Scott's soft, busy mouth on her neck, then he shifted slightly down…and even farther where he stopped to place soft kisses on her breasts. He then gave her left nipple a quick lick before taking the firm bud into his mouth.

She arched her back and gripped his hair, holding his head in place. But with little effort and a naughty grin he moved to the right and gave her other breast the same attention. A few seconds later he again shifted down, leaving a path of light kisses from the space between her breasts to her stomach where he paused to nuzzle her bellybutton and kiss the skin.

Yes. He definitely knew how to use his delectable mouth in other ways.

Her skin—every part of her—turned hot as he shifted lower still, now pausing at a spot extremely close to *her*, pulsing and wet in a way she'd never experienced.

She again gripped his hair and started to lift her hips in an undeniable invitation when Scott stopped and leisurely made his way back up.

After another thorough, deep, delicious kiss, he nuzzled her left ear and whispered, "Show me what you want me to do."

Campbell opened her eyes which locked instantly with his, smoldering with lust and a hint of challenge.

Without breaking their eye contact, she grasped his right hand and guided it down to *her*, ready and waiting for him. And as he slowly, casily, slid his warm finger inside of her she moaned out of satisfaction and yearning since she wanted *all* of him.

Their hungry mouths joined while she moved with his finger and clung to him, never wanting him—them—to stop, but wanting and craving the release.

He abruptly ended their kiss and said, "I can't do this anymore."

She forced her eyes open and squinted at him. "What's wrong?" Based on feeling *all* of him against her thigh, nothing in the slightest felt wrong.

He gently removed his finger and eased off of her. "My finger inside of you isn't enough. Give me a sec." He sat up.

A drawer opened, followed by a wrapper being opened.

Campbell smiled, but it changed to another moan of head-blurring satisfaction that matched his while he slid inside of her. Went as far as he could possibly go.

He paused and rested his forehead against hers. "*Holy shit*, that's so much better."

"Yes," she breathed. "You fit me perfectly."

Another new experience she never wanted to end.

"You read my mind," he murmured as he started to move inside of her.

Tangling her fingers into his hair, she matched his slow thrusts that gradually increased in speed and intensity. As did their kisses. White hot and ravenous.

A warm tingling began to build deep inside of her. She slid her hands down Scott's back and stopped when she reached his firm butt where she pressed him closer. Deeper.

His groan became lost in their busy mouths.

The tingling continued to build to the point her mind turned foggy. She never wanted this to end, but couldn't and didn't want to stop the intensity.

Scott lifted his head, then reached behind him to grasp her left hand still holding his tight cheek. Before she knew it, her hands were locked with his and he had her arms above her head. The slight change in position and their bodies moving perfectly together added to the fire within.

Her muscles tightened around him. Seconds later she let go, her moan surrounding them and replacing their heavy breathing. After a few more powerful, synchronized thrusts, she felt Scott's release, but captured his moan in a greedy kiss.

They stayed joined as one while catching their breath.

Scott freed her hands, and she instantly wrapped her arms around his lean waist.

He buried his face between her neck and hair. "You—that—felt way better than I imagined it would. And I have a damn good imagination."

She giggled. "I definitely have to agree with you." She hugged him tight. "I finally understand the meaning of mind-blowing sex."

He lifted his head and eased out of her which made her groan but from displeasure.

"Mind-blowing." Scott shifted to his left side and propped himself up on his elbow. He then unleashed his infectious grin. "Have I mentioned how much I like your honesty?"

"Well, actually that's not what I meant."

His grin faded. "Okay. *Ouch.*"

Campbell shook her head. "No, it was mind-blowing." She

reached up and outlined his addictive lips with her thumb. "I've had orgasms...but this was the first time I've had one while *having* sex."

His forehead formed a deep V. "Are you serious?"

"Completely." She gave him a naughty smile. "So I get it now. How amazing it can be?" In more ways than one, too, and with the right man.

"Campbell, it should always feel like that." He sealed his words with a deep, but soft kiss. "I need to get rid of something. I'll be right back."

He sat up and stood.

Campbell rolled onto her stomach to watch him walk into his bathroom, right off of his room. She nibbled her lower lip at the sight of him. And he was all hers the entire weekend.

She sure as hell would not let herself think about what would happen come Monday.

Losing the heat of his warm body locked and moving with hers caused a chill to hit her skin and she shivered. It made her waste no time crawling under his thick, cozy, forest green comforter and sinking into his enormous, comfy bed.

She laughed at not only burrowing under the comforter, but also at the fact her tingling skin made her entire body quake with *awakening* for the first time since losing her virginity to someone who'd never been worthy. Compared to Scott, her ex—the only other man she'd physically been with—had been a total zero in bed.

But she'd been too foolish and naïve to know any better.

"Did you get cold?" Scott asked around a laugh before joining her in his bed.

"I'm always cold."

He laid his head beside hers and grinned. "I have to disagree with you on that." He gently brushed aside wisps of hair on her face. "So never having *mind-blowing* sex before today. Is that what you meant when you said you'd never been with a real man?"

She lifted her shoulders. "It's one reason." The absolute truth, too.

"I'm sorry it's taken you until the age of twenty-eight to get it. That's not right." He scooted closer. "But I have to admit I'm feeling pretty damn good about myself right now."

She laughed with him, also scooted closer, and nuzzled his nose. "Or maybe you just got lucky the first time around. It had been a while for both of us."

He narrowed his eyes. "That sounds like a challenge."

"Think you might be *up* for it?" she asked while fighting a grin.

Scott slowly nodded, then gently rolled her onto her back. "I think you can tell I'm definitely *up* for it."

She wrapped him in her arms.

Yes. She definitely could.

He kissed the tip of her nose. "I also have all the time in the world to show you how much I love a good challenge."

Smiling, their mouths became one.

Campbell released a tiny sigh and once more let go of everything but them.

Chapter Nineteen

"IT'S REALLY LOOKING bad out there," Campbell murmured. "I think I pulled into your garage just in time."

Scott continued to absently run his fingers through her long hair while she curled deeper into his side. "I think I have to agree with you." And not only because of the rotten weather they could see outside his bedroom window.

Yeah. He hadn't been with a woman in an absurdly long time, but it didn't change the fact being with Campbell had blown his mind. *Twice.* And fitting perfectly together didn't come close to accurate. Even now, curved into his left arm and side, it's like she belonged right there. As well as sheathing him in her warmth and wetness that made his vision blur thinking about it.

She turned, rested her chin on his chest, and focused on him with those beautiful, bright blue eyes he'd now seen filled with an entirely different type of passion. *Twice.*

"When and where did you get your tattoo?"

She wanted to talk about his tattoo? Really?

He released a quick laugh at her surprising him yet again. "When I was stationed in Germany." He slid his right arm behind his head. "A bunch of us, including my good buddy Ian who's actually moving to Denver from Grand Junction, drank way too much beer one night and, by dawn, ended up with tattoos." He grinned. "It was a great night."

She smiled, hesitated, then asked, "I'm guessing it was before you were deployed?"

"Yeah." Also known as when he'd still been a boy. He pushed a lock of hair behind her ear. "Ian will be here next week and staying with me while he looks for his own place."

She placed a light kiss on his chest. "Then I guess we really do have to make the most of this weekend." Another kiss, only farther down. "What do you think?" She kissed his stomach.

He suppressed a groan and said, "I think you're going to wear me out."

Campbell raised her head and stared at him with wide eyes. "Do you want me to stop?"

He grinned and brought her back up until they were nearly nose-to-nose. "*Hell* no. But I think I should go check on my brilliance happening in the kitchen."

She sighed. "I'm sure it's fine, but I suppose I can briefly let you go."

Scott started to reply, but the sound of a nearby phone ringing stopped him. Maybe coming from his office right next door? Where they'd dropped and left her belongings.

"Do you hear that?"

She frowned while nodding.

"It's your phone since mine"—he pointed at the floor—"is down there still in my jeans." He caught her gaze. "Should you get it? There is a blizzard going on across most of the state."

Campbell looked over her shoulder at his bedroom doorway. Then the ringing stopped.

She faced him. "I'm sure it's fine. Probably just my roommate."

Darkness flashed through her eyes. It happened so quickly

Scott wasn't certain he'd seen it correctly. But she brought back her smile as her eyes lit up with mischief.

"I guess I'll need to move?" She barely touched her lips to his. "Or you can move me."

He slipped his hands under the blankets and slid his arms around her soft, firm, pliant, naked body. Her mouth opened against his.

Okay. They were going to wear each other out. But there were way worse things in life.

Campbell shifted until she was straddling him. Her hair formed a curtain around them.

He'd positioned her in the perfect spot when the ringing started once more.

Scott halted their kiss and opened his eyes that instantly connected with hers. Which flashed with the darkness before she sat up and again looked over her shoulder.

"Campbell, it's okay if you need to answer your phone." Though she did look absolutely fantastic sitting upright and straddling him. "I'm not going anywhere." He paused before adding, "Except downstairs to check on dinner."

She shot him a quick smile and climbed off of him. And if he could watch her do that the rest of his life, he'd die a happy old man with the hard-on of a sixteen-year-old virgin.

Scott rolled onto his left side and grinned while she pulled her thick sweater over her head, then grasped her hair in a loose ponytail to free the locks from under the collar.

She glanced at him over her left shoulder. "I'll be right back." She strolled out of his room and went left, into his office.

He rolled onto his back and stared at the ceiling.

There was no way in hell he'd be able to stop seeing her after this weekend. He'd suspected as much before today, but now it had become a fact.

Thirteen weeks. Surely they could keep it professional—like

they'd already been doing—until May? He'd interacted with her enough during class, and graded a few of her assignments and quizzes, to know she happened to be a sharp, insightful woman. A natural A-student.

Student.

Scott mentally quashed the word. He then sat up, stood, and grabbed his jeans.

He didn't need or want to think about anything beyond the right now. And right now, through tomorrow, he and Campbell had each other's undivided attention. For the most part.

The darkness flashing through her eyes drifted through his head while he pulled on his T-shirt. Something about her reaction didn't feel right. Between his time in the military and being a cop, he had the instincts. Yeah. He'd only been a cop for three years, but despite the path not being his, it was still in his blood. He also couldn't shake the suspicion there had to be much more to the ex-husband story. More instinct. On that thought, he headed for his doorway.

When he reached his office, he poked his head inside. To find Campbell sitting back on her heels near her belongings while holding her phone.

"Is everything okay?" he quietly asked.

She jolted and whipped around.

"Sorry." He leaned into the doorframe. "I didn't mean to scare you."

A smile replaced her surprised expression.

"Oh, it's fine." She held up her phone. "It was just my room-mate. Like I thought. Making sure I'm okay since I'm not at home during a blizzard. I'm texting him back."

Scott tilted his head left. "Didn't he call you?"

"Yes." She met his gaze. "But he also texted."

He slowly nodded before giving her a slow grin. "What are

you going to tell him?" And was she telling *him* the truth? If not, she could be considered a damn good actress.

But maybe she'd acquired the trait out of necessity?

She shot him a wicked smile. "That I'm staying with a *very* good friend this weekend."

"Certainly not a lie." But in that moment Scott wanted to be more than her "*very* good friend." He had a strong feeling she felt exactly the same way.

She pointed at him. "You just had to get dressed to check on your brilliance?"

Scott straightened and stepped back. "Cooking naked. We'll try it next time."

"I won't forget you said that." She stood. "I'll be downstairs in a minute."

After a long, lingering glance at her sweater stopping at mid-thigh of her shapely legs, Scott turned and went toward the staircase.

Maybe the whole ex-husband story was none of his business. He had no reason not to believe her roommate had been the one trying to reach her. She had said the three of them were close. She'd even called the guys her "Denver family." But if this weekend did end up being the beginning of something real, Scott needed to know the full story. Especially since she appeared to still be somewhat haunted by whatever had happened with the guy. Scott also liked her. A whole hell of a lot more than he should considering the situation. How would he get her to talk about it, though? Like she'd said last Saturday, she didn't like talking about her past anymore than he liked talking about his time in combat.

Scott racked his brain for an idea while absently stirring their dinner. Until warm, thin arms now clothed in a long-sleeved blue shirt encircled his waist.

Campbell placed her chin on his shoulder. "It smells amazing.

Are you ever going to tell me the name of your brilliance? It looks like soup which is perfect for this weather."

"You're close." He dipped the wooden spoon into the crock-pot, turned slightly to his left, and carefully held it up. "Guess again."

She leaned forward, blew on the liquid, cautiously sipped, then closed her mouth around the chunk of meat.

Scott took a deep, quiet breath.

The fact watching her do something so innocuous made his entire body buzz had to mean he hadn't just been out of the game for too long. He'd been the walking dead.

"That's so good." She subjected him to her blinding smile which always reached her eyes. "It's a beef soup. Or stew?"

He set the spoon down. "Stew."

Self-control. He did possess it. But why did almost everything Campbell did come off as intimate and sensual? Or maybe it was him. Or more accurately, them.

"Are you hungry?" he asked, though it came out a tad gurgled, so he cleared his throat.

"Not yet. But I'm thirsty." She nuzzled his neck. "Nonstop kissing has that effect on me."

If they spent the rest of the weekend kissing nonstop—among other things—he wouldn't have a complaint in the world. But he said, "I can offer you apple juice, orange juice, milk—"

She burst into laughter. "You don't have to go through your entire beverage list again."

"Or wine," he finished, which made her laugh even more.

"Wine sounds perfect."

Minutes later, they were approaching his couch.

As they sat close together, Campbell's shirt slipped off her right shoulder, exposing the soft skin and her tattoos—and an idea hit with such force he paused.

Courage, hope, and strength. In that order.

Alphabetical, but possibly done with another kind of intent?

She scooted back, shifted onto her left side, facing him, and curled her legs beneath her. She then sipped the white wine he'd bought that was similar to what she'd ordered last Saturday.

Scott faced her, hesitated, and pointed at her right shoulder. "Your tattoos must also have a story." He clasped her free hand and linked their fingers. "I have a feeling it's a way more *intriguing* story than mine."

She lowered her gaze to her wine. Which meant he had to be on the right track.

"I'd love to hear it," he quietly added. And so much more. But this was a place to start.

She took another sip of wine while staring at their joined hands.

Keeping his eyes trained on her, he drank some of his beer… and waited.

She finally lifted her head. "Scott, I know what you're really asking." She gave him a tight smile. "I despise talking about it because it reminds me of how stupid I was, but I'll tell *you* since I know you won't judge me."

He frowned. "Judge you? For making a mistake? Campbell, I can't believe anyone in your life would do that."

"It wasn't just one little mistake," she mumbled under her breath. She sighed and shook her head. "I met my ex at a coffee shop in downtown Durango during a thunderstorm when I was twenty." She released a humorless laugh. "It set the tone for our relationship." She turned and looked out his living room windows. "I haven't liked storms in years. Rain or snow." She glanced at him with a tiny smile. "Until today."

He returned her smile, but remained silent.

"Anyway"—she sipped more wine—"he was tall and charming and beautiful and for some reason that day he chose me. And I fell *so* hard."

Scott nodded.

"At the time, I was a full-time student at Fort Lewis College. The school down there?"

"Yeah, I've heard of it." Her admission, however, meant his instincts had been right.

Leaving school did have something to do with her ex who Scott was beginning to despise since he had a rotten feeling as to how this story would end.

"He was a student, too," she continued. "At the time, his dad was the county district attorney." Her eyes rolled upward. "I really thought I'd hit the big time being a part of his powerful, wealthy family."

Scott narrowed his eyes. "But your ex was an entitled jackass?"

"Among other things." She went back to staring at their still joined hands. "He was my first everything, and I stupidly fell for everything he said to me."

He angled his head down and left to catch her eyes. "Campbell, stop being so hard on yourself. You were twenty-years-old and it sounds like you were swept off your feet by this guy."

Scott had known plenty of assholes like Campbell's ex. Felicity had also been married to and fooled by one of them.

"Yes." She hesitated before saying, "But I was so stupid I got pregnant and married him."

Scott froze as her confession settled around them.

Okay. He hadn't expected her to say she'd been pregnant.

"I eventually left school. But fortunately I miscarried and made sure I never became pregnant again." She stared at him. "I know how horrible that sounds, but it was for the best because, of course, he turned out to be entitled…among other things."

His jaw tightened. "Did he hurt you?" The thought made him clench his beer bottle.

Felicity had confessed to him after drinking a little too much wine one night her dickhead of an ex had become physical with her once.

Also known as her impetus to finally leave the bastard and come back to the U.S.

The passage of time hadn't stopped Scott from wanting to fly to London, hunt the guy down, and rip his British head off of his body. Just like he felt now about Campbell's ex.

"Physically, no."

He relaxed his grip on the beer bottle. Still, he waited for the inevitable.

"But he always had to know how I spent my day, who I was with, and who I talked to, specifically if I'd talked to other guys. Even when I was pregnant." She lifted her chin. "If I didn't answer my phone, he would call and text until I did, then demand to know what I was doing or who—"

"You were with," Scott finished, back to gripping the beer bottle.

"All of it was so exhausting," she mumbled before taking another sip of wine. "I reached a point where I did everything in my power to answer my phone to avoid having to defend myself. And I would avoid talking to other guys—even friends of my brother's I'd known for years—as much as possible." She sighed. "My ex was controlling, jealous, and possessive which he hid behind his good looks and charm, and family's name and wealth." She frowned. "He was the total cliché and I fell for it."

Scott squeezed her hand. "You're not giving yourself nearly enough credit." Their gazes connected. "You got the hell away from him. That's all that matters." He grinned softly. "Courage, hope, and strength?"

"Yes," she breathed. "One day we were fighting about me wanting to go back to school since he wanted me to get pregnant again. Something inside of me *snapped*. I'd had enough." She looked away. "I knew leaving him wouldn't be easy and it wasn't. He made sure of it."

Probably the main reason it had taken her longer than necessary to leave the asshole. But Scott said, "He couldn't—wouldn't—let you go?"

She nodded. "Exactly. He also found petty reasons not to sign the divorce papers."

Also not surprising. Scott still hated the fact she'd gone through all of that and another realization hit. "But when he finally did, you left. *He's* the reason you left Durango."

She fell silent.

Scott leaned into the couch cushions while staring at her. "That was the only way you could get away from him? Leaving your family and friends and the place you grew up?"

Now he really wanted to tear the sonofabitch apart.

"I eventually had to get a restraining order because he kept showing up at my mom's house and following me when I left just to run errands, which was rare." She smirked. "But the order meant nothing to him and his dad had a lot of power."

Shit. Her story had started to sound like an episode of a true crime documentary, only she'd managed to get away from her crazy ex and lived to tell about it. The thought prompted him to put aside his beer and close the tiny gap between them.

She set her wine glass in the tray on his ottoman. "That's the ugly, true story as to how I ended up in Denver what will be two years ago this summer."

Scott cupped her face and gave her a gentle kiss. "You have nothing to be ashamed of."

She stared up at him with her aquamarine eyes that had dimmed quite a bit. "Thank you."

They shared another, longer kiss, and he lowered his hands to her waist.

"So I'm guessing he's gone for good?" he asked. "Now that you're here?"

She nodded. "His parents finally realized he needed serious help and took him somewhere never disclosed. It happened very quietly and quickly."

Fine. But being jailed for violating a restraining order would have been a shitload better.

"I left the area while he was gone. His dad is now in private practice, but the entire family is still in the area. I know he did eventually end up back in Durango." She slipped her arms around Scott's neck. "But I'm here in Denver with you."

He pressed his forehead to hers. "That you are." He wouldn't change that fact, either. "Reliving dark moments is tough. I get it. Believe me. But I'm glad you told me everything."

She buried her face in his neck. "Me, too. It actually felt good to tell you."

Maybe having talked about it would help her shed more of the darkness in the long run.

Hearing the entire ex-asshole story had also solved the mystery of Campbell seeming a little *off*; there being much more to her than what she presented.

Scott held her tight and close and again breathed in her scent. Only this time into his soul.

"Are you hungry yet?" Though he'd be fine staying like this with her for a while longer.

She leaned back just enough to catch his gaze. "Only for you."

He laughed. "You're determined to kill me."

Campbell nuzzled his nose. "Slowly and gently. It won't hurt a bit."

"And on that note"—he kissed her and loosened his hold—"I definitely need to eat."

He stood, but then Campbell caught his hand.

"I have an idea."

"You want to eat naked together."

She laughed. "Maybe we'll try it next time." She angled her head toward his T.V. "We should watch a movie. I know which one, too. If you have it?"

He raised his eyebrows. "A second ago you wanted to kill me slowly and gently with sex. Now you want to watch a movie?" He pointed at her. "You're sending me mixed signals."

She picked up her wine glass and settled back into the cushions. "How about we agree on the movie first, then killing each other slowly and gently with sex?"

He crossed his arms. "I'll only say yes to this if I agree with your movie choice."

"*Dead Poets Society*. I've never seen it."

His mouth inched opened. "You've never seen that movie?" Of course, when he thought about what she'd said to him after the first day of class, this really wasn't surprising info. "Okay. We have a deal. But I should warn you that the movie doesn't end—"

"Happily?" She narrowed her eyes. "Knowing you, I had a feeling that was the case."

Knowing him.

He flashed her a quick grin before heading for the staircase.

At this point, they'd barely started on the getting-to-know-each-other path. Her telling him the whole story about her ex-dickhead had been a huge step, for sure. It's not like he hadn't shared the darkest moment of his life earlier in the week. It was only Saturday evening, too. They still had a lot of weekend left which might include Monday. Because Scott had absolutely no idea when he'd again have her alone like this for an entire weekend, he planned on making use of every single minute until the second she had to leave.

Until they had to return to reality.

Chapter Twenty

CAMPBELL STOPPED SHOVELING the short path to the front door and glanced at Scott.

She grinned at him wearing her red hat while he steadily snow-blowed his driveway. She'd pulled on his black beanie cap, but he definitely looked cuter in hers.

A break in the storm had prompted him—them—to drag themselves from bed and remove the ten inches or so of snow which had already fallen. Another ten or so had been predicted to fall between today and Monday morning. And like he'd said and she knew from growing up in Durango, ten inches of snow was way easier to remove than twenty.

Her grin turned soft as she continued to watch him; his handsome face, with just the right amount of late-morning scruff, set in concentration. Suddenly, everything became crystal clear while she stood in the frigid air, surrounded by snow that reached her knees.

The book nerd connection.

Their conversations and texts about books.

His devotion to his daughter, and how he interacted with her and vice versa.

His loyalty to his mom and sisters.

The way he interacted with his students.

His infectious grin and sense of humor.

His delectable mouth and the way he used it.

The way their bodies fit and moved perfectly together.

The way he'd listened to her as she shared *most* of her humiliating past. There'd been no judgment. Only support and relief she'd managed to get away from her ex-bastard. But it really hadn't been easy. In fact, it had required a pretty desperate action she hadn't confessed last night.

At the same time, did Scott really need to know the rest? The answer, however, landed heavily in her mind because of another fact.

She was falling in love with him. Way too soon and quick? Probably.

Campbell went back to shoveling.

After this weekend, how could she feel any different? And Scott Mayhew wasn't her ex. But a she and him were the definition of complicated until the semester ended in May.

As she hurled a shovel full of snow to her left, she shook her head.

It happened to be the dead of winter at the beginning of February. So May—springtime—felt like eons from now. Sometimes they even had summer-like weather by mid-May.

They'd have to "hide" their relationship for three months? It wasn't fair.

Her phone inside her coat pocket started to buzz, and she halted.

She'd decided to keep it with her in case Lance, who had texted her yesterday evening, or Alyson or her mom called or texted to check in. Lance hadn't been the phone calls yesterday.

Yes. She'd lied to Scott. It had been easier since she couldn't go there…even though six calls from a blocked number in less than twenty-fours couldn't be a good sign. But how the hell could he have found her? Only her mom and brother knew where she'd gone. The other three calls had come in after she'd put her phone on silent before joining Scott in the kitchen last night. She hadn't discovered them until this morning.

Her heart hammered her chest while she withdrew her phone and looked at the screen.

Campbell's shoulders slumped at seeing Alyson's name.

"Hi," she answered on a quick breath after removing her gloves. She then slowly inhaled the icy air into her lungs to settle her heart rate. She shoved her gloves into her coat pocket and asked, "How'd it go yesterday?"

"It actually wasn't too bad," Alyson answered. "We used my 4Runner instead of the van. David was our driver because he and Randy decided to close the club yesterday and today."

Campbell grinned. "That's good. You've been snowed in ever since you got home?"

"Yes." She laughed. "And as a newlywed, I'm *not* complaining."

Campbell laughed with her.

Outside of the newlywed aspect, she could relate to what Alyson had implied.

Heat warmed every part of Campbell as the memories from yesterday and early this morning with Scott filled her head.

"Snowed in is why I'm calling," Alyson continued. "We've been watching the weather reports here and there. With this second round dropping another ten inches—at least—by morning, I've decided to give us a snow day. We also didn't have orders come in for Monday."

The snow-blower fell silent.

Campbell glanced at Scott watching her with a tentative smile she answered with a blinding one at hearing Alyson's decision.

Like she'd hoped, she wouldn't have to leave him before the next round of snow hit.

"I just got off the phone with Jilly. She and Jackson are stuck in Houston until DIA reopens, hopefully sometime tomorrow." Alyson sighed. "Between this storm and them being upside down on time, I have no idea when she'll be back at work. But it sounds like they had a fabulous time." She laughed. "She can't wait to tell us everything."

"I can't wait to hear everything."

Scott pointed at her and mouthed, *"What's up?"*

Campbell said, "I should let you go. Thanks for the call and snow day. I'm glad yesterday wasn't completely awful for you and Hayley."

"Of course. And you're okay? Stuck inside with your roommates?"

Her gaze locked with Scott's. "I'm great." Blissful, really. "Life is good." Idyllic was a much better word. "I'll see you Tuesday morning."

She ended the call as Scott trudged through the snow, right for her.

"You're giving me that blinding smile of yours." He stopped within hugging distance. "You must have received some pretty good news."

"I did." She grasped the front of his coat, and tugged him down and forward. "I have a snow day tomorrow." She pressed her lips to his which escalated to a kiss hot enough to melt all the snow surrounding them. "Have you heard anything?" she asked when they came up for air.

"No," he breathed the word. "But I'm sure I will. Shannon texted that Peyton definitely has a snow day tomorrow."

Campbell reluctantly released his coat. "Is she back to one-hundred percent yet?"

He nodded. "Sounds like it. I'll give her a call tomorrow." He slipped his arms around Campbell's waist. "I'm finished and you" —he looked at the path—"are not nearly finished." He gave her a pretend glare. "Aren't you the slacker."

She wrinkled her nose. "I'm removing snow the old-fashioned way."

He kissed her forehead. "True. But you need to hurry it up. I'm starting to go through withdrawal at not being naked and plastered against you." He stepped back and glanced at the flurries starting once more. "And I think the second round is arriving."

Campbell grinned. "You know, you could be a gentleman and help a girl out."

Her phone began to buzz and she absently looked at the screen—*blocked number*.

Campbell's smile left her mouth as a chill not related to the outside temperature enveloped her, causing her to shiver.

She tapped ignore and shoved her phone back inside her coat pocket. She then, due to a terrible habit she'd developed from long ago, glanced up and rapidly looked at her surroundings.

Nothing but a white sea of snow and a few of his neighbors also shoveling.

"Hey." Scott angled his head down to catch her gaze. "What's wrong? Who called you?"

No, no, *no*. It absolutely couldn't be him. It was impossible he could have found her. Talking about him last night had brought everything back and had made her paranoid. That's all.

She needed to get a grip.

"Campbell, where'd you go?"

She blinked several times and forced her mouth into a smile. "My fingers are frozen and I need the bathroom. I'll be right back."

Once inside Scott's house, she walked into the living room, withdrew her phone, and stared at the screen.

There had to be a way to block a blocked number. Since she didn't have time to figure it out right at this moment without causing more curiosity on Scott's part, she had no choice but to simply turn off her phone and leave it that way indefinitely.

She'd talked to Alyson. She'd texted with Lance last night. Blaine was away, working. The only other person who might call her would be her mom…and possibly her brother. The fact she hadn't heard from either of them had to mean they were fine. Snowstorms like these were nothing new in the Durango area.

The front door opened.

Campbell pressed the two buttons, swiped right, and her phone went dark. She once again stuck the device inside her coat pocket, but this time she zipped it closed.

She whirled toward Scott, staring at her with raised eyebrows.

"I thought you had to use the bathroom."

"I do." She tried on a smile. "I had to warm up my hands first." She held them out. "Do you want to help me with that?"

He narrowed his eyes.

Campbell held her breath until he closed the gap between them.

Scott removed his gloves and tossed them onto the couch. "Campbell, what's going on?" He gently folded her hands inside his and rubbed them. "Who's calling you?"

She lifted her shoulders. "I don't know." Completely the truth, too. "Wrong number, I guess. It's just starting to irritate me because whoever it is won't stop calling."

He stared at her. "Then you should answer it and tell them they have the wrong number."

Yes. If she really and truly believed it was a wrong number, she would have done exactly that by now. But she couldn't say those words.

If she did, it would mean verbally acknowledging the fear her ex *had* found her.

No. She couldn't and wouldn't go there, especially right now.

"I figured out how to block them. It's fine. I promise." It wouldn't be a lie once she had time to block the unknown caller. She then gave Scott her best naughty smile since they absolutely needed a subject change. "I have an idea that's way better than watching a movie."

He sighed. "I'm getting the feeling you're not telling me something."

Campbell kept her own sigh in check. "Scott, everything's okay." And, dammit, it was okay. It *had* to be okay. She clutched the front of his coat and brought him even closer. So close she brushed her lips against his. "Please stop being so serious. This is our last full day together until who knows when." She gave him a soft kiss which he hesitantly returned. "You said you're finished with the driveway. Right?"

He slowly nodded. "But someone else didn't finish the path."

"Fine. I'll be outside in a minute. Or"—she leaned forward— "I can be more useful upstairs, crawling into a hot bath and waiting for you."

His mesmerizing chestnut eyes flashed with a strange combo of desire and frustration. But she knew if she could get him refocused on the now, the frustration would vanish. She would also make certain it didn't reappear the rest of the day and night.

"*You're* trouble," he murmured. "I'll be upstairs in a little bit."

Once again alone, Campbell released a sound breath.

She really did need to get a grip.

Years of paranoia had returned and caught her off guard today. No doubt lounging in a hot bath with Scott—and doing other, decadent things—would eradicate the feeling.

One full day left of having him all to herself. The man she was falling in love with.

Nothing would stop this weekend from ending the way it had started yesterday afternoon. Perfectly.

SCOTT WATCHED Campbell's body move up and down in deep sleep. She was curled onto her right side; her bare, smooth back facing him with her long hair fanned across the pillow.

How could it already be Monday morning?

Neither one of them had anywhere to be that day. He'd received his snow day notification the previous evening while dozing in bed with Campbell after their rather erotic bath. As exhausted and spent as his entire body felt, he still hadn't had enough of her. And soon she'd have to leave. Return to her house and prepare for reality called Tuesday morning.

They'd both have to prepare for reality tonight.

Then Ian would be here with his horse of a dog. Then Scott would have Peyton come Sunday. Then…what? He and Campbell would see each other during class and probably chat afterward like they'd been doing. Back to texting, for sure. But not really seeing her—being alone with her—for more than two weeks wasn't enough. At the same time, it had to be enough.

For now.

He reached out and gently ran his fingers down her bare arm, over the deep curve of her waist, paused at the blankets, then reversed his direction.

She stretched, mumbled something incoherent, and snuggled deeper into the pillow.

Scott scooted closer.

He hated the thought of letting and seeing Campbell go at some point today. Especially since the mysterious calls from Saturday and yesterday had rattled her.

He wasn't deaf, dumb, and blind.

Yeah. At some point, she'd turned into a good actress and a fast thinker. But after hearing the ex-dickhead story, Scott suspected those were traits she'd learned to protect herself.

No woman—no one period—should have to live like that. Obviously, the mysterious phone calls had brought back bad memories. He believed she had no idea who was calling, but the fact she kept trying to ignore the calls, probably hoping they'd stop on their own, had to mean she possessed lingering fear her ex hadn't left her life for good.

Why she felt she had to lie to him about it, Scott couldn't comprehend.

Maybe she didn't want him to worry? Or come across as over-reacting? Or acknowledge out loud the possibility it could be her ex?

She'd made it sound Saturday night the asshole had no idea she now lived in Denver. It seemed as if she had nothing to worry about. But that kind of fear—the kind which gets into the psyche and makes itself comfortable—wasn't easy to shake.

It hadn't been easy for him to shake that level of fear when he'd returned from combat. A wholly different experience and type, but fear nonetheless. He'd also had help from his family and *brothers*, and wanted to be the one who helped Campbell get rid of her fear, once and for all.

She stirred, shifted onto her back, and rolled toward him.

Scott grinned softly at having a damn near uninhibited view of her bare front side.

Her eyes fluttered open, and their gazes caught.

"Hi," she murmured. "What time is it?"

He scooted even closer. "I don't know and I really don't care." He had no desire to continue his current train of thought, either.

Monday morning had arrived, and she'd be leaving at some point. Everything else could wait since she was here with him and had absolutely nothing to fear.

"I like your honesty," she said around a full-body yawn. "Did it finally stop snowing?"

"It looks like it," he answered, keeping his eyes trained on her. "But I'm not ready to face the day just yet. Are you?"

She laughed quietly. "Not until I have to."

"Excellent." He rolled her onto her back and barely touched his lips to hers. "Campbell, I know after today it's going to be tough seeing each other. For many reasons."

Her smile faded while she nodded.

"But I hope you'll believe me when I say you can trust me." He sealed his words with a kiss. "And that I only want *you*." Another, longer kiss. "And that we'll figure this out."

She opened her mouth to reply, but he silenced her with a kiss which swiftly became greedy and more than a little desperate.

Within minutes, and after a quick visit to his nightstand drawer, Scott pressed himself inside of her since she was once again ready for him.

Her moan joined his, and she wrapped her arms and legs around him, hugging his body closer to hers. So close he became as far as he could be inside of her which made his head buzz.

"I don't want to leave today," she whispered between a breathless kiss while matching his slow, deep thrusts. "This weekend didn't last long enough."

"I know," he whispered back. "And I don't want you to leave." He buried his face between her neck and hair, and breathed in her scent that was now less floral and more *them*.

A place and action which had become a favorite of his since Saturday.

Not too long after, her muscles began to tighten around him, so he slowed to a stop and lifted his head.

Her eyes flew open.

The passion he'd seen many times over the course of the weekend stole his breath.

"What are you doing?" she asked. "Don't stop now."

He grinned. "Maybe I want to kill you slowly and gently with sex."

She lifted her chin. "I guess we do have all morning." She then squeezed *him* tight.

He pressed his forehead to hers. "You're not playing fair," he managed to say as she squeezed him yet again and shifted beneath his body.

Her warmth. Wetness. Tightness.

Dark-blonde hair fanned across the pillow.

Her hypnotic blue eyes filled with desire while staring up at him.

All of it more than what he needed to finish what he'd started.

At feeling and hearing her release that joined his, Scott knew he'd reached the point of no return. Campbell Grey had hooked him, and he sure as shit wouldn't let her go.

Chapter Twenty-One

THATCHER GREETED Campbell the moment she stepped inside the shop.

She paused to give his head a rigorous rub. He responded by licking her fingers.

"Hi there. How were the roads?"

Campbell straightened at Alyson's voice. Her boss sat behind the counter while holding a piece of paper which had to be their daily order sheet.

"Not too bad." Campbell approached the counter. "Much better than yesterday."

"You went out yesterday?" Alyson laughed. "You were way more ambitious than me."

Only because she'd had to drive herself home. She certainly hadn't wanted to be out.

Campbell walked behind the counter and stored her purse.

"Jilly texted me early this morning,"Alyson continued. "She and Jackson should be home later today. She even said she'll come in for a little bit tomorrow."

"That's great. I'm sure they'll be glad to finally be home."

"They will." Alyson carefully eyed Campbell. "There's something different about you."

She removed her hat and coat, and faced her boss. "Like what?"

Yes. She'd spent most of the weekend wrapped around an irresistible man who she was falling for—had fallen for?—but it's not like Alyson could see that by looking at Campbell.

Alyson squinted at her. "Are you wearing different makeup? You're glowing a bit." She pointed at Campbell's head. "Your hair looks different, too." She grinned. "I like all of it."

Campbell had chosen to fix her hair like she'd worn it on Saturday. She'd also chosen to wear a tad more makeup, too, since today happened to be Tuesday. Class day. The time wouldn't pass fast enough until she saw Scott in a couple of hours, either. The "glowing" could only be due to how, and with whom, she'd spent her weekend. As the memories inundated her mind, her face and body turned warm. Almost hot.

"Wait a minute," Alyson murmured. "It's Tuesday."

Campbell pointed at the paper Alyson still held. "What have we got today?"

Her boss faced her. "How was the snowy weekend at home with your roommates?"

She smiled. "Great. But it was just me and Lance. Blaine was working. He'll be home tonight." She cleared her throat. "Can I see what we have today?"

Alyson set the paper down and crossed her arms. "When you tell me how you really spent the weekend." She angled her head toward Campbell. "Your hair. The makeup. The glow. It's also Tuesday." She paused before adding, "And please don't take this the wrong way, but in the time you've worked here, I've *never* seen you like this."

Clearly, Alyson Preston possessed the superpower of sensing

when an employee spent the weekend in bed with a scrumptious, addictive man.

"Campbell, what's going on with you and Scott?"

She could continue to lie. Deny everything. But she didn't want to lie. She'd become head-over-feet crazy for Scott Mayhew, and vice versa. Yes. She now truly understood what it meant to be physically in sync with and crave a man. Yet, that's not all they shared.

"Your silence is speaking loudly."

Campbell blinked and refocused on her boss, staring at her with blatant concern.

"I know it's none of my business," Alyson quietly said. "You're adults. I'm just your boss. And you certainly don't have to give me any details. But please tell me you're being careful?"

Fully understanding Alyson's question and recalling the story about her college friend, Campbell opened her mouth to reply, but the phone started to ring.

She closed her mouth so hard her teeth clicked.

Alyson tore her gaze from Campbell and picked up the receiver. As her friendly greeting replaced the silence, Campbell stored her hat and coat under the counter with her purse.

Dammit. It wasn't fair she and Scott had to be so…forbidden.

She frowned.

They were adults. Single adults who could separate the professional from the personal. Would it be easy? Not really. But it's like he'd said yesterday before pulsing inside of her.

We'll figure this out.

He'd also said he only wanted *her,* and she'd be a fool to walk away now.

Alyson put the call on hold and set the receiver down. "It's for you. A customer who's worked with you in the past."

Campbell absently nodded.

"I'm sorry." Alyson slid off of the stool. "I'm sure I've overstepped, so I'll be in the back, getting caught up on paperwork." She pushed the piece of paper in Campbell's direction. "Orders that came in last week for today. Hayley can do deliveries when she comes in this afternoon."

Alyson headed into the backroom while Campbell suppressed a sigh.

Though she truly appreciated her boss's concern, it didn't feel warranted. Everything between her and Scott would work out just fine.

She picked up the receiver, took the call off hold, and answered, "This is Campbell. How can I help you?"

Silence, followed by, "Hi, *Campbell*. It's me."

She froze as the all-too familiar deep voice penetrated her head. A voice she'd briefly loved and now loathed. A voice she'd tried to forget and had never planned on hearing again.

Campbell gripped the receiver and started to lower it from her ear.

"Don't hang up. I just want to talk to you."

His request chilled her body to the point she shuddered.

Was he *watching* her? And how the hell had he found her?

She walked as close to the shop windows as the phone cord would allow and scanned the area. Nothing and no one. Just a slushy, quiet street with a few parked cars.

"I didn't want to call you at your job, but you're not good at answering your phone."

Her breath slowed while the realization surrounded her.

He had been the persistent, blocked caller. But how had this happened? She'd done everything right since leaving Durango. She'd also been in Denver for over a year-and-a-half.

Why now?

"Can we talk in person?"

She lifted her chin. "No." She bit out the word. "I'm hanging up."

"One hour. That's all I'm asking."

"That's crap and you know it. How did you even find me?" she quietly asked. "You know what? It doesn't matter. Just stay away from me." She started to lower the phone a second time.

"I know," he continued as if she hadn't spoken, "all about your new life."

She squeezed her eyes shut.

How could this be happening? And just when her new life had started to snap into place?

At the same time, the bastard had always been eerily good at ripping her world out from beneath her feet when she least expected it.

"I think you can spare one hour from your *glamorous* Denver existence."

She remained silent.

"Or I'm in the neighborhood if it would be easier for me to come into Daisy's Bouquets."

He was out there somewhere, watching her.

Dread slithered up her spine while her stomach twisted. And there was no way in hell she would ever allow him to be inside of Daisy's Bouquets; her second home and place she loved, along with the women who'd also become her Denver family.

She swallowed the bile rising up her throat, then managed to say, "I'm off at five. I can meet you then." She had no other choice.

"I don't think I can wait that long to see you in person. How does eleven sound?"

Eleven—*no*. He knew about her class, too?

Her heart pounded her chest as she said, "I can't believe you're doing this to me again."

"Don't be dramatic. And you can miss one class, Miss Over-achiever."

Campbell pressed her lips together and looked at the floor.

Scott. What would she tell him? Even though he hadn't pushed when it came to the damn calls that had been from her ex-bastard, Scott had known something wasn't right.

"Or I could catch up with you at that so-called college. It's your choice."

She gritted her teeth, then said, "Fine." She couldn't have her ex on the campus, another place she loved being, and so close to Scott. "There's a coffee shop in the Highlands on Thirty-Second Avenue. I'll be there at eleven. You get one hour. No more."

"I'm looking forward to it."

She slammed the receiver down with enough force that Thatcher lifted his head to look at her from where he sat on his dog bed.

"Everything okay?" Alyson's raised voice reached Campbell from the back.

She took a moment to breathe deeply through her nose before answering, "Yeah. The guy copped an attitude when I told him we don't have sunflowers right now."

Dammit. She had to get rid of him—again—but how? Another restraining order would be a huge waste of her time. Call his parents? It could work. Maybe if she threatened it that would be enough? They had stepped in before and taken him somewhere to "get help."

She shook her head.

Like the restraining order, it had apparently worked miraculously.

No matter what, she had to keep him away from the places and people she loved, especially Scott…even if it destroyed her heart and soul which had taken her years to repair.

"SCOTT?"

He stopped at Johanna calling his name while he walked by her office.

She waved him forward. "I need a few minutes of your time."

Well that sure as shit didn't sound good. Still, he grinned and stepped into her office.

"Can you close the door?"

Scott stared at her for several seconds before doing what she requested.

His instincts went into overdrive while he sat in the empty chair in front of her desk.

What could this be about? It seemed far too serious to be promotion related.

The promotion which no longer seemed like the best choice for him right now.

"I feel like I'm back in middle school and got called into the principal's office."

She cracked a smile. "Did you have a nice, long, snowy weekend?"

Mind-blowing and unforgettable were much better words. But he said, "I did. You?"

"I was able to get caught up on some work while my husband dug us out yesterday."

Silence fell while she peered at him.

Scott shifted in his seat. "So what's up?" And why could she be staring at him like that?

Like she wanted to use her eyes to drill a hole into his head and read his mind.

"I received a call not too long after I arrived," she began, "from a gentleman who's in your American Literature class. Because of what he was calling about, he wanted to remain anonymous."

Scott raised his eyebrows. "Okay."

She hesitated, then said, "He called to report that you're having an inappropriate relationship with a woman in the class."

His breath left his lungs while he met Johanna's piercing gaze.

"A woman by the name of Campbell Grey."

He maintained eye contact with his boss while mentally going though every swear word in his vocabulary.

"Do you recognize her name?"

Holy shit, this couldn't be happening. How could it be happening?

He slowly nodded. "Yeah. Sharp student. Sits in the back. Participates a fair amount."

There could be no way in hell the kids—and they were mostly kids—in that class had picked up on his and Campbell's connection. Especially during class time. Even their after class chats had been innocent. Always about books and reading…with the exception of Thursday.

Had someone seen and overheard them? Then again, it's not like they'd been standing *that* close together. They'd also been talking quietly. Until right as she was leaving and mentioned looking forward to the reading assignment.

"I told him what he was saying was a serious accusation, given the college's policy, and to give me more information," Johanna stated. "And that proof would also be required."

Scott narrowed his eyes.

Something about this didn't feel right at all. Suspicious and way too personal.

"So what exactly did this student say?" And had it actually been a student? *His* student?

"He did report spotting you two together over the weekend at your residence."

Scott's body turned cold, but he managed to give Johanna a baffled expression while continuing to make eye contact with her.

"Said he also happens to live in your complex." She sat back.

"Of course, I don't believe a word of it for many reasons. The first one being he doesn't have proof."

Scott quietly released a slow breath.

Okay. A massive miracle, for sure.

"Reason two is that he was so specific with your student's name. I'm thinking he's a jealous boyfriend or husband. Perhaps she's liking your class a little too much?"

His boss not believing the caller didn't change the fact someone had been watching him and Campbell at his home —*jealous boyfriend or husband.*

He halted when he remembered the strange phone calls Campbell had received.

Johanna shook her head. "Reason three is that he couldn't tell me a thing about the class outside of the name. My probing questions then made him hang up quite abruptly."

What if the caller had been a former, unstable ex-husband?

"Scott, if for some reason the guy—whoever he is—pushes it, I will completely have your back on this." She gave him a tiny grin. "Reason four being you're a wonderful instructor, and have an impeccable teaching background here and at Red Rocks."

He forced himself to return her grin. "Thanks, Johanna." But the guilt shrouding him from her complimentary words and support landed heavily on his shoulders.

Scott knew in his gut the call hadn't come from a student in American Literature. But as violated as he felt at being watched at his own home, he'd crossed into jeopardizing his career and everything he'd worked for the second Campbell had stepped into his home that Monday night. The wrong person knew he'd crossed the line, too. He also couldn't shake the ominous feeling Campbell might be in trouble when he recalled everything she'd told him about her ex.

Scott stood. "I need to prepare for class. I appreciate you telling me."

"Certainly." She pointed at him. "I can't believe it, but someone doesn't like you. Because of that, I recommend erring on the side of cautious. On another note"—she straightened—"I'd like to set up your interview for tomorrow at four o'clock. Does the time work?"

Interview? He couldn't even think about that right now.

"Can I get back to you on the time?" He turned and opened her office door. "I have a friend coming into town tomorrow who's going to be staying with me. I need to get his ETA."

Johanna nodded. "Thursday will work, as well. Let me know when you can."

"Yep." He strode out of her office and went directly to his a few doors down.

Once inside, he closed the door and removed his phone from his jacket pocket.

Yeah. He'd be seeing Campbell in less than an hour, but this couldn't wait. It's not like he'd be able to talk to her right away when he saw her, either.

"*Shit*," he muttered when she didn't answer her phone, forcing him to leave a message.

Scott then followed up his voicemail with a text version.

I really need to talk to you. Please call me ASAP.

He set his bag on his desk and sat in the chair.

She'd told him about her ex's jealousy and possessiveness. How difficult he'd been when it came to signing the divorce papers. Unwilling to let her go. Supposedly being taken somewhere for *help*. Then there were the mysterious phone calls Campbell wouldn't answer. She'd even looked a tad fearful on Sunday while scanning Scott's street after ignoring another call. His street where they'd been seen—watched—at his home.

Where his little girl stayed with him every other week.

Scott's jaw tightened.

Now the "anonymous" call to his boss? It all pointed to her ex-sonofabitch *not* being gone for good.

Scott leaned back and stared at his phone while willing Campbell to text or call him back.

If her ex did end up being behind this shit, Scott would figure out a way to help her face him once and for all.

Chapter Twenty-Two

CAMPBELL SPOTTED her ex-bastard the moment she stepped inside the coffee shop a few doors down from where Daisy's Bouquets had lived this time last year.

Her gaze locked with his ice-cold blue eyes as he actually smiled.

She clenched her teeth.

Chatter from people at other tables and the barista steaming milk surrounded her as she marched to where he sat in a back, corner table.

His smile grew when she stopped behind the empty chair.

She tightened her hands buried inside her coat pockets into fists to stop herself from doing something really *dramatic* and obnoxious—like smacking the smile off of his face.

"You're lookin' good." He gave her a long, slow once-over. "Your hair is longer."

Campbell lifted her chin, but remained silent.

He pointed at the empty chair. "You can sit down. Do you want some coffee?"

"No," she enunciated while grudgingly taking a seat. "I won't be here long."

He released an exasperated sigh. "Why can't you let shit go? It's been two years. And I'm not here to fight with you."

Campbell leaned forward. "Then tell me why you *are* here or I'm leaving." She narrowed her eyes. "How did you even find me?"

Dammit. She'd done everything right.

He gave her his revolting, smarmy smile. "Baby, you know a good magician never reveals his secrets."

Another round of bile inched up her throat at his smile and words. She also fully understood what he wouldn't say.

"Though I will admit," he conceded, "it sure wasn't easy…*Campbell.*"

She ignored his words and stated, "You used your dad's connections and money."

Still, she'd considered that before leaving Durango to disappear into the sprawling, Denver metro area. As he continued to smile, a realization almost knocked her off the chair.

She'd completely and stupidly underestimated his unstable dark side, and now he'd found her. Was sitting right across the table from her saying "I win" without using those words.

Like the first time around, though, she wouldn't go down without a fight.

"Speaking of your dad," she casually began, "I'll bet he has no idea where you are right now." Somewhere he wasn't welcome and didn't belong. "But I'm sure he'd like to know."

Her ex-bastard picked up his cup and took a drink. "I wouldn't bet on that."

What the hell did that mean? But she fell silent.

"Mommy and daddy dearest are pissed at me and"—he raised both hands—"cut me off," he finished with air quotes. "Some mistake I met in a bar one night went whining to the cops that I got rough with her."

She shuddered at the fury flashing through his eyes and across his face. He'd never been rough with her, but she had no problem believing what the woman had said about him.

"Total bullshit." He shrugged. "The parents will get over it eventually. They always do."

Campbell lowered her gaze to the table.

How the hell would she get rid of him this time? His parents had stepped in previously. It had, however, required her and her mom making a lot of noise and getting a lawyer involved. Her mom couldn't know he'd found Campbell, either. She didn't deserve to go through this a second time. Campbell also didn't deserve it, but she'd been the one who'd foolishly fallen for this manipulative and narcissistic bastard sitting across the table.

Outside of his blond-god good looks, smooth, deep voice, and ability to use charm, what had she seen in him? A question she really couldn't answer when she thought about Scott.

A *real* man.

"But after the parents wrote me off," her ex easily continued, "I received good news."

She forced herself to look up and again meet his icy blue eyes.

He smiled and leaned forward. "About you, of course."

Yes. Of course. It also answered the *why now?* question.

"So I packed up some shit, closed out a bank account, and headed this way." His smile deepened. "I had to get here before the storm."

Before the storm.

That day last week when Scott had asked her to get snowed in with him, she'd sensed something foreboding was on its way. She'd chalked it up to not liking storms, but what if she'd sensed her ex. This unrecognizable person who she'd once loved.

Or had she?

If fate hadn't been on her side the day of her twenty-first birthday, they'd have a child. The worst way to spend any birthday. But if not for the miscarriage, she'd be doing everything in her power to protect a daughter or son right now. As it stood, she had several people in her life she had to keep him away from. And one of them *did* have a daughter.

She had to do something. But what?

"Look," he said around a sigh, "I know shit between us became insane."

Only because he was insane.

"But you have to know, on some level, it's always been you." He gestured at their surroundings. "The second I saw you in a *different* coffee shop, in a different city."

She needed to get out of here and far from him so she could think. She also needed to return Scott's text and call. By now, he had to be wondering what had happened to her.

"I spent months looking for you and I'm here because I want to be with you."

Campbell mentally groaned.

Would she ever be truly rid of him?

He frowned. "I can't say I'll be able to call you—"

"You need to listen to me very carefully," she enunciated. "I want you to leave. Go back to Durango where you belong. Actually"—she released a humorless laugh—"you can go straight to hell for all I care." She stood. "If I see or hear from you again, I will get the police involved."

He gave her a ghost of a smile. "And you're forgetting how patient I can be."

Campbell stepped back.

She'd known her threat wouldn't phase him. It sure as hell hadn't in the past. But it was all she had at this precise moment.

"I'm also going to remind you I know *everything* about your new life."

His words, which sounded like an unspoken threat, hung between them for several seconds. She then turned on her heel and marched from the coffee shop.

He'd stressed *everything*. Why? What had he really been saying?

Campbell removed her phone from her purse while she speed-walked to where she'd parked her car.

Scott was in class at this moment where she also belonged.

Tears burned her eyes as she imagined missing the quiz and in-depth class discussion on the two Kate Chopin stories she'd absolutely loved. Just like *The Awakening*.

The Awakening.

After last weekend, she understood Edna even more. Discovering herself emotionally, mentally, and physically. Campbell had only needed to let go of who she'd been to become the woman who'd driven away from Scott's home yesterday afternoon.

She slid into her CR-V and slammed the door shut.

Now she was on the verge of spiraling back into the woman who'd left Durango because of her stupid mistake who wouldn't let *her* go.

She sniffed, blinked her eyes clear, and went into the texting thread with Scott.

I really need to talk to you. Please call me ASAP.

Although she had no idea what could be on his mind, he happened to be absolutely right. They needed to talk ASAP. And not just about her ex-bastard tracking her down and not leaving.

With a deep breath she typed, *I'm sorry I didn't make it to class. I'll explain everything when I see you. Meet me at the Starbucks near City Park when you're finished.*

Because her ex had to know what she drove, she needed to get the hell out of the Highlands while he remained inside the coffee shop. She knew this because of where and how she'd parked. He had to know where she lived, too. Had to have been, like he'd done in Durango, following her since he arrived in Denver before the storm—

Her breath caught in her throat when she reached a stoplight.

I know everything about your new life.

She briefly squeezed her eyes shut.

Oh, no, no, *no*.

Campbell accelerated into the intersection when the light turned green.

She couldn't, however, deny the obvious when she remembered the call she'd received while standing close to Scott outside his home.

Her ex-bastard had been watching them. He knew where Scott lived.

Panic invaded her insides to the point her heart thumped against her chest.

Though he'd never done anything dangerous—just a manipulative need for control and playing mind games—she couldn't stand the thought of him knowing about her and Scott and where Scott lived…with his five-year-old daughter half the time.

Her stomach hitched and she forced herself to breathe deeply through her nose.

She couldn't lose her head right now. She had to *think*. One thing at a time.

Go to Starbucks and wait for Scott. She was supposed to be in class, so Alyson wouldn't expect her back in the shop until around one o'clock. When Scott arrived, she'd tell him the whole truth. Then she'd have to walk away since he'd probably be shocked and hurt by her confession. She'd get through the rest of the day, go home, and figure out what to do next.

She'd have to do all of it without shattering into a million pieces.

With the exception of meeting with Scott, her huge, costly mistake would be somewhere watching her and patiently waiting to make another move.

A couple of tears slid from her eyes at the dismal, unfair image.

Chapter Twenty-Three

"I HAVE A QUESTION," the girl who sat next to Campbell in the back stated.

Only today Campbell hadn't made it to class. Considering the way Scott's work day had started and coupled with his suspicions, it couldn't be a good sign.

He managed a friendly smile. "I'm sure I have an answer."

His phone inside his pants pocket had buzzed a couple times during class. A better sign, for sure. But he couldn't check it until he ended class after answering his student's question.

"Why can't we read more Kate Chopin or another female writer instead of the next guy?"

He slid his hand into his right pocket and grasped his phone. "I'm glad you liked Kate Chopin so much, but Booker T. Washington was an influential black writer and *Up From Slavery* is an important piece of American literature." He withdrew his phone. "But we'll definitely be reading and discussing more female writers this semester. On that note, chapters one and two are due Thursday. There will be a quiz. Happy reading."

As students left the classroom, Scott focused on his phone.

He released a quick breath at seeing Campbell had texted him back. Twice. But her first message did nothing but add to his concern and confusion. Her second message had been letting him know she'd arrived at the Starbucks.

This wasn't a good time for him. He had office hours right after this class. Unless, of course, there happened to be an emergency. Between Campbell's cryptic message, not coming to class, and his instincts working overtime, this did feel damn close to an emergency.

With that thought, he quickly packed up his laptop bag and strode from the room.

Nothing about the way this day had started and where it seemed to be going felt right.

Scott's misgivings only tripled in strength the second he stepped inside the Starbucks and spotted Campbell sitting at a table away from the windows.

She was staring at her cup, then reached up and swiftly swiped her cheeks and nose.

His heart splintered at seeing her looking nothing like the woman who'd reluctantly left his house yesterday. And after the longest, hottest goodbye he'd ever experienced.

He headed toward the table.

Campbell glanced up, her big, beautiful eyes damp and dim and filled with defeat. The complete opposite of how they'd looked this time yesterday. Her cheeks were also an entirely different type of flushed with a hint of tear stains.

Finding her this way, combined with everything else, could only mean one thing.

Scott sat in the empty chair and leaned forward. "Campbell, I think I know—"

"My name isn't Campbell."

He halted as her unexpected confession hung between them.

A burst of laughter from a nearby table sounded as if it were miles away.

He squinted at her. "Excuse me?" He could not have heard her correctly.

She sighed. "I mean, legally it's my name. *Now*. I changed it before I moved to Denver."

Scott continued to stare at her.

What the hell was happening here?

"It's not the name on my birth certificate."

He sat back and remained silent while his brain frantically processed what she'd said.

"I know it sounds crazy and desperate," she hurriedly continued, "but before his parents finally got involved because they had to, my ex wasn't leaving me alone. Nothing my mom or I or my brother did to try and keep him away from me worked. He didn't care about the restraining order. Because of his family's prominence and growing up in the area, he had friends everywhere, including on the police force." She learned forward. "They worshipped him, and I was just *overreacting*."

Okay. Based on what she'd already told him, none of this sounded surprising. It still didn't stop him from saying, "He became fixated on you to the point you felt you had no other choice but to change your name, as well as leave Durango? Campbell, that's not—" He shook his head. "That's not even your name."

Holy shit, had this day gone in an entirely surreal direction.

She lifted her chin. "It's now my name. Do you want to see my driver's license?" She reached for her purse. "I don't have my social security card on me. It's at home."

Scott reached across the table and placed is hands on hers. "No. That's not necessary. I'm just"—he released a slow breath—"processing. I think I'm allowed."

She pulled her hands out from underneath his and picked up her cup. "You are. And I'm so sorry, Scott. I should have told you on Saturday while I was telling you what happened with my ex.

But Campbell Grey is legally my name. No one here knows the truth because I left the other woman—the other me—in Durango."

He caught her gaze. "Why did you tell me the truth?"

She drank some of her coffee, set the cup down, and said, "Because I'm falling for you, and you need and deserve to know everything."

Under entirely different circumstances, Scott would have loved hearing that confession coming from her since he felt the same way. But his brain had reached overload.

She released a humorless laugh. "Changing my name was a huge pain in the ass and all for nothing." Her lower lip quivered. "He still found me. It's the other thing you need to know."

Scott narrowed his eyes.

Which meant his instincts had been right and the asshole had to be the reason she'd missed class today. He was back and had made himself known.

His jaw turned to steel before he asked, "What is he capable of? Be honest with me."

She sighed. "He just wants to get back together which is *nothing* new."

Her response hadn't answered his question, but Scott stayed silent.

"Between what I told you about my name and what I'm about to say," she quietly added, "I know you're going to run in the other direction. But I'm almost certain he knows about us." She paused before saying, "And knows where you live."

He slowly nodded. "I know it." He again reached out to clasp her hand. "And, yeah, I'm definitely on overload right now, but I'm not about to run in the other direction."

"What do you mean you know?" Her forehead formed a deep V. "How could you know?"

Now he needed to be honest.

The second he finished telling her about the call to his boss, what color Campbell's face possessed vanished as her eyes became round.

"Oh, my God," she mumbled. "Scott, I'm so sorry."

"Don't apologize." He squeezed her hand. "It's not your fault, and Johanna made it clear she didn't believe him. But you're going to have to call—"

"The police? So simple, right?" She finished her coffee and grabbed her purse. "Scott, I have no idea where he is, what he's driving, or where he's staying. He's in complete control."

"And we'll figure it out. I know people, too." Namely Ian, Denver PD's newest detective who would be headed this way tomorrow, but Scott also still had a few buddies on the force.

She again pulled her hand free and stood. "I'll drop the class when I get home tonight."

Scott stared up at her as his heart dropped into his gut. "Campbell, you can't do that. I know how important being back in school is to you. If you'll just trust me—"

"I promised you last week," she softly stated, "that I wouldn't do *anything* to jeopardize your career and life with Peyton. And I meant every word."

He also stood. "You don't have to drop the class."

"I need to get back to work." She stepped backward. "I swear to you I'll fix this."

"Will you wait a second?" He reached for her hand, but she turned and sprinted outside. "*Shit.*"

Acutely award of people at a nearby table watching him closely, Scott followed the same path Campbell had taken, only a tad slower. But at seeing her CR-V already leaving the parking lot, she apparently was going the same speed she'd left the Starbucks.

He muttered another choice swear word while climbing into his SUV.

As he stared blankly at the dashboard, he replayed the last few minutes.

Campbell Grey wasn't her real name. A beautiful woman full of surprises. But *shit*. She'd changed her name? Certainly unexpected information, though not where he needed to focus. At least, not at this moment. And, yeah, it made him want to rip her ex-husband's head off, but Scott couldn't stop her from dropping the class. The fact her unstable ex had come to Denver, picking up where he'd left off on his fixation with her, needed his full attention.

Who the hell was this sonofabitch?

She'd never said his name or his family's name, and Scott hadn't been interested enough in the shit bag to ask. Until now. With the right person on top of it, he could get all the info he wanted. Especially if the asshole came from a "prominent family" in a relatively small city.

He reached into his pocket and withdrew his phone.

"Hey," Ian answered. "Saw that Denver got buried over the weekend. But the weather's still looking damn good for a road trip tomorrow. Stella and I are even going to listen to the book you recommended a while back."

Scott had actually recommended several books to Ian, but he said, "Sounds good. So I need a huge favor. Specifically, your official detective status."

Silence before, "Okay. What's going on?"

Scott started the engine. "I need all the info you can find on a guy and family in the Durango area. The catch is that I don't have any names. Only that the guy's dad was the county's DA about eight or so years ago."

"It'll be easy to track down names and what you need based on just that info." Another pause, then, "Are you going to tell me what this is about?"

Scott backed out of the parking space. "When you get here."

"Okay. I'll be in touch soon."

Scott headed in the direction of the campus. Though he really wanted to go to Daisy's Bouquets, pull Campbell into his arms, and hold her until someone pried them apart. It had to be what she needed most, too. That and her ex-dickhead to leave and never come back.

Felicity's ex had been a worthless sack of shit, but he'd let her go with almost no fight. Campbell's ex, on the other hand, appeared to be in an entirely different category of worthless.

Scott gripped the steering wheel remembering how shocked and defeated she'd looked before racing out of the Starbucks.

She'd said, *"I swear to you I'll fix this."*

Not alone, she wouldn't. Before Scott could help, he needed to know her ex's full story. As did a close, trusted friend who happened to be a cop.

There had to be a way to get rid of this guy for good. Send him back to whatever black hole he'd emerged from recently where he needed to stay the rest of his damn life. Maybe the answer would come after Ian did some digging? After they talked about what he'd found?

And thank God Peyton was with Shannon and Adam this week.

The relief inside of him so strong he expelled a deep, steady breath.

In the meantime, all Scott could do was be patient until Ian called him back with answers, then they'd figure this out and Campbell would never again have to deal with the bastard.

Chapter Twenty-Four

CAMPBELL'S lower lip trembled while she moved the cursor to the button which would officially make her no longer Scott's student.

Tears slid from her eyes, turning her laptop monitor into a gray, wet blur.

It was better this way, especially for him and his job.

She and Scott had surpassed the point of no return when she'd arrived at his house on Saturday. Actually, they'd really passed it last Monday before she'd left his home. By dropping the class, they could unapologetically be together. No more hiding. Unbelievably, he'd made it clear before she'd raced out of the Starbucks he wouldn't be running in the other direction.

So why did her heart feel as though once she clicked the button it would break apart?

She sniffed twice and absently wiped her cheeks.

When she'd signed up for the class back in November, it had been another huge step forward into her Denver life. A life she had fallen in love with at some point. She'd loved being in college, too. Dropping out of Fort Lewis College had nearly crushed her heart, mind, and soul. But she'd done it out of devotion to the baby growing inside of her, and wanting to be a wife and mother. She'd always planned to go back to school. *Always.*

Life, however, had taken her down a completely unexpected path. But Campbell had still planned on going back to school.

Last year had been amazing in so many ways, she'd wanted this year to be even better. The best one yet since moving to Denver. Between dating someone for the first time since her ex-bastard and being surrounded by love in the shop and at home with her roommates, she'd decided to ease back into college by taking required American Literature.

Another round of tears hit her eyes and she squeezed them shut.

She'd surprisingly fallen in love with the class...and her instructor who loved books and reading and talking about books as much as she did.

Only a few parts of the Scott Mayhew package she'd fallen for, too.

She sniffed twice and swiped her nose.

Campbell couldn't stand the thought of not being in his class and it had almost nothing to do with them. She'd loved being back in a classroom, and having homework and taking quizzes and participating in class discussions about what they'd read. Scott also happened to be a really good teacher.

Her ex's smarmy smile and arrogant demeanor while they'd been in the coffee shop that morning appeared in her head.

By then, he'd already called Scott's boss. *Always in control.* Now she knew for a fact what he'd really meant by he knew "everything about her new life."

She gritted her teeth as despair quickly reverted to fury.

None of this was fair.

What more could she do to get away from him? More importantly, why wouldn't he let her go? What more could she do or say to make him understand she didn't want him? Then again, she wasn't dealing with a reasonable, rational person. Maybe it meant she'd have to think outside the box on how to make him go away for good. But where the hell could he be?

Campbell stood, stepped toward her bedroom window, barely opened two blinds, and peeked through the slit.

She slid her gaze left and slowly scanned the entire street turning dark from twilight.

Nothing but lawns covered in twenty inches of snow. Frozen trees with snow and icicles on the branches. Plowed sidewalks. A slick, snow packed street with a few parked cars.

She frowned.

Could he be in one of those cars? It didn't look like it due to their darkness. The temperature had fallen to below twenty degrees. To stay warm, the engine would have to be running and none of them were. With his penchant for sneakiness, she couldn't believe he'd be that obvious, either. So where the hell could he be? And how had he been watching her and Scott on Sunday without being noticed in a sea of snow?

Her phone burst into song which made Campbell jolt and whirl from the window.

His incessant calls had stopped since she met him at the coffee shop, but instead of bringing relief the pause in calls seemed even more…eerie. Deliberate. He had reminded her how patient he could be, so she hesitated before reaching for the device on her desk. With a deep inhale, she picked it up and—her shoulders drooped at the caller's image and name.

"Hi, Mom," she answered while leaning against her desk.

She hated the fact her ex had her once again tied up in anxiety over his behavior.

"Hi, Sweetie. Did you and your roomies get all dug out?" She laughed. "Denver ended up with ten more inches than us."

Campbell sat in her desk chair. "Lance was on top of it yesterday when I got home."

Silence fell on her mom's end, followed by, "Home from where?"

Dammit.

She shook her head and came back with, "Work." She cringed. "I had to go in and take care of something. Did Evan help you get all dug out?"

Yes. She and Scott could be a *them* when she dropped the class. But until then, her mom didn't need to know. Campbell also wouldn't tell her about her ex until she had a plan in place.

"He and the new love of his life came over and helped. I made them dinner as their payment. How's the class going? And work? We haven't talked since last week. I'll be honest I was getting a little concerned." She sighed. "Bad habit, I know. I'm still glad you answered."

Had her mom developed a sixth sense superpower, too?

Campbell stared at her laptop monitor. "I'm sorry I haven't called. Life's been a tad crazy with the class and working full time." And falling for a man who would soon no longer be her American Literature instructor. Her vision blurred yet again and she blinked her eyes clear. "But everything's fine." She placed her hand back on her wireless mouse. "I hate to get off the phone so quickly, but I'm swamped with homework."

A couple of quick knocks on her bedroom door caused her to jump and she looked over her right shoulder.

"You okay in there?" came Blaine's voice. "Lance and I are here and have wine."

Damn. She needed to get a grip.

"Blaine and Lance need to talk to me about something. I'll call you in a few days."

Hopefully by then she'd have a plan in motion to get her ex-bastard permanently out of her life.

"Okay," her mom slowly said. "You're sure you're alright?"

Campbell eyed the cursor still over the button, paused for several seconds, then clicked.

With a shaky breath, she replied, "Yeah. It's been a long day. That's all." A message popped up asking if she was sure she wanted to drop the class. "Love you. Give Evan a hug."

She clicked continue as her mom said, "I will. Love you, too."

You have now been removed from the class appeared while she ended the call.

"Campbell? Honey? Can we come in?"

Her sorrow returned with a vengeance.

She managed to close the college's webpage, then her laptop, despite her wet eyes.

Her bedroom door eased open and Blaine poked his head inside. At that moment, her phone again started to ring, but seeing the newest caller's name only made the tears come faster.

Blaine's eyes widened while he pushed the door open. "What the freak happened?" He glanced at Lance standing beside him. "This is a code red situation."

Lance nodded. "I'll be right back with the bottle."

Campbell's body shuddered from the emotion streaming from her eyes she couldn't stop.

Blaine rushed toward her, set two wine glasses on her desk, and sat on her bed's edge. His gaze dropped to her phone which fell silent. "Whoever that was cannot be worth this. What's going on with you?"

She sniffed several times.

Lance reappeared with the bottle of wine and sat on the chest in front of her bed.

Her roommates focused on her with raised eyebrows.

Campbell's phone dinged and lit up from a text.

I really want to talk to you. Please call me.

"Who's trying so hard to get a hold of you?" Blaine persisted.

Lance handed her a tissue.

At this point, she had nothing to lose by telling her roommates—the closest people she had to best friends—everything. With her unstable ex out there somewhere, they needed to know.

She wiped her nose and cheeks with the tissue. "It's Scott."

Smart, successful, handsome, charming, funny, book nerd, ex-military, single dad Scott who wanted to be with her as much as she wanted to be with him.

Of course her ex-bastard had chosen now to invade and upend her life a second time.

"Why does that name sound familiar?" Blaine swung his gaze between her and Lance.

Lance's mouth inched open. "Your American Lit instructor?"

Blaine leaned forward. "Professor Hottie is calling and texting you?" He gasped. "Is *he* the mysterious, very good friend you were with last weekend?"

Campbell re-read Scott's message full of kindness and concern she'd didn't deserve. As such, she couldn't bring herself to do what he asked. She also needed to come clean with Blaine and Lance because they, too, deserved to know everything. Maybe they could even help her when it came to the topic of getting away from her ex for the last time.

Blaine reached for and grasped a wine glass. "Honey, we love you and you need to talk to us. What's happened?"

She pressed her lips together, instantly tasting wet saltiness from her tears. She then lifted her chin and said, "Yes. I spent last weekend with Scott at his place."

Their eyes went back to round.

"But that's just a fraction of the reason I can't stop—" Her voice cracked on the words.

They remained silent.

She picked up the other wine glass, took a quick drink, and started from the beginning.

The real reason she'd ended up in Denver over a year-and-a-half earlier with a new name.

SCOTT GRABBED his ringing phone right beside him on his couch, but sighed at seeing Shannon's name.

Why wouldn't Campbell call him back? He thought he'd made it clear he wasn't pissed about anything she'd told him or the situation. Shocked shitless about her name? Definitely.

"Hi. How's Peyton?"

But he still hadn't run in the other direction.

"It's me, Daddy."

At hearing his little girl's voice, he smiled and cleared his mind to concentrate on her. And the fact she was safe and sound with her mom. "Hi, baby. How was school today?" He put aside the papers he'd been trying to grade since calling and texting Campbell.

"Fine. We couldn't play outside 'cos of all the snow."

"That's no fun. How's your snowman, Olaf, doing?"

She giggled, and Scott's smile deepened.

"He lost his carrot nose. Mommy and Adam think a big bird stole it. But we gave him a new one."

"I'm sure Olaf is very happy to have his brand new nose."

"Uh-huh. So Mommy and Adam are getting married, and I'm going to be a flower girl."

Scott halted.

"Mommy said I'll look like a Disney princess that day."

Holy shit, three out of the many women in his life had given him absolute whiplash today.

"I have to go. Mommy needs to talk to you now."

He gave his head a hard shake before saying, "Alright. I love you. Call you tomorrow."

"Love you."

Phone jostling followed Peyton's words.

"I honestly didn't think she'd say it quite like *that*," Shannon stated. "Are you okay?"

Scott stared at the floor.

No, he sure as hell wasn't okay and it had nothing do with his ex's news. But he said, "It caught me a little off guard since you didn't seem convinced it was what you wanted when we last spoke. But I'm fine, Shannon. Truly. Congratulations." He meant every word, too. "Sounds like you guys had a pretty memorable weekend." So had he, only in an entirely different way.

Everything had seemed so damn clear this time last night. Now…not so much.

Shannon laughed. "I figured if I could still stand the sight of Adam after getting snowed in an entire weekend due to a massive blizzard, marriage with him was worth a shot."

Scott smirked. "How romantic of you."

"No ring yet," she continued. "And no date. But we have some ideas. We're even talking about a destination wedding."

He started to reply when another call hit.

It had to be Campbell. Or possibly Ian.

"Hey, can we talk later? I have another call coming in that I need to take."

"Rushing to get off the phone with me again?" she teased. "If I genuinely liked you, I might start taking it personally."

"And it's always a pleasure, Shannon. Hug Peyton for me."

He ended the call with his ex and accepted the one from Ian.

Not who Scott really wanted to be on the other line, but an important call nonetheless.

"Hi," he answered. "You got something for me?"

"I have a *shit ton* of info for you," Ian replied. "Can you talk right now?"

"Yep." Scott leaned forward, rested his elbows on his knees, and mentally braced himself.

"Your guy's name is Paul Harmon, only child of James and Marlena. Real big shots in that entire area, but especially Durango."

Okay. It's what Campbell had basically said on Saturday and at Starbucks earlier.

"He's your typical entitled, rich asswipe who got away with way too much crap because of his last name."

Scott frowned. "Like what?"

"Mostly drunk driving and vandalism. But he's also managed to avoid serious trouble from complaints by a few women about his rough side. He's definitely a bastard," Ian added.

Scott narrowed his eyes.

Campbell had told him on Saturday her ex had never hurt her. Yet, the thought of her with such a sonofabitch made him want to punch a wall.

"And then there's the ex-wife and that ugly story."

He straightened and gripped his phone.

"A woman by the name of Brittany Tate turned Harmon, daughter of Judy and Bruce Tate. Dad's not really in the picture. Lives in Steamboat. She also has a younger brother, Evan."

Scott's breathing slowed.

Brittany Tate Harmon. Her real name that was of course nothing like Campbell Grey.

"According to my source in the Durango PD—who wants to have my children because I'm that charming—it was a whirlwind romance and she became pregnant. Then they got married, but she miscarried soon thereafter and stayed with the guy. From what my source implied, sounds like staying with him was easier than leaving because she *belonged* to him."

Scott clenched his teeth. Still, with the exception of sharing her real name, everything Ian had said matched what Campbell had told him on Saturday.

"When she did finally get away and decided to divorce the asshole, he had trouble accepting everything and—"

"Wouldn't leave her alone," Scott finished.

To the point she'd changed her name and relocated to Denver to start a new life.

"You got it."

Leaving the bastard had been the antithesis of normal.

"She did get a restraining order, but with guys like that, and because of his family's connections, it didn't mean a damn thing. And no one on the force talked about it."

She'd said at Starbucks she'd been accused of *overreacting*. The order still didn't mean a damn thing to the guy. But Denver wasn't Durango.

"His parents finally stepped in," Ian continued, "got him to sign the divorce papers, then shipped him off to some unknown city and place to *get help*. My source said he was gone for months, too. But here's where the plot really thickens—while he was gone the ex-wife left the area. All her mom and brother have said, and only when someone asks, is that she took a job out of state. But they've never said where."

Scott stared at his ottoman while everything Ian had told him swirled through his mind.

Paul Harmon had caused Brittany Tate enough trouble for one lifetime. Campbell Grey seemed to want nothing more than to build a life here in Denver. A life where she didn't have to worry about her ex showing up whenever he felt like it, supposedly wanting to get back together.

"I'm sure you can guess that when the ex came back from wherever he'd been, he wasn't too happy to find out Brittany Tate Harmon had left the area."

Scott slowly nodded as he remembered something else Campbell had said earlier.

I have no idea where he is, what he's driving, or where he's staying.

"Paul Harmon had been keeping a pretty low profile until a month ago or so." Ian paused and it sounded like he was flipping through papers. "Another woman went to the police about his rough side, but the charges—"

"Were dropped." Scott shook his head. "What the hell's with this family?"

"I don't know. Maybe they're worshipped for shitting twenty-four karat gold bricks and sharing the wealth? But that's everything on your guy in a nutshell. Now it's your turn. Do you actually know this jackass?"

Scott started to reply, but stopped when a thought nearly knocked him sideways. But he'd have to come clean with Ian to move forward with an idea taking shape.

"No," he admitted before adding, "But I do know *her*. She's actually here in Denver and now going by a different name."

Silence fell on his buddy's end.

"And *Paul* is also here."

Ian sighed. "I guess that explains why he was keeping a low profile. He was biding his time while looking for her." Another pause, then, "I think I can also guess how you know her."

Scott sat back. "We can talk about it later. What you need to know is that he's pulling the same shit he did in Durango, and she's determined to fix it on her own. But she's rattled." A mild word, for sure. "She also doesn't know where he is, what he's driving, or where he's staying."

"Understood. I'm on it and will call back when I know more. I'll see you tomorrow, too. Stella and I will get an early start."

"Wednesdays are my full days." Scott also had to talk to Johanna about the interview, something he couldn't face tomorrow. Possibly not at all. "If you can get into town around noon, I can meet you here and let you in. Then head back to work."

"Sounds good."

Scott ended the call and a second idea hit him. But he needed to talk to Campbell.

He called her again…and she didn't answer.

Shit. Why did she keep avoiding him? Was it embarrassment? It didn't make sense.

He went into their texting thread and typed, *You have to know that I'm not angry. I also need to talk to you. Please call me back.*

Scott stared at his phone. The longer he sat there with no response, however, a third idea came to him. Certainly not his first choice, but necessary if she kept avoiding his calls and texts. Hopefully calling her at Daisy's Bouquets wouldn't cause her coworkers too much curiosity.

Chapter Twenty-Five

THE CLOCK on Campbell's bedroom wall changed to four o'clock and her phone rang.

Blocked number for the umpteenth time.

She silenced the device while somehow stopping herself from hurling it across her room. It wasn't her phone's fault her ex-bastard had started playing his mind games.

If Campbell answered his calls, he won.

If she didn't answer, he won.

If she turned her phone off, he won.

If she destroyed her phone out of fury and frustration, he won.

Always in control. And she still had no idea how to get rid of him for good because she had no idea how he could be found.

She burrowed deeper under her blankets and tried once more to focus on *Jane Eyre.* Since she no longer had homework, she'd decided to pick up where she'd left off on the authors Scott had recommended after the first day of class which now felt like a year ago.

Scott. The man she loved…who she'd been avoiding for over a day.

Blaine suddenly appeared in her doorway. "I heard your

phone ringing again. I can put myself in charge of it if that would help."

Her eyes turned bleary at his offer and at remembering how amazing and non-judgmental he and Lance had been after she'd told them everything, including her real name.

"I can't let you do that." She released a humorless laugh. "And if I do, he wins."

"Honey, there's no way he could know your roommate has your phone."

She wiped under her eyes and sniffed. "I would know. But I love you for offering."

"Love back at you. By the way, there's someone here to see you."

Campbell frowned and shifted upright.

Who on earth would be here to—

Scott replaced Blaine in her doorway.

Their eyes snapped together, and he gave her a soft smile.

She scrambled from her bed and stood.

His smile deepened as he gave her a swift once-over.

That's when she remembered she wore purple sweatpants, her fraying Fort Lewis College sweatshirt, thick slipper socks, and had her hair piled on her head in a messy knot.

She mentally groaned, then asked, "What are you doing here?" She gestured at her room. "How did you get my address?"

Scott leaned against the doorframe. "It's nice to see you, too."

"I warned you she's not at her best today," Blaine said from behind Scott. He then pointed at Scott and fanned his face. "I'm sure you won't need me, but I'll be downstairs if you do." With a final fan, Blaine turned and disappeared from view.

"He seems like a nice guy." Scott released a quick laugh. "He wouldn't let me in until I showed him my driver's license. Though he admitted after he let me inside he did recognize me from my faculty bio picture, but still wanted to make sure."

Campbell's face became the temp of an electric burner turned to high.

Scott's smile turned affectionate.

"Please answer my questions."

He walked inside her room and closed the door. "You weren't answering your phone or returning my texts, so I called Daisy's Bouquets. Alyson told me you called in sick. When I asked for your address, she hesitated. But after swearing to her my intentions were honorable, she obviously gave it to me. That's how I'm here."

Campbell lifted her chin. "Yesterday was a rotten day and I…" Her voice trailed into silence. "I just wanted to stay home." Where she'd be safe and *he* couldn't get to her.

Scott sighed. "I understand and I'm not here to judge you. I was worried." He pointed at her bed. "I also need to talk to you. Do you mind if we sit?"

Campbell's posture relaxed while she took in his rumpled hair, weary eyes, and scruff lining just under his cheek bones and jawline—concern for her embedded in his handsome face.

"I'm sorry I haven't called or texted you back." She lowered herself to her bed's edge. "I was avoiding you…*life*. I have no excuse but that."

"I had a feeling." He came around and sat close beside her. "That's not the only reason I'm here, though. I wanted and needed to see you. I also really hope what I'm about to tell you doesn't piss you off." He released a quick breath before saying, "I know everything." He grasped her right hand and linked their fingers. "Including your ex's name…and your real name."

She nodded.

Of course he did. With what little she'd told him, it probably hadn't been too terribly hard to uncover the full story.

"Gotta love Google," she mumbled under her breath.

"Actually, my friend Ian was the one who uncovered what I didn't already know."

Campbell peered at him. "Ian. The one who's moving to Denver?"

"Yep." Scott squeezed her hand. "He's a cop. Detective now."

"Oh." She pressed her lips together before saying, "I told my roommates everything last night." She stared at their joined hands. "I had to because *he's* out there, watching—"

Her phone started to again ring.

Campbell's shoulders slumped.

Scott reached for her phone and looked at the screen. "Blocked number." He narrowed his eyes flashing with anger. "Blaine said he heard your phone ringing again." He lifted his gaze to hers. "How many times has the sonofabitch called you today?"

Her eyes became wet once more. "I don't know. At least a dozen."

Scott silenced her phone, flipped the switch to silent, and put it inside his coat pocket.

"You doing that means he's winning."

"No," he countered. "He won because I have no doubt he's somewhere nearby, watching this house, and knows you didn't go to work today."

She pulled her hand free and tried to stand, but Scott stopped her by cupping her face.

"Campbell, I don't know you as well as your roommates do and of course your family. I'll also never know what you went through to start over in a new city. And I hate the fact you dropped American Literature. But I've heard and seen enough to know hiding from life in your bedroom isn't the real you."

Her lower lip began to tremble.

"Courage, hope, and strength. In that order. *That's* the real you."

At seeing the affection and determination in his perfect chestnut eyes, she took a slow, steady breath.

He was right, of course. About everything. Her ex-bastard had already won because she'd allowed him to get inside her head and had reacted by shutting down.

Something she'd sworn to never again allow when she'd left Durango.

"Since I have no doubt the asshole is close and watching," Scott continued, "I want you to stay with me."

She froze.

Has she heard him correctly?

"I have an idea." He gently rubbed her bottom lip with his thumb. "It's in the spirit of keeping friends close but enemies closer. You have to trust me, okay?" He guided her head to his chest. "And Ian who's at my place with his horse he calls a dog."

Campbell smiled and deeply inhaled Scott's familiar, delicious scent. "I trust you completely." She also couldn't get rid of her ex-bastard alone.

Past events had made that an unfair and disheartening fact. At the same time, she couldn't help but feel a spark of negativity when it came to him leaving her alone for good.

She'd changed her name and moved to a major metro area with a population of nearly three million people and her ex had still found her because of his dad's connections and money.

"Scott, I don't know how a person beats a living, breathing version of the devil."

He tightened his arms around her. "Timing." He kissed her forehead. "Ian and I will tell you our idea tonight." He leaned back to catch her gaze. "If there's anything about it you don't like, tell us and we'll—"

"I want him out of my life for good, so at this point I'll do anything." Every part of her meant those words. "I love my life here in Denver and I already gave up one life. I can't and won't do it again. Not because of him." The complete truth, too.

"And that sounds like the *real* you."

She pulled away and straightened. "How long am I staying with you?" If he actually said the word forever, she'd be beyond okay with that answer.

"A couple days? It really all depends on your ex."

Whatever that meant. But she absolutely trusted him and his friend.

"Okay. Be prepared for Blaine to put up a fight, though." She stood. "He and Lance told me, after I told them the truth, that my ex would have to go through them to get to me."

Scott grinned. "I'm liking your roommates more and more because it's clear how much they love you." He leaned forward. "As does Alyson."

Yes. They did. But how did—

Campbell stepped back. "I'll be ready to go in a few minutes. But I'll have to follow you in my car because I *am* going to work tomorrow."

His grin deepened.

She went to her closet.

Scott's feelings for her didn't matter at this moment. She— they—needed to concentrate on ridding her life of the devil for the last time.

Only then would her Denver life as a different and *awakened* woman truly begin.

———

SCOTT FOLLOWED Campbell into his house from the garage, but several loud, deep barks stopped her in her tracks.

"Stella, knock it off!"

Ian's Bernese Mountain Dog—who probably reached Campbell's waist and weighed more than her—bounded toward them with her mouth hanging open.

Scott gently propelled Campbell forward and closed the door behind him.

As Stella excitedly sniffed Campbell who cautiously pet her head, Ian headed for them.

"Don't let her bark or size fool you," his buddy said while giving Campbell a friendly smile. "She has the demeanor of a kitten on catnip."

Campbell switched to rigorously rubbing Stella's head which earned her several enthusiastic finger licks.

"I'm Ian Stafford." He held out his hand which Campbell grasped. "You must be *the* Campbell Grey I've been hearing so much about."

Campbell's face turned that still appealing shade of red while she slid her eyes, which had brightened a bit, to Scott and back to Ian.

"Guilty." She released his hand. "I'm sure everything Scott has told you is true, too."

Ian's smile doubled in size. "I sure as hell hope so."

Scott narrowed his eyes. "Ease up, will you? We'll be right back. Think you and Stella can stay out of trouble for a few minutes?"

"I should actually take her for a walk now that you're here." Ian scratched Stella's head but stared at Scott who nodded that he understood what his friend really meant. "I think she can wait a little while longer, though."

Scott clasped Campbell's hand and led her up the stairs.

When they entered his bedroom, she stopped and gave him a soft smile.

"I get to stay up here with you?"

He dropped her bag on his bed and sat on the edge. "Well, it's either stay up here with me or share the couch with Ian and Stel-la." He winced. "Even *I'm* not that brave."

She fought a smile while shaking her head.

Scott reached out, grasped her hands, and tugged her until she stood between his legs. He then slid his arms around her waist and buried his face in her stomach hiding underneath her thick sweatshirt. "I know I said this on Saturday, but I'm really glad you're here."

She wound her fingers through his hair. "That makes two of us."

He breathed her into his soul, paused, and looked up. "Campbell, you have to know—"

Stella's loud, deep barking reached them upstairs, followed by a yelp, followed by a blood-curdling scream, followed by Ian yelling "Stella, no!"

Scott's deep frown matched Campbell's as she stepped backward.

What the *hell*?

He stood and darted from his room with Campbell right behind him.

"Who the hell are you and where's my brother?"

At hearing Felicity's raised voice, Scott raced down the stairs —but halted at seeing his sister backed against the front door, clutching Princess Belle, while glaring at Ian standing between her and Stella licking her big, wet mouth.

Felicity spotted Scott and her shoulders relaxed. Until her gaze landed on Campbell, standing to the left of him.

His sister's eyes flashed with outrage and shock.

Shit. Just what Scott didn't need or want at this exact moment.

Felicity straightened while hugging Princess Belle to her chest. "Will you please tell me what the *bloody* hell is going on around here?" She pointed at Ian. "His enormous animal just tried to eat my dog while you were upstairs with—" She stopped, took a deep breath, and gave Campbell a tight smile. "I do hope you know I genuinely like and respect you. You're a lovely woman." She focused on Scott. "But she's your student and shouldn't be here."

Ian's eyes widened and he looked at Scott. "*Student?*" He leaned forward. "You conveniently left that part out, Professor."

"And who exactly are you?" Felicity asked again.

Scott sighed and finished walking down the stairs. "Felicity, this is Ian Stafford. I know I've told you about him. He's from Grand Junction and was in my unit."

Her posture relaxed a fraction as she curtly nodded.

"He's relocating to Denver and is staying with me while he looks for a place. Ian"—Scott glanced at his buddy—"this is my nosy, mouthy sister, Felicity."

She glared at Scott at the same time Ian stuck out his hand.

"It's nice to finally meet you."

Felicity hesitated before grasping Ian's hand for a whopping split second.

"I'm sorry Stella startled you." Ian rubbed his dog's head. "She doesn't mean any harm."

"A dog that size should be better trained."

Ian frowned at Felicity and angled his head back.

She focused on Scott. "I came by to check on you because you haven't answered or returned my calls or texts today."

Because he'd been hoping to avoid talking to her. But he said, "It's been a hectic day."

"Only because of me," Campbell interjected while coming down the stairs. "Felicity, I know how this looks." She stopped at Scott's side. "But I'm in love with your brother."

Scott looked sharply at Campbell, concentrating on his sister.

A taut silence surrounded them...outside of Stella's panting.

Yet another round of whiplash caused by a woman in his life. But this whiplash made Scott grin and link his fingers with Campbell's which he gently squeezed. Though he wanted to respond to her confession in a much more visceral way.

"And I'm not his student anymore."

Felicity's gaze went from Campbell, to him, and back to Campbell.

"The reason I'm here," Campbell quietly added, "is because I have an ex-husband who's…being difficult right now. And Scott and Ian—who's a cop—have an idea on how to help me." She stepped forward. "Alyson and Jillian don't know about any of this, but I will tell them as soon as I can."

Scott eyed his sister still tightly hugging Princess Belle staring at Stella.

Felicity sighed. "I certainly understand what it's like to have a difficult ex-husband," she murmured. "I also know my brother will do everything in his power to help you." She eyed Ian. "I suppose I should also thank *you* for helping my friend."

Ian smirked. "Please don't trouble yourself."

Felicity tore her gaze from Ian to again concentrate on Campbell. "Is there anything I can do to help?"

Campbell shook her head.

Felicity opened Scott's front door and said to him, "Next time, just return my calls and texts." To Campbell, she said, "Please call if you need me." She gave Ian and Stella a cursory glance before leaving.

Another round of silence fell as Felicity closed the door behind her.

"So that was the famous Felicity Mayhew." Ian shuddered. "I've been in the box with sociopaths who were more charming and friendly than your sister."

Scott slowly nodded. "Yep." When she happened to be in a mood like her current one, it really wasn't hard to believe his friend's observation.

"Stella and I are going to go on that long walk." Ian attached her leash to her collar. "When we get back, we'll talk about the *difficult* ex-husband."

Seconds later, Scott and Campbell were alone. For the first time since she'd left Monday afternoon. Back to reality which had gone in a way neither of them had expected.

She faced him. "I'm sorry. I didn't mean to blurt out—"

Scott silenced her with a long, deep kiss that lasted until they needed to pause for air. Then her phone still inside his coat pocket started buzzing.

He withdrew her phone. "Blocked number. This asshole definitely doesn't give up."

Campbell held out her hand. "I can take it." She stared at her phone still buzzing. "Maybe I should even answer it."

"No. Not yet. He has to be close by." Scott shrugged out of his coat and put her phone in the right pocket. "It's the other reason Ian took Stella for a walk."

Campbell's eyes widened.

"He knows what your ex is driving."

Her mouth inched open.

"So I say let the bastard squirm for a bit." He tossed his jacket on the staircase railing. "Based on everything you've told me and Ian found out, it has to be driving him crazy you're here with me and another guy."

She hugged her arms to her chest and sat on a step. "I'm so sorry about all of this. I honestly thought I'd done everything right and he'd eventually get bored and move on."

"Unfortunately, the dark side of obsession doesn't work like that." Scott sat beside her. "And please stop apologizing." He placed his arm around her shoulders and hugged her to him.

She curled into his side. "Can we stay just like this until Ian and Stella are back?"

Scott rested his chin on her head. "Yeah."

She'd told Felicity, "*I'm in love with your brother.*"

He hugged Campbell tighter, opened his mouth—her phone started buzzing yet again.

His jaw turned to steel.

Her relentless ex had to be somewhere nearby while he watched, called, and waited.

Now wasn't the time for Scott to share his feelings for her. But if everything went the way he and Ian hoped, it would be soon.

Chapter Twenty-Six

CAMPBELL STARED at Alyson and Jillian. "You want to promote me to manager?"

She hadn't known what to expect when she'd walked into the shop—after a somewhat dreamlike and unexpected Wednesday night—following her "sick day." But a huge promotion that would come with a pay increase to match?

Was she still asleep in Scott's comfy bed and curled into his warm, strong arms?

Jillian gave her a huge smile that reached her dark eyes weary from the jet lag. "Hayley told us yesterday she's doing a summer semester in Spain program. She won't be leaving until May, but she said if she loves it, which we're sure she will, she'll probably stay for the fall semester, as well."

Campbell couldn't help but grin. "Good for her. That'll be so much fun." She'd planned on doing something similar when she'd been Hayley's age and a full-time student.

"It means we need to hire and train someone before she leaves," Alyson inserted. "After talking it over yesterday, Jilly and I want to hire two part-time employees and not just because of how busy we've become the last year or so."

All because Alyson and Jillian had crashed a Felicity Mayhew wedding, and Alyson had crossed paths with Felicity's younger brother.

Her irresistible younger brother Campbell loved. Feelings he hadn't reciprocated at any point last night. At the same time, did he really have to say the words? His actions since Tuesday at Starbucks had certainly spoken louder than words of love.

Jillian's smile deepened. "Jackson and I had such an amazing time in Argentina that we're already talking about our next trip. Two weeks in Indonesia this summer." Her grin slipped a fraction. "That is, if his mom is still doing as well as she is right now."

Campbell nodded. "I'm sure she will be, too."

She'd met Jackson's mom, who'd been diagnosed with terminal cancer in September, at Alyson and David's bachelor-bachelorette party right after Christmas and she had looked good.

"And David and I," Alyson quietly threw in, "want to start a family."

Campbell returned her soft grin.

"We're not ready to start now," she hastily added. "But we will be soon."

Jillian reached across the work table and clasped Campbell's hand. "We're going to need you more than ever from this point moving forward. That deserves the right job title and salary."

Campbell pressed her lips together before murmuring, "Thank you so much."

As thrilling and surprising as their words were, all of this meant she'd have to tell them the truth. Like Scott and her roommates, she dearly loved and trusted her bosses and they deserved to know everything.

"We also respect the fact you're back in school," Alyson stated.

Campbell's gaze locked with Alyson's who now knew she and Scott were *something*.

Jillian squeezed her hand. "We'll obviously continue to work with your class schedule."

More incredible news. She did still have to tell them about American Literature.

"I appreciate that. Really." Campbell hesitated before saying, "But you guys should know I had to drop my class, so I'll be here all day again on Tuesdays and Thursdays."

Jillian arched her right eyebrow while Alyson's mouth drifted open.

"Going back to school this semester wasn't meant to be." Not too far from the truth, either. "I would like to try again, though. Maybe in the fall?" She lifted her shoulders. "With the raise you guys are going to give me, I could even enroll at Metro or CU Denver." But first she had to get her life back, once and for all.

"*Absolutamente.*" Jillian released her hand and straightened. "It sounds like you're accepting the promotion?"

Campbell laughed and nodded. "Of course I am." Another huge step forward.

Alyson and Jillian came around the table.

She shared a tight group hug with the women.

As they released each other, Campbell took a deep breath and said, "There's something I really need to tell you guys, but right now isn't the time."

Their grins transitioned into slight frowns.

"Can we close the shop for lunch and talk then?" She couldn't stand the thought of her ex-bastard out there watching her and her bosses out in public having lunch together.

Alyson glanced at Jillian who shrugged.

"We can do that." Alyson focused on Campbell. "Sounds pretty serious."

The shop phone started to ring, and Jillian headed for the desk.

Ian had been unsuccessful at locating her ex's vehicle in

Scott's townhome complex or surrounding neighborhood; their idea simple enough. Catching her ex watching her—them. Being somewhere he didn't belong. So either he hadn't been nearby after all or was still damn good at being sneaky.

Always in control.

"Is it about Scott?" Alyson leaned forward. "Is he the reason you dropped the class?"

She sighed. "Yes…and no. To both questions."

"Campbell, it's for you." Jillian placed the call on hold. "A client who's worked with you in the past."

Alyson's frown deepened. "That sounds familiar."

Campbell lifted her chin. "I'll take it out in the shop. Thanks."

She marched to the phone sitting on the counter.

Damn him and the past repeating itself and his need for control and his obsession with her. She being the one thing in his life he couldn't have.

Recalling how Alyson's and Jillian's faces lit up with love and excitement while talking about David and Jackson—who loved and adored them an equal amount—Campbell narrowed her eyes while staring at the blinking button on the phone panel.

Though Scott hadn't said the words last night, she knew in her heart, mind, and soul how he felt about her. For the first time in her life, she had exactly what she wanted.

Friends who'd become family.

A job she loved, despite the occasional tough couples and wedding coordinators.

A *man* who wanted and adored her as much she wanted and adored him.

Yes. She'd had to give up American Literature because of her ex-bastard. But college wasn't going anywhere. Maybe she did belong at a four-year university, like Metro or CU Denver, studying business. She did truly love the idea of starting and running her own independent bookstore. And Alyson and Jillian were definitely great role models when it came to women owning and running a successful small business in a major city.

Campbell picked up the receiver.

Enough was enough.

She hit the blinking button and quietly said, "Okay. You have my attention."

Her ex laughed.

Campbell shivered at the deep, condescending sound.

"I reminded you how patient I can be. But having your attention isn't good enough."

Of course not.

"What do you want?"

"You know exactly what I want." He released an exasperated sigh. "Britt, why can't you let shit go and give me—us—a second chance."

"Don't call me that!"

"It's your name!" he snapped back. "This whole thing is stupid. Especially you being with Mr. *College Professor*."

"Don't talk about him," she enunciated.

"Whatever." He paused, then said, "How's that class going, by the way?"

She gripped the receiver. "If all you did was call to gloat, I'm hanging up."

"Don't be dramatic. And since it sounds like you now have nowhere to be at eleven o'clock, meet me at that same coffee shop. We need to talk. In person."

Knowing Scott and Ian's plan, she wanted to tell her ex-bastard to go straight to hell where he belonged. Scott and Ian had also mentioned being able to track all of his damn calls to her phone. But she had *his* attention right now, and a plan started to take shape in her head.

"You're right." She frowned at saying those words. "We do need to talk in person."

Silence fell on his end.

"But privately."

More silence.

"Are you again '*in the neighborhood*'?"

A pause, followed by, "I'm closer than you know."

Disgust mingled with contempt caused her to clench her left hand into a fist.

"Then I'll come to you. Eleven." A thought occurred to her and she asked, "What are you driving?" Ian had told her last night, but obviously her ex couldn't know she knew.

"A gray, piece-of-shit Chevy SUV I had to buy from some loser client of my dad's."

Campbell froze.

"The parents took my BMW when they cut me off."

Dammit. That's why Ian had been unlucky last night.

On top of his sneakiness, her ex-bastard was driving a completely different car than what Ian had found in his research —the BMW.

"I'll park where you'll actually be able to see me," her ex added. "See you soon."

The line went dead, and Campbell set the receiver in the cradle.

She needed to text Ian her idea, but Scott had to be at work, getting ready for American Literature. She couldn't call or text him about this. No matter what he said she'd already, though indirectly, caused enough of a stir when it came to his college-teaching career.

Yes. He'd be pretty upset after the fact since what she would be doing wasn't *the* plan. She'd also have to make Ian swear not to say a word to him until absolutely necessary. Scott's displeasure with the change in plans would still be better than disturbing his career any further.

"Campbell?"

She whirled in the direction of Alyson's voice.

"Everything okay with that client?"

She forced her mouth into a smile. "Yeah. He just had questions about Valentine's Day bouquets. And costs." Surely she wouldn't go to hell for all the necessary lies she kept telling Alyson. The thought, however, reminded her of another lie she had to say. "I just remembered I have to run to the campus about my tuition refund before lunchtime."

Alyson crossed her arms. "So that means we're not going to chat today?" She peered at Campbell. "It sounded like you had something pretty important to tell us."

Campbell lifted her shoulders. "It can wait." Just a little while longer.

Alyson stared at her a few seconds more before heading into the backroom.

Campbell immediately removed her phone from her back jeans pocket to text Ian. If he didn't reply right away, she'd call him.

She had to face her ex. If she didn't, she'd never be truly free of him.

SCOTT RAN a hand thought his hair, then rubbed his eyes.

For the life of him, he couldn't concentrate on his student's essay on Malala Yousafzai. Fantastic influential person. Really well-written paper, too. But his mind happened to be elsewhere. He also wanted to be somewhere else with a specific someone.

Campbell had needed to go to work today. It still hadn't been easy to watch her drive away from his townhome, alone, earlier this morning.

Because the shit bag was out there, watching her. Probably calling her nonstop, too. But Ian also happened to be out there and had told Scott after Campbell left that he would be stopping by his new place of employment to get some local help.

Her ex-asshole seemed to have mastered hiding in plain sight.

Scott stared blankly at his laptop monitor.

He knew he'd made the right choice walking away from the police force when Shannon became pregnant with Peyton. In a situation like this, though, it was incredibly hard to be here since he wanted to be standing with Ian and his new partner at this moment.

A knock from his office doorway made him glance sharply to his left.

His student from the morning Mondays and Wednesdays English Composition class gave him a shy smile. "Hi. I'm—"

"Kinsey. I know." He smiled. "What's up?"

She walked into his office and sat in the same chair she had a couple of weeks earlier. "I just wanted to say thank you." She went into her backpack and withdrew a paper she held up. "I've never *ever* gotten an A on a paper."

Scott made the connection and said, "It was extremely well-done and thoughtful and convincing." He laughed. "It made me want to listen to rap music for the first time in my life."

She smiled as her face became crimson. "Really? That's so cool." She pushed a lock of hair behind her ear. "I loved writing it."

"I could tell." He straightened. "I know you said you hate writing, but I wouldn't be so quick to dismiss it. You did a great job."

Her smile deepened. "Okay." She slid the paper inside her backpack. "I heard that your American Lit class is really good. Do you, by chance, teach it in the summer?"

He shook his head. "That's nice to hear, but no. I'm only teaching it in the fall." He paused before adding, "With the exception of this school year." And if he hadn't agreed to take on the class this semester, he may never have met a smart, beautiful, passionate woman who looked like Cinderella and preferred stories with happy endings.

Now that Scott knew Campbell's full, unhappy story, her penchant for happy endings and strong identification with Edna from *The Awakening* made absolute sense.

Kinsey stood. "Alright." She flung her backpack over her shoulder. "I guess that means I'll be taking American Lit in the fall. Thanks again for the A and helping me choose the topic."

Taking American Lit in the fall.

"Of course. I'm looking forward to reading your next essay." He meant every word, too.

With another shy smile, Kinsey left his office.

Scott went back to staring at his laptop monitor and the realizations hit.

Okay. The hours upon hours of grading were the definition of tedious and tapped into his time with Peyton, but maybe he could get some help with that. And the atypical hours and schedule *did* work with his single-dad life. He also, when not distracted by unforeseen twists in his personal life, looked forward to every single class. Specifically, the teaching and talking with his students and witnessing their light-bulb moments which were always fulfilling. Because like Felicity had stated the first week of the semester, Scott really did love being in the trenches. Just like their dad. With that thought, he stood and headed for Johanna's office.

She looked over at him after he knocked on her doorway. She then removed her glasses and sat back. "I know what you're about to tell me."

Scott walked inside and closed the door behind him. "Mind-reading. I wish I had that superpower." Especially as of this week.

"I'm sure my husband wished I didn't have that ability." She placed her glasses on her desk. "I knew you were having second thoughts about going after the Assistant Chair position when you said you'd get back to me about scheduling the interview…and never did."

He slowly nodded. "I'm sorry. This week has been full of surprises." That was putting it mildly. "Johanna, we both know the position will probably go to Darcy. She has to be the one in this department also going after the job."

His boss's silence only supported his instincts.

"She's been here for years which shows her dedication to the school." He lifted his shoulders. "This is only my second semester here. I also haven't been teaching that long." He smiled. "And I love it. All the grading aside, I'm not ready to give up being in a classroom full-time for an administrative job." Felicity would probably never let him forget she was right.

Johanna returned his smile. "Okay. I'll let the dean know you've decided to withdraw your interest." She leaned forward. "But keep in mind I'll be retiring someday. That means there will again be an opening in this department."

He stepped back. "Take over the position of chair? Try to fill *your* shoes?" He opened the door. "Not a chance in hell."

She laughed. "I was thinking more along the lines of the Assistant Chair taking over for me which would once more leave that as the opening."

Scott shrugged. "I'll keep it in mind. In the meantime, I need to get to American Lit which reminds me. I have a request."

"I'm all ears."

"Do you think starting in the fall semester I could get a TA to help me with the grading? Maybe someone who's also interested in being an English teacher someday?"

Johanna smiled. "It shouldn't be a problem. We can offer it as an English elective. But I would have someone in mind and talk to the student in April so he or she plans their fall schedule accordingly."

He returned her smile. "I can do that." He already had a few ideas. Possibly Kinsey? "I'll see you later." Though not his initial vision, having a TA would definitely be a substantial help.

As Scott headed for American Lit, however, his thoughts went back to Campbell and her dropping the class. Their relationship, connection, and feelings for each other aside, she'd been a great student. As an instructor, he genuinely despised the fact she wasn't in the class anymore. And all because of her worthless ex's behavior. Yeah. He and Campbell had crossed the line *big time*. But Scott firmly believed if not for her ex, they would have gotten through the rest of the semester without disaster striking. Maybe a little naïve thinking that way, but it's how he felt.

Scott set his laptop bag on the desk in the classroom as students filtered inside. He exchanged quick smiles with several of them.

As he opened his bag, his phone inside his pants pocket started to ring.

"Oh!" The guy who also liked *Dead Poets Society* pulled his phone from his backpack. "Yours going off reminded me I have to silence mine. Thanks, man."

Scott withdrew his phone, silenced the ringing, and halted when he saw Ian's name.

Shit. He needed to answer the call and class hadn't officially started yet.

He turned to walk out into the hallway—but was stopped by the girl who Campbell *used* to sit beside in the back.

"So I had a hard time reading and focusing on *Up From Slavery* and will probably choke on the quiz today. That means I *will* need extra credit."

Scott looked at his phone, now buzzing in his hand, and back at his student.

"Dooo…you need to answer it?"

Yeah. He sure as shit did. But he happened to now be standing in the classroom with his students sitting at their desks and had to be a professional.

He shoved his phone back inside his pocket.

Hopefully Ian would leave a message or text. While the students took their quiz, Scott could step out into the hallway and find out what was happening.

"No. It's fine. So extra credit. I still think it's a little early in the semester to have this conversation. I also feel you need to have more faith in yourself, but what are you thinking?"

She launched into watching *Dead Poets Society* and other ideas she had.

Scott forced himself to focus on everything she said.

Chapter Twenty-Seven

AS CAMPBELL APPROACHED the gray SUV where her ex-
bastard happened to be waiting for her, she clutched her phone
inside her coat pocket.

Ian had told her not to meet her ex until he texted that he and
his partner were close, but she had yet to hear from him and
eleven o'clock had arrived. If she didn't follow through with
meeting up with her ex now, he'd remain in control, and Ian and
his partner couldn't be far.

Ian had also requested *she* do something sneaky as a way to
seal her ex-bastard's fate.

With a shaky breath, Campbell opened the passenger-side
door and slid into the SUV.

She faced her ex who faced her, as well.

Even "cut off" by his parents, he managed to ooze wealth and
arrogant sophistication dressed in an expensive, thick, black
leather jacket and jeans; his blond hair underneath a black cap.
His cold, cobalt eyes shielded by designer sunglasses.

She knew firsthand this particular devil preferred to wear
Armani.

He pointed at her head. "I hate it when you wear your hair up like that." He reached toward her, and she pressed herself against the door which earned her a heavy sigh. "I've never hurt you and I'm not going to start today."

Her posture relaxed a fraction. "Physically, no. But you figured out other ways."

He turned toward the steering wheel. "I also hate this dramatic *new you*."

"And I hate the fact you're here in Denver." She leaned forward. "I agreed to talk to you in person—alone—because this has to stop. You can't keep doing this to me."

He started the engine. "If you'd stayed in Durango where you belong, we wouldn't be here. Denver is just another shit hole of Colorado. And how many damn times do I have to say all I want is for you to give me and us a second chance. When did that become a crime?"

Delusional.

She was trying to reason with a person who didn't think like normal people. But she couldn't back down now. Her future, no matter where it happened or with whom, depended on her fighting him every step of the way.

"You're not listening to me. *Again.* How many times do I have to say all I want is for you to walk away? To let me go?" She gestured at their surroundings. "What more can I do to show you I want to be as far away from you as I can possibly get?"

He put the SUV into reverse.

Campbell's already racing pulse catapulted into overdrive. "What are you doing?"

He backed up, then pulled out of the parking spot.

Dammit.

She briefly closed her eyes at once again stupidly underestimating her ex-bastard.

Hopefully Ian and his partner were close. They also had the SUV's description.

"We're going somewhere where we can be alone and talk." He shot her a condescending smile. "It was your idea, *Campbell*."

She slowly buckled her seat belt as he drove away from where he'd parked, a few spots up from Daisy's Bouquets.

Calm. That's what she needed. Just to stay calm. Her ex had never physically hurt her and she had no choice but to cling to his statement he wouldn't start today.

"We are alone and we were fine talking where you parked," she stated.

"It wasn't private enough." He settled back into the driver's seat. "Gotta say, I like having you alone for the first time since"— he glanced her way—"the night before you left me."

She clenched her teeth while staring out the windshield.

"Truthfully, what you did to me was kinda cruel. Moving out while I was at work, then having me served with divorce papers when you were back at your mom's?" He paused before adding, "I think cowardly might even be a better description than cruel."

She eyed him. "You knew it was coming. Stop playing the victim." She also held on to the fact it had taken him months to finally sign the damn papers and only after his parents had been forced to get involved. "We're *never* getting back together, and I will *never* stop fighting to get away from you." She straightened. "Pull over. I want out. Right now."

What the hell had she been thinking? She absolutely wanted to get rid of him for good, but not at a risk this high. And what had happened to Ian?

"I'll pull over and let you out when I feel like it. And what are you going to do, *Campbell*? Change your name again and move to another city? The definition of dramatic." He braked at a stoplight and faced her. "It was losing our kid that changed you." He shook his head. "You're still blaming me for that, aren't you?"

She remained silent.

Yes. The stress of being married to a jealous, possessive,

controlling bastard had more than likely caused the miscarriage. Still, the huge loss had ultimately saved *her* in the long run.

"Why can't you let the past go? We also could have tried again. Many times." He pointed at her. "And I know I made mistakes, but no matter how highly you think of yourself, you weren't perfect, either."

The light turned green.

Campbell slid her fingers as covertly as possible to the buckle release button.

"I know you were screwing around behind my back."

Of course his delusional, jealous mind still thought she'd cheated on him multiple times.

"You weren't giving it to me anymore."

For the life of her, she couldn't understand what she had ever seen in this person. This so-called man whose blond-god good looks couldn't hide the ugliness inside of him. So much for him being taken somewhere to "get help." But for all she or anyone else knew, his parents had dropped him off in some city on this planet with cash and a credit card, and simply walked away.

As much as she hated it, she couldn't stop a spark of sympathy for Paul Harmon.

"And you obviously had no problem giving it to the college professor all last weekend."

Campbell whipped her head in his direction and narrowed her eyes.

"It had to be the best sex of his pathetic life," he muttered while running a red light.

"Stop talking about him and let me out of this damn car!" she snapped while pressing the buckle's button.

"You can't seriously be into that guy," he said as if she hadn't spoken. "Speaking of guys, how many more are going to show up in your life?" He braked at a red light he couldn't run because of the car in front of them. "You live with two guys, you're screwing your college professor, and now there's the dude with the big-ass dog."

Oh, my God. He really did know everything.

"Miss Overachiever sure is busy nowadays."

She had to get away from him, get Ian on the phone, and—

Lights started to flash behind them, followed by a siren, quick and piercing.

She glanced at her ex, his head tilted up while he looked in the rearview mirror.

Relief shrouded her when she glanced over her left shoulder and saw the unmarked police car with the flashing light on its roof. Due to the sun's glare, she couldn't tell if it was Ian and his partner. If those two weren't in the car, the reason they'd been pulled over by other officers caused her to release a quiet breath before she focused on her ex.

"I guess you shouldn't have run that red light."

He gripped the steering wheel as the light turned green. "If I were you, I wouldn't do or say anything stupid." He followed the car into the intersection, but went right instead of straight. "It'll be my word against yours." He stopped behind a parked car on the side street and shoved the SUV into park.

She smirked. "And this isn't Durango, you arrogant, entitled bastard."

Before her ex could reply, the back driver's side passenger door opened—and Ian slid into the backseat.

Campbell's eyes widened, though he gave her a friendly smile.

Another round of relief made her relax against the passenger door.

"Sorry we're late." Ian scooted until he sat at the opening between the front seats. "The shitty traffic in this city is going to take some getting used to." He turned his smile on her ex. "Hi. I'm Ian. I'm sure you recognize me." He pulled out his badge, then added, "It's actually *Detective* Ian Stafford with the Denver PD." He laughed. "I'm really liking the sound of that."

The unmarked police car pulled up alongside the SUV, ultimately blocking them.

"And that's my new partner." Ian waved at the older gentleman who smiled and waved back. "So you ran a red light back there, Paul Harmon."

Her ex's jaw became rigid.

"This SUV of yours," Ian smoothly continued, "has also been spotted in a few different places where it didn't belong." He glanced at Campbell. "Complaints from neighbors we didn't discover until today." He went back to concentrating on her ex. "But there was never anyone in the vehicle when patrol officers checked out the complaints." He nodded. "You're good. I'm definitely impressed. It takes a shit load to impress me, too."

"I'm flattered," her ex replied. "Can you give me the damn ticket so we can go?"

Ian's smile doubled in size. "Oh, you're not going anywhere." He angled his head toward Campbell. "She definitely gets to leave. But I'm sure she'll want to press charges first."

"For what?" Her ex stared at her. "What the hell have you told him?"

"She didn't have to tell me anything," Ian answered for her. "All the damn phone calls to her cell since you got into town last week told me more than enough. My partner and I stopped counting when we reached fifty."

Campbell's breathing slowed.

She'd suspected the number to be high, but more than *fifty*?

"Between your addiction to hearing her phone go to voicemail," Ian said, "and this vehicle being spotted in neighborhoods where Miss Grey happened to be at the time, and her being in your car with you against her will—"

"She wanted to talk to *me* alone!"

Ian caught her gaze and asked, "Is that what really happened?" His stare turned piercing; what she needed to say crystal clear in his dark eyes.

"I did suggest we talk privately"—she looked at her ex—"but I never agreed to go anywhere with him. And when I asked him to pull over and let me out, he refused." She withdrew her phone from her coat pocket and showed it to Ian. "I also recorded everything like you told me to do."

Her ex's mouth hardened while he shook his head.

Ian grinned and straightened. "Then that cinches it. Is there anything you'd like to say to him before I happily haul his ass out of this vehicle and read him his rights?"

Campbell lifted her chin. "I'm sure I now have your complete attention, so you need to listen very carefully." She leaned forward. "From this day on, I will do everything I can to keep you away from me and out of my life. I don't care what it takes."

"My partner and I will gladly help her with that, too." Ian gave her a warm smile. "As will our many Denver PD colleagues." Ian again waved at his partner who lifted his arm and tapped his watch. "I think I'm being told to hurry up. It is getting close to lunchtime. I also need to squeeze in looking for a place Stella and I can live before this busy day is over." He raised his eyebrows. "The big, rambunctious dog you had to see me walking yesterday?"

Her ex stayed silent.

With a final glance at the *boy* who'd turned her life upside down, then stalked her to the point she'd resorted to desperation, Campbell opened the door, slid out of the vehicle, and slammed it behind her.

She deeply inhaled the frigid February air into her lungs as Ian hauled her ex from the SUV and handcuffed him. While Ian launched into his rights, she turned and walked to the sidewalk, still icy and somewhat snow packed from the storm which felt like a lifetime ago.

Everything she'd done and sacrificed to get away from her ex, combined with years of dealing with his possessiveness and harassment and watching him get away with it, for the most part, left her shoulders with such intensity she burst into laughter…that quickly turned to tears.

Now she, Campbell Grey, fully understood the meaning of the word *awakened*.

Chapter Twenty-Eight

SCOTT TAPPED his foot while he waited for the front door to open.

Based on the number of cars parked at Campbell's house, he had to be the last one to arrive. Had probably also been the last person to know everything that had happened because he'd been at work, forcing himself to concentrate on his American Literature class.

Which he'd ended fifteen minutes early.

The door flew open.

Ian grinned. "Good. You're here. I need to go walk Stella, so can I have—"

"You're a dick." Scott shouldered his way past Ian.

"That wasn't necessary." Ian closed the door. "I called. You didn't answer. I left a message and texted you. What's the problem?"

"You didn't tell me a damn thing in that so-called message and text."

In truth, he hadn't heard the entire story until calling Ian seconds after ending class. Scott had then wasted no time getting to his SUV and driving—more like racing—to get here.

He veered left, into the living room, but stopped at seeing Campbell on the couch, sitting between Alyson and a woman with dark, almost black hair. Her roommate, Blaine, sat on the coffee table in front of her with a big, burly guy beside him. Her other roommate?

Campbell stood when Scott stopped at the coffee table. "Please don't be angry."

He crossed his arms. "Correct me if I'm wrong, but what happened today wasn't the plan." He focused on Ian. "And who I'm really pissed off at is *you*."

"I told him not to tell you." She frowned at Ian. "But you called him anyway."

Ian opened his mouth, but Scott said, "Why would you tell him to keep me out of it?"

"Because you were working and I didn't want you to worry." She leaned forward. "I don't care what you say. I've caused you enough trouble at your job."

Scott released a slow breath and ran a hand through his hair.

"And you clearly have no faith in my abilities as an officer of the law," Ian stated. "My partner and I were on top of the situation. *Obviously*," he added under his breath. "Paul Harmon is right where he belongs." He laughed. "He of course lawyered up, but his parents aren't feeling generous with their time or money or connections, so he isn't going anywhere." He glanced at Campbell and back at Scott. "She was great, by the way. You should be proud of her."

A taut silence followed Ian's compliment. Which caused Campbell's face to turn that all-too appealing shade of red.

The concern and tension and frustration which had consumed Scott after talking to Ian left him in another slow breath.

"It was nice meeting all of you…despite the circumstances." Ian thumbed over his shoulder. "I'm being completely serious when I say I have to go walk Stella or you'll walk into something at your house that's far worse than what's happening here. I also have to get back to the station and deal with the not-so fun parts of being a cop."

Scott followed him to the door and reached into his front, right pocket for his keys. "You can leave them with my neighbor right across from my place." He cracked a smile. "If she invites you inside for coffee, please say no. I don't need you corrupting a retired teacher who watches my daughter when I'm in a bind."

Ian took the keys. "Am I going to see the most beautiful redhead I know before I leave?"

"Not if I can help it." Scott paused before adding, "Thanks for what you did today."

As concerned and frustrated as Scott had been after talking to Ian, Campbell had undoubtedly been in capable hands when it came to his long-time buddy.

Ian smiled. "I'm going to expect more than words of thanks since you'll have your house to yourself most of the night." He opened the door. "My partner invited me over to his house to have dinner with him and his family. All I ask is that you tear yourself away from the lady long enough to walk my dog. Think you can handle that, Professor?"

"It'll definitely be hard, but yeah. I can handle that."

Ian laughed and stepped outside, closing the door behind him.

Scott turned and headed back into the living room.

His gaze connected with Campbell's.

She looked so damn good and perfect, and safe and sound in her house. He wanted nothing more than to pull her into his arms and hold her the rest of the night, well into morning. But too many eyes watching them closely stopped him from going right to her side.

The woman with the dark hair stood and held out her hand. "I'm Jillian Castillo, Campbell's other boss." They shook hands. "I know quite a lot about you, Scott Mayhew."

He slowly nodded. "Which has to include my unforgettable moment at the Ritz-Carlton wedding last year?" He caught Alyson's cringe before she also stood.

Jillian grinned. "*Si*. And every single thing I've heard about you has been flattering."

"Thanks. But for the record, my life isn't typically this *interesting*." He glanced at Campbell who looked away, fighting a grin.

Alyson wrapped Campbell in her arms. "I know Ian said you needed to go to the station tomorrow to make your formal statement, so just take the day off."

Campbell having the day off would be damn perfect since Scott didn't work on Fridays.

Jillian gave her a hug when Alyson withdrew. "We're really glad you're okay."

Campbell smiled tightly. "Thank you for coming over. And I'm so sorry I didn't tell you the truth about everything sooner." Her lower lip quivered. "I promise this won't happen again."

Not if Scott and Ian and everyone else in Campbell's life had a say. What she'd just said, though, meant she'd told her bosses the ugly ex-asshole story.

Alyson grasped Campbell's hand. "We know. We also love you. You can call if you need us." She released her hand. "We'll see you Saturday for another"—she looked at Scott—"fairy tale, Felicity wedding."

Scott smiled. Hearing his sister's name, however, reminded him he needed to give her a call and smooth over what had happened yesterday. But that time wasn't now.

Someone else needed his attention the rest of the day and he wouldn't let her down.

After quick goodbye waves to him and Campbell's roommates, Alyson and Jillian left.

The big, burly guy stood and nodded at Scott. "I'm Lance.

Campbell's other roommate." He looked at Blaine who also came to his feet. "I need a drink. Stat. You?"

Blaine nodded. "I know the most *amazing* spot for day drinking." He gave Campbell an affectionate smile. "We'd invite you two, but I have a feeling that isn't necessary. I'm sure you'll also be spending the night elsewhere again, so check in with us later?"

She smiled as they gave her quick hugs. Then Scott and Campbell were finally alone.

Silence settled between them while they stared at one another.

She stepped forward. "My ex called me at work and something inside of me snapped. *Again.*" She lifted her chin. "After years of dealing with him and his crap, I'd had enough so I agreed to meet him. That's when I found out he wasn't driving the BMW."

Scott stepped forward. "Ian told me that's why you called him. He also said he told you not to meet up with the bastard until he and his partner could get there." He paused before adding, "But you went without hearing from Ian."

She sighed. "Scott, I had to face him. Show him he wasn't in control anymore." She shook her head. "I just stupidly didn't expect him to drive off with me in the car."

"But thank God Ian and his partner were there and the jackass ran a red light." Scott closed the gap between them. "Ian told me about the recording, too." He cracked a smile. "Nicely done."

She reached up and massaged what felt like a deep V in his forehead. "You're still upset."

"Only because I wasn't there." He loved her.

Hearing from Ian everything that had happened had sealed Scott's feelings. He also still couldn't stomach the thought of her being trapped with her unstable ex inside the guy's vehicle.

Yeah. She'd told Scott the bastard had never hurt her, but almost everyone had a breaking point. Especially guys like her ex.

She softly grinned. "I love that you wanted to be my knight in shining armor."

"I guess I'm old fashioned that way." He slipped his arms around her waist. "I am proud of you, though." Despite the tenuous situation she'd put herself into, he meant those words.

"Thank you." She slid her arms around his neck. "And the way I see it, you *were* there."

Scott stared at her. "What do you mean?"

"Ian. You're the one who rightfully involved him."

He hugged her tight. Still, it didn't change the fact he wished he'd been there to help Ian arrest the sonofabitch and toss his ass into a jail cell.

"I like Ian a lot." She snuggled Scott's chest. "It'll be nice to get to know him better when he officially lives in Denver."

"He's really a huge pain in the ass."

She laughed.

"But a damn good friend. More of a *brother*."

"I know," she murmured. "So do you forgive me?"

He leaned back which forced her to lift her head from his chest. "On two conditions. First, no more secrets. I'm not sure my neck can take more whiplash after this week."

She frowned. "Whiplash?"

"Never mind. Condition two"—he pressed his forehead to hers—"is that you come home with me where I can keep you in my sight for most of the weekend."

"What about Ian?"

"He'll be busy finding a place to live. Once he does, it's back to Grand Junction to finish packing and move here."

"Then I agree to both of your terms." She angled her head back. "There's someone I have to talk to before we leave."

He gently pushed a few stray hairs behind her right ear. "Your mom?"

"Yes," she murmured. "But then I'll be all yours."

Scott pressed his lips to hers for a kiss they managed to keep on the soft and chaste side.

She withdrew from his arms, swiped her phone off the couch, and headed for the kitchen.

He lowered himself onto the loveseat and inhaled his first head-cleansing breath since early this morning when Campbell had been curled in his arms. The smart, beautiful, passionate woman now officially his and who needed to hear his feelings while he had her all to himself.

Scott would owe his buddy more than a "thanks" for making himself scarce after this day.

"I HAVE A QUESTION," Scott asked.

Campbell, stretched out next to him on his ridiculously comfy couch, snuggled his side. "You want me to take my clothes off?"

He laughed. "Later. Definitely." He paused, then said, "How did you come up with the name Campbell Grey?"

She lifted her head and caught his inquisitive gaze.

"I get it's nothing like your real name, but where did it come from?"

She rested her chin on his chest. "Campbell is my mom's maiden name."

He nodded. "Okay. It's making way more sense. But Grey?"

"This will probably sound extremely sad and depressing," she slowly began, "but when I decided to change my name—to let go of Brittany Tate Harmon—I was in a pretty dark place in my head. I really don't like the word black so I went with *gray*."

His expression transitioned into a combo of affection and sadness. "And the British spelling came from…?" His soft voice trailed into silence.

She lifted her shoulders. "I've just always liked that spelling of the word."

His mouth eased back into his infectious grin. "Good to know. So what do your mom and brother and friends in Durango call you?"

"Campbell. But it took us a *long* time to get used to it. My mom and brother still occasionally slip and call me Britt." Just like her ex-bastard had on the phone. Thinking of him made her confess, "And I didn't have friends in Durango. At least, any friends who were mine."

Scott's grin vanished. "Because of your ex?"

She remained silent.

"*Wow*. He really is the definition of a piece of shit." Scott shook his head. "I'm going to say one more thing having to do with him, then we're finished with that topic."

"Fine with me. I just wish we'd never have to think or talk about him again." But she and Scott knew she'd be at the mercy of the justice system for a while. "It'd be nice if situations like this did happen fast, like in the movies and television shows."

"Yep. And the last thing I'm saying about it is that I'll go with you tomorrow to the station." His grin came back. "Next, much better topic. What are you doing Valentine's Day?"

Her eyes widened. "Oh, my God. It is next week, isn't it?"

Where in the world had the last few weeks gone?

"Believe it or not," he added under his breath. "Last year, I accompanied a striking little redhead to the ice skating rink where she damn near out skated me."

Campbell giggled.

"I'll have Peyton again this Valentine's Day…and you." He shifted Campbell up until they were almost nose-to-nose. "Think you might want to join us?"

His question, which was so much more than an invitation, hung between them.

"I'm in love with you, too," he quietly continued, "and you

and Peyton need to get to know one another."

Her smile grew.

Yes. She'd suspected Scott felt the same way for her as she did for him. But absolutely nothing on this planet topped hearing him say the words, especially after this day.

She nuzzled his nose. "I would love to join you and Peyton on Valentine's Day." Every single part of her meant those words she then sealed by pressing her mouth to his.

As their kiss gradually intensified, his phone, nearby on the ottoman, started to ring.

They broke apart.

Campbell scooped up the device and handed it to him.

"It's Shannon. Or it could be Peyton calling me on her mom's phone." He shifted upward which forced Campbell to also sit up. "Do you mind if I answer it?"

"Of course not." She brought her knees to her chest as he answered the call.

A giant smile infused his handsome face while he said, "Hi, baby. How was your day?"

Campbell hugged her knees and grinned.

"Olaf lost his nose *again*?"

She relaxed into the couch cushions and a tiny sigh escaped.

The first time she'd been here, nearly two weeks ago, she'd wondered what it would feel like to be a part of Scott Mayhew's cozy, warm, single-dad world overflowing with love.

"A Disney cruise?" Pause, then, "I'm sure you'll meet all the princesses."

Now she knew, without hesitation, this was exactly where she wanted to be and belonged.

"No, I won't be able to go on the cruise with you." He faced Campbell, grasped her right hand, and linked their fingers. "So you'll have to get me Goofy's autograph. Can you do that?"

Campbell buried her face in the cushion to muffle her

laughter.

"No, I don't need to talk to your mom. Love you. I'll call you tomorrow."

She peeked at him as he ended the call. "*Goofy's* autograph?"

"He's a cool, tall dog." Scott tossed his phone onto the ottoman. "I've also always felt he's completely misunderstood." He grasped her other hand and pulled her into his lap. "I guess Shannon and Adam—her now fiancé—decided to get married this summer on a Disney cruise."

Campbell squinted at him. "I thought you said she feels marriage is unnecessary."

He shrugged. "Shocked the shit out of me, too. But I'm happy for her. *Them*."

She stared at him. "You're really okay with her suddenly wanting to get married?"

"Why wouldn't I be okay with it?" He kissed the tip of her nose. "She and I were meant to be Peyton's parents. No more, no less." He again brought back his grin. "Back to Valentine's Day. Do you like fish?"

She held up her hand when she recalled the conversation with her mom. "Actually, while we're on the topic of vacations, your spring break will be here before you know it."

His grin slipped. "It should be your spring break, too."

She fingered the collar of his shirt. "Scott, I promise I'm going back to school. Probably this fall, only this time I'm going to enroll at Metro or CU Denver."

"I went to both of those schools and loved them equally."

"And Al and Jilly promoted me to manager, so I'll be able to afford—"

"They gave you a promotion?" He angled his head back. "How long have you been holding on to that pretty important info?"

She hesitated, then said, "It happened this morning. Right

before my ex—"

"Got it," Scott mumbled. "That's fantastic, Campbell. Really."

She sighed. "I'm not sure I truly deserve it after keeping so much from them." She winced. "I lied a lot to Alyson just in the last week or so. But she and Jillian were amazing about it." She focused on Scott. "They had no right to be, either."

"And you have to stop being so hard on yourself." He caught her gaze. "You did what you felt was necessary to have a life that was *yours*. No one can fault you for it."

She nodded, though it would probably take time for her to feel fully free from the guilt of not being honest with her bosses and roommates much sooner.

"Okay," Scott stated. "No more serious. You mentioned spring break, and I'm *intrigued*."

Campbell fought a grin while shaking her head. "I'm going to Durango that week because I haven't been there since I left. I need to see my mom and brother."

The feeling had never been stronger than at this moment, at the end of a rather emotional day, which had included an emotional conversation with her mom where Campbell had sworn to never keep anything from her again.

"I get it." Scott brushed his lips against hers. "I'll be pining for you while you're gone."

She gave him a mischievous smile. "Or you could go with me."

Their gazes locked.

"I love you and want you to see where *Brittany* came from, which includes meeting my mom and brother."

The corner of his mouth lifted in a tiny grin. "I'd love that."

"And maybe she'll even make us whoopie pies."

"Fantastic. But it's reminding me I finished the ones you brought on Saturday and will probably need more before then."

She laughed before their mouths came together once more for

a brief but deep kiss.

"I'm also pretty sure I have Peyton that week."

Campbell adjusted herself to straddle his lap. "So she'll come with us."

He placed his hands on her waist. "I guess that means I'm going to Durango for spring break with the two most important, beautiful ladies in my life."

They shared a longer, deeper kiss…until Campbell stopped and sat upright.

"Did you ask me if I like fish?"

He gave her a pained expression. "Really? That's what you're thinking about?" He released a quick breath. "I'm taking Peyton to The Aquarium on Valentine's Day and to eat at the restaurant there. It's why I asked if you like—"

"Yes, I like fish. Where were we?"

Stella started to snore from where she was sprawled out at the bottom of the staircase.

Scott grasped the bottom of Campbell's sweater. "Excellent. Ian's horse is asleep and won't need to be walked anytime soon." He gently pulled her sweater up and over her head, then tossed it across the living room.

Campbell responded by removing his shirt which followed the same fate as her sweater.

She swiftly, and in between delectable kisses, ended up stretched out beneath him.

Their mouths slowed to light kisses and eventually stopped.

With his infectious grin, Scott murmured, "Show me what you want me to do."

Campbell unbuttoned his jeans. "Only if you promise to never stop saying that to me."

His grin deepened. "I agree to your terms."

After removing their remaining clothing, she showed him *precisely* what she wanted.

"DADDY, I want Cinderella to tuck me in, too."

Scott handed Peyton Coco the pink elephant. "Honey, her name is *Campbell*."

Campbell laughed as she approached Peyton's bed. "It's really okay. I actually love that name." She lowered herself to the bed's edge and returned Peyton's big hug which caused Scott to smile softly. "I had so much fun with you naming all the fish we saw tonight."

That had, primarily, been given names from *Finding Nemo* and *Finding Dory*.

"Will you read me a *Pete the Cat* story?"

He leaned down. "Not tonight, baby. Tomorrow for sure." He kissed her temple.

"You can't forget, okay?" She hugged Coco to her tiny body. "Night, Cinderella."

Scott shared a quick, quiet laugh with Campbell.

Once they were back downstairs in the living room, he handed Campbell a gift bag.

She stared at him. "Scott, between the shop being *crazy* busy because of Valentine's Day and being with you all weekend, I never had a chance to get you something."

He sat and gently tugged her down. "Not a big deal." He pointed at the bag. "Open it."

Fighting a smile, she shook her head and reached into the bag. She withdrew her copy of *Sense and Sensibility*, then peered at him. "Thank you?"

He laughed. "I promise there's more inside. I just wanted to give it back to you since I finished it while you were working on Saturday."

"*And*?"

"The Dashwood sisters lived happily ever after."

"Reading a book that ended happily clearly didn't send you into cardiac arrest, either."

He shot her a pretend glare, then angled his head toward the bag. "Keep going."

She reached into the bag a second time and withdrew *The Awakening*.

"Thought you might like your own copy."

She gave him a quick kiss. "Thank you. I love it."

"You're not finished yet."

Laughing, she again reached into the bag and withdrew her *real* present. "*Delta of Venus: Erotica*." She slid her gaze to him. "How do you say the author's name?"

"*Ahnaheess Neen*. Another influential female writer whose work was pretty controversial." He leaned forward. "What's in that book makes Kate Chopin's stories tame since some of it is intense." He grinned. "The deal is, we have to read the stories I marked together…when I don't have Peyton. So we'll have to wait until next week."

She gave him a naughty smile. "I do like the title."

"Excellent. There's one more book inside the bag."

Her smile grew while withdrawing the final book—and she burst into laughter.

"*Pete the Cat: Snow Daze.*" She continued laughing.

"It's a *riveting* story about a massive storm resulting in numerous snow days."

She put all the books and bag onto the ottoman, then ended up cradled in his lap.

"It's perfect," she murmured. "This entire night was perfect."

"I'd have to agree with you," he replied, lowering his mouth to hers.

Campbell stopped him by placing her fingertips on his lips. "And thank you for helping me understand the meaning of the word *awakened.*"

Understanding the meaning of happy endings, Scott grinned before their mouths fused.

Author's Note

I hope you enjoyed Book Three in the Timing is Everything Series that will end with *This Time It's Forever*. Each book can stand alone, but it's recommended they're read in series order for maximum enjoyment.

And if you have a moment, please leave a rating and brief review at wherever you purchased the book. Authors always appreciate and need honest reader reviews.

About the Author

Christine Miles is a full-time writer living in Albuquerque, New Mexico.

An avid reader and writer since elementary school, her passion for literature inspired her to pursue a BA in English and an MA in Creative Writing. She writes YA and Adult Contemporary Romances with sassy, independent heroines and swoony heroes who love them for their strength.

When not writing romances, she loves traveling, binge-watching shows on streaming apps, reading mysteries and thrillers, listening to music, and spending quality time with her family, friends, and dog.

You can find her on Facebook and Instagram. Sign up for her newsletter to get ARC's and updates at www.christinemilesauthor.com.

facebook.com/ChristineMilesAuthor

instagram.com/christinemilesauthor

amazon.com/author/christinemilesya

bookbub.com/authors/christine-miles

goodreads.com/christinemilesauthor

www.ingramcontent.com/pod-product-compliance
Lightning Source LLC
Chambersburg PA
CBHW061607190726
48288CB00007B/2207